D1175938

After Lucy

After Lucy

Brenda Langmead

ROBERT HALE · LONDON

ISBN 0 7090 7431 X

Robert Hale Limited
Clerkenwell House
Clerkenwell Green
London EC1R 0HT

2 4 6 8 10 9 7 5 3 1

Typeset by
Derek Doyle & Associates, Liverpool.
Printed in Great Britain by
St Edmundsbury Press, Bury St Edmunds, Suffolk.
Bound by Woolnough Bookbinding Limited.

Chapter One

Kate heard the front door close. Fergus was back from his nightly checking-up call on his mother. 'A granny flat', the estate agent had called the converted outbuildings next to their Victorian house, but Maggie had turned that name down at once.

'I'll be a granny to whatever you're cooking up in there,' she'd said cheerfully, patting Kate's bump, 'but I'm damned if I'm going to be labelled Granny by everybody else from the postman to the dustmen. That place will be "The Cottage" as long as I'm living in it.' She'd been cheerful in those days. The 'before' days.

It was like thinking back to another life now, remembering times when they'd all laughed together. Now there never seemed to be a genuine, straightforward atmosphere to any of their exchanges. No matter how trivial the subject matter, Kate could never think of what she was saying to Maggie for wondering what Maggie was thinking, how Maggie was feeling. She knew that the same constraints affected Fergus and Maggie too. She saw it on their faces. Odds were that it had been like that for Fergus tonight. But at least Maggie hadn't kept him there long. Either that, or Fergus had refused to be kept.

He took her by surprise and came straight upstairs once he'd locked up instead of pottering about for ages as he usually did. Kate tensed as she heard the creak of the first stair and found herself wishing that she'd put the bedside light off.

Hot on the heels of her reaction came shame. What a desperate way to behave towards her husband. This was Fergus, whose shoulder she'd wept buckets on, Fergus who'd sat through the awful night-hours with her when neither of them could sleep for grief, Fergus who'd somehow managed to pull her back from the brink of the madness that had threatened in the early days. He was not someone whose approach should be dreaded, even momentarily.

'Not asleep yet?' he said softly as he came into their room. He was already shrugging off his sweatshirt which he tossed in the vague direction of the chair in the corner. Trainers followed the shirt.

'Just as well I'm not!' she said ironically, momentarily at ease with herself again, and he grinned at her, acknowledging his noisiness. 'You weren't long. Was she all right?'

He pulled a face. 'Pretty much as usual. I wouldn't go so far as to call it all right. Ready for bed, anyway. She said she was turning in as soon as I left. She asked if you would bring her some ham from the delicatessen for lunch tomorrow. I said I expected that would be all right. Will it?'

Kate stifled a sigh. 'Of course it will. Doing her shopping's no problem. But her being afraid to put a foot out of doors is. When on earth is she going to go out again, Fergus?'

Fergus was peeling off his jeans. 'God knows. But after last time I don't think it's worth pushing her into anything, do you?'

Maggie had only left her cottage twice in the past four months. The first time had been to be taken to the doctor's in such a state of trembling agitation that he had tactfully given her house calls to renew her prescriptions since then. The second time had been as a result of Fergus getting tough and insisting that it was time his mother pulled herself together. His bullying forced her into going to what had been her favourite café to meet a friend for a cup of tea. The only result of that attempt to sort things out had been an anxious phone call from one of the staff to say that Mrs Callender was very distressed, and would someone come and collect her? Fergus was in the middle of afternoon surgery by that time. It was

Kate who had to deal with the situation and remove a shuddering, terrified Maggie from the table in the corner where her friend was trying, desperately embarrassed, to cope with her. Fergus was right. There was no point in forcing another situation like that.

He was having an uncharacteristic fit of tidiness and going round picking up his scattered clothes. Kate watched him, remembering, as though from another lifetime, how once the sight of Fergus wandering around in the raw would have had her randy as anything. Now, nothing. Maggie was not the only one with problems. Would any of them ever be the same again?

'I'm going to have a quick shower,' Fergus said. 'Won't be long.'

He disappeared into the bathroom. Kate's thoughts turned once more to Maggie. She wished she didn't have to keep thinking about her. She would never have tolerated the idea of living with Maggie on the doorstep if she hadn't liked her. Inviting her down from the north to live near them had seemed a good thing to do. Fergus's chance to buy into partnership in a Lichfield veterinary practice was going to put hundreds of miles between Maggie and them. She was lonely after Fergus's father died, they knew, though she didn't complain. Once they moved south, they couldn't have visited much, given the hours and weekends Fergus would be working, and Maggie didn't drive so the journey would have been a hassle for her.

On their side, it helped to have the proceeds from the sale of two houses, since they were moving to an area of much higher prices. Kate intended, too, to go back to work after she had the baby. They wouldn't expect too much of Maggie in the way of grandchild-minding, though she was eager to be involved, but having her there to supervise could be an advantage.

So much for careful forward-planning. Bitterness welled up in Kate. All those sensible provisions made before the move, and here they were, left with what? Lucy dead – the word still jolted her, even in the silence of her mind – after fourteen short weeks. The three of them trapped in proximity that circumstances had made painful instead of pleasurable. And, as far as she herself was concerned, the tormenting, shameful feeling that without Maggie's presence in the cottage, Lucy might still be alive.

Instantly the rational part of her set about the routine business of attempting to dismiss the thought. She despised herself for thinking it. Cold reason told her it wasn't true. Lucy would have died whoever had been sitting unknowingly downstairs in the house at the moment when something – none of the so-called experts knew what – made her stop breathing. The doctor had said so. Kate had read it in the leaflets they had given her. The coroner had reinforced what everyone else had said. Cot death was like that. Unexpected and cruel. Bitterly, bitterly cruel. But no one was to blame. Lucy had not been the victim of anyone's neglect – not Maggie's, not Fergus's, not even Kate's, though heaven knew Kate felt the most guilty of all.

If it hadn't been their wedding anniversary . . . if they hadn't planned before Lucy's birth that they wouldn't be the kind of boring parents who never left their child or spoke of any other subject but her . . . if Maggie hadn't been only too eager and willing to look after her beloved Fergus's child single-handed. . . . Distraught, Kate hurled herself over in the bed and thumped the pillow. The ifs were endless, and utterly pointless.

She tried to concentrate on Fergus's noisy activity in the bathroom. He was whistling. Her throat flooded with bitterness. How could he whistle in that carefree fashion when her own mind was hell-bent on relentlessly dragging her through yet another ghastly replay of that awful night when Lucy had died? She wanted to be like Fergus, accepting what had happened, determinedly looking towards the future and working back to happiness . . . not forever desperately searching for a clue to explain what had happened to Lucy, finding each time some new thing which, had they or had they not done it, might have kept her alive.

It happened on their wedding anniversary. That was the final cruelty. Never again would an anniversary dawn without bringing with it the memory of the telephone ringing in the room where they had planned hours of glorious unbroken sleep after the taxing nights broken by Lucy's demands, demands that were now so very precious in retrospect.

They had been so ridiculously happy in their luxurious hotel bedroom, like kids let out of school. The tape in Kate's mind began as it always did with the 'before' time, as though she had to experience the carefree 'then' in order that she shouldn't spare herself the full horror of what came afterwards.

Herself coming out of the bathroom, Fergus lying in bed, his hands clasped behind his thatch of dark unruly hair, his deep-set blue eyes on her with a wicked look she knew well.

Fergus saying 'You know what this feels like? It feels like a dirty weekend. Whose tasty young wife are you, in that scrap of a thing I've never seen before? Bet you daren't let me work out its price per inch!' That sexy little growl in the back of his throat, his grin broadening and his voice going into ladykiller mode. 'Come here, woman! I'll have it off you!'

Herself chasséing across the room, catching his mood as she always did in those days, then diving into the bed and into his arms. The kisses and the laughter. Then the telephone ringing. Fergus reaching over her to pick it up.

Her mind was going into slow motion now. She'd thought it was Maggie, of course. Who else would ring them? But not for one moment had she anticipated anything other than a query about the whereabouts of some item of Lucy's extensive equipment.

Fergus rigid with shock, the colour washing like a tide from his face, herself scrambling out from underneath him to crouch naked and shivering, her ear close to the receiver, catching phrases here and there, knowing that something was wrong at home . . . dreadfully wrong. The two of them staring speechlessly at each other as Fergus at last put the phone down. Herself terrified to ask. Fergus finally forcing himself to tell her what the night duty doctor whom neither of them knew had told him, not knowing how to start, how to form the words, how even to conjure up a voice. The packing, the journey back through the darkness,

9

all of it hideously unreal, until the car turned into the drive where the doctor's car was still parked.

Reality coming hurtling towards them then as they went past him and a white-faced Maggie, who seemed to have shrunk and become an old woman since they left only hours ago. Up the stairs, nearer and nearer to Lucy's room. Across the pale cream carpet, right up to the white cot where everything was so still, so silent. Then, belief.

Kate took a deep, shuddering breath, realizing that she had been holding her breath as she inevitably did while the ghastly silent loop of film replayed itself in her mind. She sat up until her breathing quietened, the racing of her heart calmed down and the awful pictures in her mind faded. It was four months since that day. Look forward, not back, she told herself desperately over and over again like a mantra, wondering if it would ever be possible.

She was lying down again by the time the bathroom door swung open and light fell across the bed before being extinguished. She heard Fergus open the curtains to allow for the chink of night sky he liked to see. Then he padded round to his side of the bed and slid in beside her, smelling of the posh soap she had put in his Christmas stocking, and tasting of toothpaste as he leaned over to kiss her goodnight.

'All right?' he said in her ear, as he always did before settling down.

Because she was not all right, she turned towards him with an incoherent murmur and buried her face in the hollow of his neck.

'Hey! What's this?' Fergus's voice was soft as his arms went round her. 'What's all this?' he repeated, his hold on her tightening.

Memories were still haunting Kate's mind as she clung to him, desperate to banish them. Why, when there were so many lovely mental pictures of Lucy in all her tender freshness, should it be Lucy as she had been on that awful night when they stood looking down on her in her cot that returned with such persistent cruelty?

Struggling against her feelings, Kate didn't at first realize that Fergus had misinterpreted her turning towards him. Only gradually did she become aware that his tone had been not so much of concern as of half-disbelieving, delighted surprise. That his hands were following a path of caresses that was familiar and yet frighteningly strange, like something seen through the wrong end of a telescope. It was not the unthreatening comfort she needed that Fergus had in mind, but sex. Sex after the months of abstinence with the two of them dead to all positive feelings. Sex, and all it implied of life, when she felt full of death.

She froze against the eager tenderness of his kisses on her eyes and her cheek and her mouth. She knew now why she had so incomprehensibly wished earlier on that her light had been out and herself asleep when he came upstairs. Subconsciously she must have read the signals and sensed that this was coming – known, too, how frighteningly little she would welcome it.

'Fergus –' she whispered, trying to turn her head away, a different kind of panic rising in her now.

His lips closed hers. 'Don't talk,' he said against her mouth, his voice stifled but urgent so that she knew he was utterly determined. 'We've done enough talking.'

They had not made love for almost four months. Lucy's death had drained them of all but the unbearable emotions of loss and pain and grieving. They had talked it through, because sex had always been a good and strong part of their marriage, finding grim comfort in the fact that they both felt the same awful sense of hiatus, agreeing that it was to be expected that a devastating experience such as they had gone through was bound to have its repercussions and it would all sort itself out eventually.

More theorizing gone down the drain, Kate thought wildly now. She had naïvely assumed that the two of them, who had always been so well attuned, would come alive in that way with perfect joint timing. But Lucy's loss wasn't the same for both of them. How could it be? Fergus hadn't carried the precious burden of an unknown child for nine long months. He hadn't

11

given birth to her. His body hadn't nourished her. He hadn't at the height of his grieving had to cope with breasts that went on producing milk and aching with the need to feed a child who no longer existed. They were different people with different emotions and different needs. She needed Fergus's arms round her, needed his calm, comforting words when she felt she was ready to drop off the edge of the world. But she did not need to be touched in the way he was touching her now. Her distaste at what had once been such a joy shattered her.

Her husband, she kept telling herself. He was her husband whom she loved. She knew what long, barren unhappiness had led up to this tentative approach to the loving that had once fired them both. How could she meet his reaching out to her with the flat statement that she was dead inside, she wanted nothing of him?

All this raced through her mind while she steeled herself to let things happen, unable to make the faintest response to the loving that had once filled her with joy, wondering if she could contain her awful revulsion for as long as it took.

It was a lovemaking that was like no other. A faint, ghostly third party was present, coming between Fergus's hand and her body, his lips and her own. Every touch was clouded and numbed with memories of Lucy – her birth, the tug of her feeding, the warm, velvet softness of her skin. Instead of the once-familiar joyful pounding of the blood, Kate's veins ran chill with knowledge of the dangers of loving and the pain of loss.

She was enduring what had once been a delight, and at the same time hating herself for reducing what was between her and Fergus to mere endurance. Then, as Fergus's breathing intensified until it seemed to roar in her ears, she was suddenly screaming and bursting into a paroxysm of violent sobbing, thrusting him away from her with all her strength, arms and legs flailing at him. Fergus half-fell, half-jumped out of bed. 'For God's sake, Kate! What the hell's the matter?'

Words tumbled out then, incoherent, jumbled, too fast to be followed. Everything he did reminded her of how Lucy had been conceived and she couldn't bear the thought of that happening, not yet. She wasn't fit for it, couldn't cope with it, couldn't bear it. She was dead inside – didn't he know that? – and she couldn't bear his intrusion, anyone's intrusion, into the deadness of herself. She barely understood herself, so how on earth could Fergus understand her?

She expected anger. It would have been logical and absolutely right for him to be angry with her. He had put the light on by now, and she saw that he was indeed and understandably angry. But as he looked at her convulsed face she saw the anger die down and he actually began to reach out to the snarling, spitting creature that she had become, ready to take her into his arms and comfort her yet again. And she couldn't bear his goodness. She retreated to the edge of the bed like a wild thing, shouting at him to leave her alone.

'I've been leaving you alone for long enough, Kate,' he said vehemently. 'What do you expect me to do? Stand by and watch our marriage go down the pan? Let you dwindle before my eyes until there's nothing left of the person I married?' He went into the bathroom and she heard him turn the cold tap on, heard the chink of a glass against it. He came in wiping his mouth with the back of his hand and said, 'This can't go on, you know. You must know it as well as I do. You need help.'

'Don't bloody patronize me when all you mean is you've decided I'm not being obliging enough these days,' she said bitterly.

He shamed her with his dignity. 'Yes, I love you, and yes, because I love you I want to make love to you. Once you thought that was perfectly normal. You wanted it as much as I did – as I do.'

'Things change. Once we were a normal couple with a child,' she countered, her voice breaking on the last word.

He looked at her steadily, his dark eyes enraging her with the pity in them. 'You've got to get over it, Kate.'

'Like a cold? Like a bit of indigestion?' she said savagely.

'Like the sorrow it is, but one we face together and don't allow to drive us apart. I do feel it's doing just that. Can't you see that it is?'

She didn't answer. There was no answer. He was right, and she didn't know what to do about it.

He sat down on the edge of the bed, and she tensed, ready to fly for the door, but he came no closer.

'I fished those leaflets out of the bin, the ones they gave you at the surgery. I wasn't going to push you into anything you didn't want to do then, but I thought it was crazy to throw them away. Kate, if you won't ask the doctor to refer you to someone in the profession, you could at least give one of the addresses they list a try.'

Kate had been adamant that she would have nothing to do with bereavement counselling or groups of people who, like her, had lost a child. The very thought of it was repugnant to her. She didn't want to set herself apart from the rest of humanity with a band labelled 'the afflicted'. She didn't want anyone telling her that they knew how she felt. Lucy was unique. Her loss was unique. No one knew how she felt about it.

'I go out, don't I?' she said passionately. 'I've got myself a job. Not a proper job, I know, but better than nothing, surely? I speak to people – people who don't want to speak to me half the time. People who seem to think I'm bad luck that can rub off on them. That's trying, isn't it?'

'It's papering over the cracks. Not filling them in.'

'I see. You think I should fill them in with another baby? Don't tell me you're joining that brigade. Break one, go out and buy another.' She saw the hurt of her words on Fergus's face but was too outraged, too desperate with her own misery to care. 'I could have a hundred more babies and there'd still be a gap where Lucy ought to be.'

At that moment the phone rang.

Kate found that she was shaking uncontrollably at the sudden shattering of the tension between them. She pulled on her dressing gown. Only her overwhelming desire to know that Fergus was being called out and prevented from pursuing what she saw as his hounding of her held her back from hurtling downstairs to find sanctuary in the furthermost corner of the house.

He was sitting on the edge of the bed, his back towards her, somehow vulnerable in his nakedness but as always, no matter what the hour, what the circumstances, making a calm, professional response to the call.

It was Brian Thwaite, she guessed, a dairy farmer six miles or so to the east of Lichfield. Fergus had mentioned the possibility of a call from him in the next few days.

'The one you had trouble with last time?' Fergus was saying. 'Seems determined to get them all the wrong way round, doesn't she? How long has she been down? Long enough, then. I'll be over right away. Your cowman around? Good. We'll sort her out. Don't worry.'

Relief washed through Kate, leaving her limp. He was going out, perhaps for the rest of the night. Long enough for him to forget his frustration and his plans for her. Long enough for her to drag herself back into her sanity, if she could find it.

Fergus was already starting to dress. He finished shrugging his sweatshirt over his head and came to stand at the foot of the bed doing up the belt of his jeans. 'You heard that? I've got to go over to Edingdale. A breach at Thwaite's farm. You're shaking. Will you be all right, Kate?'

'Perfectly.' She forced stillness on herself, looking defiantly at him. 'I haven't exactly given the impression of needing company, have I?'

Fergus shrugged. 'Nevertheless, I wouldn't choose to leave you at this precise moment.' His Scots accent, inherited from his father, always intensified when he was worried, and his way of speaking got more precise . . . 'even stuffier', she used to tease him in the days when they could tease each other. Somehow this went a little of the way to destroy the horrible atmosphere in the bedroom.

'You pompous ass, Fergus,' she told him, attempting normality. She always called him that at such times.

'Oh, Kate. . . .' His hand reached out towards her, then he withdrew it and she thought miserably that she had done that to him, made him stop in mid-loving action. 'What a bloody mess we're in,' he went on. 'Can I get you a drink before I go?

15

I wouldn't say no to a whisky myself.'

'I'll get one in a while if I want one. It'll give me something to do.'

His eyes held hers a moment longer, then he turned to go. 'If you're sure. . . .' At the door he paused again. 'Damned cow!' he said savagely.

'Me? Or Thwaite's?' It was a brave attempt at humour, spoiled only by a wobble in her voice.

'Oh, Kate!' Fergus said again, silhouetted against the landing light. 'Don't cry again, not now when I can't stop to be with you however much I want to.'

'I'm not crying,' she said gruffly. 'I'm sorry, Fergus. Sorry for what I said and did. Or rather for how I said it and did it. It was awful.' She paused. 'I did mean it, though. The not being capable of living normally yet.'

'I wasn't in any doubt about that.'

'And I'm very much afraid that I might do the same thing again.'

'That's why we've got to talk. But it can't be now. Shall I give Maggie a call? She'd come round, I know.'

'That's the last thing I want!' Kate said, far too emphatically. She stood up. 'Look, I'm getting up. I'm going to come downstairs and have that drink you suggested. Then I'll maybe stupefy myself with a bit of late-night television, and if you're not back by the time I feel dozy, I'll just come back to bed.'

Fergus was scribbling on the hall telephone pad as she came downstairs.

'That's the number I'll be at. Ring if . . . if you need to for any reason. Brian won't mind.'

'I expect the cow would, though.' She gave him a push. 'Go on. Stop dawdling around.'

It was a relief when the door closed behind him and she had no other feelings but her own to cope with.

Chapter Two

Maggie looked at the clock for the umpteenth time. Half past one, and Kate was still not back with the ham for her lunchtime sandwich. Perhaps Fergus had forgotten to pass on the message. Or, more likely still, Kate was sick to death of nannying her mother-in-law. Maggie wouldn't blame her. She lifted the curtain of the kitchen window and peered down the empty drive. Her hand trembled with a fierce life of its own, and she dropped the curtain impatiently.

She went across and checked the store cupboard again. Nothing suitable for sandwich-making had miraculously appeared in it.

When she thought back to the well-stocked cupboards she had kept when Donald was alive, she realized just how far she had gone on the downward spiral. Oh, she had her hair done and cleaned the house, but inside herself she was a weak, contemptible creature, and she despised herself for it. Afraid to go out, when she had lived most of her married life on a lonely hill-farm in the Cheviots, with Donald heaven-knew-where on the land for most of the day. She'd been responsible for herself in every way then, and happy to be so.

She sat down again, conscious of a too-rapid heartbeat. What could she do to stop this mounting agitation? Make a list of what she needed poor Fergus and Kate to bring her from the supermarket, if she could concentrate sufficiently? Yes, that was something that needed to be done. She only functioned through lists these days. 'Get up. Wash. Dress. Do hair. Make porridge and toast'. It was a wonder she didn't write down when she was supposed to breathe.

If only something would really occupy her mind to the exclusion of everything else. She couldn't read, nowadays. Her thoughts seemed to run on two levels, so that whatever the surface part of her mind was trying to concentrate on was constantly invaded by activity in the lower level. The lower level was full of what it imagined other people to be thinking about her, and between these imaginings were the dreadful memories of the ghastly tragedy in which she had been so closely involved, memories Dr Terry told her to put out of her mind. But she couldn't. It was the same if she tried to listen to the radio. Even when Fergus or Kate talked to her, the inward horrors kept pace with their conversation.

Today had been particularly bad. She had wakened this morning with a splitting headache, and neither the doctor's magic pills, nor the aspirins she had swallowed with her first cup of tea had done any good. She had sneaked another magic pill mid-morning, along with more aspirins, but her temples were still pounding. It was just over three hours since her last painkillers, and the bottle told her to wait four, but she was going to risk two more.

She got up and took them, then, back in her chair, closed her eyes and, as the clock that the choir had given to her and Donald as a wedding present ticked soothingly in the silence, she willed herself to relax into oblivion.

The telephone roused her. It must have been ringing for some time, because as she struggled to her feet it cut off. That was just as well, since her legs refused to hold her upright, and deposited her full length on the hearthrug. No harm, other than to her dignity, fortunately. She managed with some difficulty to get herself upright again.

From where she was standing she could see into the kitchen. She had left the top off the aspirin bottle. She went through and screwed it back on. Her eyes focused blearily on the label, and she realized that what she was holding in her hand was not the aspirin bottle. It was the magic pill one. Careless, that. Did it mean that she had taken magic pills instead of aspirins? Whatever she had had, she felt better for it. Floaty, but better.

She swayed gently on the spot for a moment or two. Her stomach did a formidable rumble. She wanted a ham sandwich. Why on earth didn't she go and get ham? Simple, wasn't it? It wouldn't take more than half an hour for the round trip – well, maybe a little bit more, given the state of her legs. For once, miraculously, she felt unperturbed at the thought of going out. A walk would clear her head of the last vestiges of the headache, though she rather hoped it would leave alone the cotton wool with which her mind felt to be stuffed. Cotton wool, in comparison with the alternative, which was a kind of limping chaos, was no bad thing.

She buttoned herself with difficulty into her coat and had two attempts at putting her hat on the right way round. She almost set off without her purse but was quite pleased with herself for remembering it before she closed the front door. At the bottom of the drive she stopped, not knowing whether she had locked the door or not. She decided she didn't care, and headed with precarious dignity down into town.

Kate was coming out of the Kitchen Shop, the wind snatching at the skirts of her coat and threatening to have the red beret off her head, when she saw Sue Bagnall coming along Market Street towards her. Sue belonged to the same choir, and she had certainly seen her too, Kate knew, but didn't want to acknowledge the fact, judging by the way she dodged into Woolworths after a stagey consultation of her shopping list. They hadn't met since Lucy died, and Sue obviously preferred to avoid a difficult encounter.

She wasn't a very close friend, but she was more than an acquaintance, and they were both members of the same choir. If Kate let it pass this time, the same miserable charade would no doubt take place when they next almost bumped into each other until somebody found the ability to put an end to it. And that somebody would, of course, have to be herself – Kate, the cause of it.

She hurried along the street and went into Woolworths. Sue was at least genuinely looking at the card racks and not skulking inside the door. Kate came up behind her and gave her a tap on the shoulder.

'Sue. I thought I saw you come in here.'

Sue spun round, looking as though she had been caught shoplifting. 'Kate—' She choked on the word and dropped a handful of cards. 'Oh, dear! Look what I've done. What a clumsy idiot.'

The two of them crouched down to retrieve the cards.

'Always somebody's birthday, isn't it?' But not Lucy's, Kate's treacherous mind told her. Sue was almost snatching the cards from her hand and Kate realized that one of them had 'To Daddy' printed in large letters on the front of it. The cards Lucy would never make, the sticky, hopeless, but incredibly dear infant-school offerings that she and Fergus would never see now, flashed through Kate's mind. Was her face betraying her feelings?

'It's Maggie's birthday next month. Better get a card for her,' she said as lightly as she could. 'Fergus never remembers.'

'Men never do, do they? We should get secretarial duties written into the marriage vows.' Sue dumped the cards back on the rack as though they were burning her fingers. Her face was red as she turned to look at Kate.

'I'm so sorry,' she said with an unexpectedly direct approach. 'I haven't seen you since . . . I don't know what to say except that I'm sorry. Desperately sorry. I saw you out there – I expect you know I did – but I was coward enough to want not to have to say anything. Nothing's right, is it? How are you? Even that's a stupid question. How can you be anything but absolutely awful?'

This was better than expected. Sue was going for the realistic approach, and at least she could be answered honestly.

'It's varying shades of awful now. I hang on to that. I've been back at work for three weeks. That seems to be the thing to do, they tell me.' She even managed a rueful smile. 'And they tell me quite a lot these days.'

'You're not teaching again?' Sue said incredulously.

'No – just doing three half-days on the desk at the Information Office – much less taxing.' They gave up on the cards and went out into Market Street again. Having brought about the encounter, Kate was suddenly exhausted and longing to get away, but Sue suggested going for a coffee, and it seemed prudent to accept.

Conversation had its usual painful, sticky patches. People seemed to think Kate would never want to speak of babies, and she had to convince them that what she resented was Lucy being dead, not other children being alive. She asked about James, Sue's son who had been born at the same time as Lucy.

Sue was obviously uncomfortable, but tried to answer normally.

'He's still a podge. But he's starting to want non-stop entertainment now. I could spend all day picking up what he throws out of the pram. Mum's looking after him today. It's unbelievably good to have a break from him. Oh, God!' Her face contorted with embarrassment as she realized what she had said and to whom. 'I'm so sorry, Kate. I can't believe I said that.'

'It's all right, really. A perfectly normal thing to say.' I'm the abnormal one, she wanted to add, the pariah, the one fate put a finger on. There was the sort of painful silence she hated.

'Look' – she said, launching herself into it – 'I really must go now. As soon as I feel like singing again, I'll be back at choir.'

Sue didn't attempt to persuade her to stay.

As Kate walked home up Dam Street, a solitary cry from one of the wildfowl on Minster Pool came from beyond the row of shops, echoing the bleakness in her mind. Life was like some huge, obscene snakes-and-ladders board, the ladders almost non-existent, the snakes huge and everywhere. Was she making any real progress at all?

She went wearily up Bishop's Walk and along Gaia Lane towards the house that had been such a delight when she and Fergus moved in. Victorian, with gracious, high-ceilinged rooms and a lovely, tree-shaded garden, it had drawn her home like a magnet in the early days as though she had a continual need to reassure herself that it was theirs. Now her heart sank as she went wearily back.

There was no sign of life at Maggie's windows. Kate was thankful to be able to walk past and put the key in her own front door. She would have to see Maggie a little later, but perhaps she would feel more up to it then.

Possibly it would have been easier between them if Maggie hadn't seemed to be having as hard a struggle to get over Lucy's death as herself and Fergus. If Kate gave way to her often irrational feelings, she resented that. How could anyone else's sorrow equal her own? Maggie's plain, transparent face seemed to be permanently pleading for forgiveness, and there was a limit to how many times you could go on saying – and believing – that there was nothing to forgive.

She hung up her coat and beret, then took her shopping through into the kitchen, unloading it on to the pine table. Damn. There was the delicatessen packet – the ham Maggie had asked her to bring for lunch. She had bought it on automatic pilot, then completely forgotten the meal it was intended for and dawdled around having coffee with Sue. She was going to have to take it round now and apologize. But she would make the excuse of being tired and wanting to go up for a rest. That would give her a quick get-out.

Maggie's door did not yield to a determined turning of the handle. Kate gave a brisk knock, and when nothing happened, picked up the flower pot on the kitchen window sill and saw the key there in its usual place when Maggie was out. But what was not in the least usual these days was for Maggie to be out at all.

What on earth had prompted today's apparent miracle? Kate let herself in and put the ham away in the fridge, scribbling a note to leave on the kitchen table saying it was there.

Then, thankful to have avoided an encounter, she locked the door and put the key back under the geranium pot. Bed and oblivion for a couple of hours before she needed to do anything about the evening meal were overwhelmingly desirable.

*

Zoe Clark, surgery receptionist for three full and two half-days a week for the past five years and self-appointed mother to all staff, looked up from her keyboard as Fergus came through the door. He had the appearance of having been pulled through a hedge every which way.

'You look like a man who needs a strong cup of coffee. Bad day?'

'Too right. And ditto last night.' Fergus slumped against the counter. 'Why do farmers never think to offer either thanks or refreshments?'

Zoe grinned. 'Which one was it today?'

'Two of them. Harper and his bull, then Davies's bloody savage of a horse.'

Zoe laughed. 'Say no more! Wasn't he the charmer that took a lump out of Martin's arm?'

'The very same, and not one whit more likable.'

'You'll be glad to get back home to some tender loving care, then.'

'If only!' Fergus said, last night still looming large in his mind. He shouldn't have said that. He hurried to change the significance of his words. 'There's not much chance of that. I'm standing in for Martin tonight. He's got some Lodge do on.'

'In that case, I'll find you a chocolate biscuit with your coffee, you poor martyr – and you're far nicer than that smarmy vet on the box,' Zoe said, getting up and following him into the back regions of the surgery. 'Fergus!' she exclaimed, catching hold of his arm, and bending down to look at the back of his thigh. 'That looks like blood on your jeans. I hope it belonged to Davies's horse, not you.'

'The swine did lash out at me at one point – and I could have sworn I hadn't turned my back on him for a split second.' He twisted futilely. 'It is sore, now you mention it. Can't see a thing, though. It'll have to wait.'

'Don't be daft, Fergus. If you leave it until the end of surgery you could have all kinds of filth in your bloodstream.'

'Can't be helped. I'm not a contortionist.' He made to move

off into the cloakroom. Zoe's hold on his arm remained relent-
less.

'I'll see to it for you. I did Martin's arm and that didn't turn
bad on him.'

'Martin didn't have to drop his pants to have his arm treated.
Thanks, but no thanks, Zoe. I'm an old-fashioned wee boy.'

'Prehistoric, more like. Do you imagine I haven't seen
enough pants dropped in my time? The view doesn't vary
much. Forget the false modesty Fergus and think of your
health, you dope.'

Fergus grinned at her determined face. 'Oh, all right, then.
You've convinced me, Granny.' Zoe, about as far from granny-
dom as anyone could be with her shining blonde hair and
cheeky grin, had married soon after her seventeenth birthday
and divorced before her twenty-first. The product of that brief
domestic interlude, Rebecca, now fourteen, was showing all the
signs of following her mother's teenage pattern, and Zoe's tales
of her battles to control her daughter entertained the surgery at
large.

Now she gave Fergus a shove in the direction of the cloakroom. 'Get in there, and I'll bring the first aid kit – and plenty
of iodine to burn the cheek out of you.'

Fergus removed his jeans and was examining the back of
them when Zoe came through the door with a bowl of steam-
ing water in her hand.

'Bit of a mess,' he said. 'Not torn, though.'

'Something to be thankful for, then.' Zoe bent down behind
him and he felt her cool fingers on his thigh, then the heat of
the pad of cotton wool and the sting of disinfectant.

'Ouch. Go easy. What's the verdict?' he asked.

'Nice bum!' Zoe said, quick as a flash. Her pert, bossy face
craned round to peer up at him, grinning. 'Well, you asked for
that one, didn't you?' She sat back on her heels, dabbing away
at his leg again. 'It's more of a graze than a cut. Won't need
stitches, but you'll have to watch it – or Kate will. How are you
for tetanus jabs?'

'Had a booster less than six months ago.'

'You'll live then. You need a dressing, which means that some time you're going to have half your pelt ripped off. OK?'

Fergus sighed in anticipation. 'You're the boss.'

'That's the way I like it.' Fingers snipped, pressed and smoothed. 'There you are. Get yourself decent. I heard the surgery door go. First one's arrived. Mrs Sinclair's Persian, the bad tempered one, according to the appointments list.'

'Another of life's little pleasures,' Fergus said resignedly, stepping carefully into his jeans.

Kate woke up with the awful out-of-kilter feeling that daytime sleeping always gave her to find the doorbell trilling.

Running her hands through her dark hair in an attempt to make it presentable, she scrambled off the bed and hurried downstairs to open the front door.

'Here we are!' Maggie said brightly. She was wearing her best coat, but it was buttoned up wrongly and bunched under her chin. Her hands were on the handle of a pram. Recognition hit Kate savagely. It was Lucy's pram. Could it be? How could it be? Hadn't Fergus put it up in the loft? But there it was, an achingly familiar pale blue Mothercare model, its raised hood towards her.

A fist clenched agonizingly round Kate's heart and she thought for a moment she was going to collapse. Then the pressure relaxed, and her heart began to race as the evidence of her eyes penetrated to her befuddled brain, into which the stupendous explanation of what she was seeing suddenly exploded.

She had been dreaming. The thought bubbled through her mind like yeast, spreading ecstatic lightness. That was it! She had been dreaming. The whole nightmare of Lucy's death she thought she had been living through had taken place in her sleeping brain.

Relief so dazzling that it seemed to illuminate the world flooded through her as she stepped eagerly down on to the drive and round to stand by Maggie so that she could look into the pram.

The sleeping child had Lucy's fair hair and the cherubic look

25

common to all sleeping children, but she was not Lucy. Nor was it Lucy's pram, Kate now realized. The pattern inside the hood was different, and she had never seen the blankets and pillow before.

The dazzling brightness drained from the world. Kate rounded on Maggie, and saw that the smile that had been on her face when she so brightly announced herself on the doorstep was fading and turning into an expression of worried bewilderment as she looked from Kate's agonized, accusing face to the sleeping child.

'What have you done?' Kate said, scarcely able to get the words out, so devastated was she by the awful contrast between what she had for one glorious moment believed, and what she now had to accept as true all over again. Then, as the full horror of it galvanized her, she seized Maggie by the shoulders and shook her, almost shouting the repeated words, 'What have you done now?'

The 'now' with its suggestion of blame for Lucy's death was cruel, but Kate wanted to hurt. Maggie was like a rag doll in her grip, still looking down into the pram.

'It's not her. It's not her,' she was saying, her words indistinct and running into each other. She went on repeating them as though they were a mantra that would make everything come right.

Kate looked round wildly. All she could think of was hiding what Maggie had done. She took the handle of the pram and carefully negotiated the step into the hall with the sleeping child. Maggie was still sagging on the drive, muttering agitatedly to herself. Kate went out again and grabbed her by the arm.

'Stop that!' she said harshly. 'Pull yourself together. We both know it isn't Lucy. You don't have to keep on saying it. Are you mad to have done this? Aren't things bad enough without you making them worse?'

Maggie was whimpering as Kate closed the front door behind her. Kate was afraid of the violence she could feel threatening inside herself. She swallowed down the dangerous mix of anger and despair, and with forced gentleness ushered Maggie into

26

the sitting-room.

'Sit down,' she told her, pushing Maggie onto the settee. She was a nasty grey colour, and her eyes looked funny. Brandy, Kate thought, before she passes out altogether and nothing can be got out of her.

'What are we going to do?' Maggie whispered once the glass was in her hand, its contents shaking and slopping over her coat.

'You're going to drink that first.' Kate tilted the glass in the right direction, and watched as Maggie sipped cautiously, then, as the drink hit the spot, took a more greedy gulp.

Was the child all right? Fear leapt in Kate's mind and she hurried out into the hall. She reached into the pram and laid the back of her hand against the baby's cheek. The mouth pursed primly and gently unfolded again. The cheek was warm. Oh, Lucy, she yearned, her eyes closing against the ache that filled her chest.

Back in the sitting-room she sat down at a safe distance from Maggie.

'Tell me exactly what happened.'

A nerve was jumping near the corner of Maggie's mouth. 'I – I can't remember. I can't remember where she came from.'

'She didn't "come" from anywhere,' Kate said sharply. 'You took her from somewhere. Where, Maggie? Her mother must be desperate. Don't you realize that?' She saw panic rising in Maggie and with an effort controlled herself. 'Start with earlier this morning. You went out – and you haven't been out for weeks. What made you do it?'

'I wish I hadn't,' Maggie said shakily. 'I wish I'd just stayed there and gone to sleep and never wakened up. It would have solved everything.'

'Look, Maggie,' Kate cut in, 'There'll be time to deal with how you feel later. But right now I must know what happened.' The implication of what Maggie had said hit her suddenly. 'Why should you go to sleep and not wake up? What had you done, Maggie?'

'Taken too many pills. Oh, not to try and do away with

myself. I just wish I had, now. I felt really bad this morning, and I'd got a splitting headache. I felt worse when I saw you and Fergus go off.'

'Why on earth didn't you tell us?'

'How could you make me feel better?' Maggie said with deadly simplicity. 'I tried to work it off around the house – but it didn't work, and I got into a muddle with the pills.'

'How many?' Kate fired at her. 'How many did you take?'

Maggie frowned and shook with the effort of remembering. 'Three lots, I think.'

Kate's voice rose. 'A one-a-day prescription, and you took three in one morning?'

'Four, I think,' Maggie said fearfully. 'I thought the last lot were aspirins, but they weren't. I just felt a bit unsteady, but suddenly I felt that I could go out . . . so I did, only. . . .' Her voice dried up and she stared down into her glass.

'Go on. Where did you go?' Kate prompted.

'I don't know. I really don't. It all started to go . . . woolly. The next thing I really remember is stopping to look at the ducks.'

'On Minster Pool? So you'd been in town?'

'I don't know. I was by Stowe. And I had the pram, then.' She looked at Kate and her face crumpled. 'I felt so happy, Kate. For the first time in so many weeks. I must have gone round the pool like I used to do, because I was on the far side going towards town. I'd forgotten what it was like to feel happy. . . .'

'There's a mother somewhere who's forgotten that too,' Kate said as gently as she could. 'Maggie, if you can't remember where you found the baby, there's going to be no alternative to ringing the police.' She saw horror flicker over Maggie's face. 'No point in panicking about it. We've got to get that child back to its mother. What time did you leave the cottage?'

'It must have been after two, because I'd been expecting you back.'

Kate looked at her watch. 'It's turned five now. That means the baby could have been missing for anything up to two and a half hours. Oh, God, Maggie. The police are going to be involved by now anyway, aren't they?' She got up and went out to the pram again, crouching to look in the shopping tray under it. If by some miracle there should be something with an address on it, it might be possible to take the child back to its home without getting mixed up with the police. Apart from a plastic carrier bag containing a couple of Pampers, the tray was empty. But in any case, the idea was a non-starter. Police all over town would be on the lookout.

The baby's legs jerked, lifting the yellow rug with its scattering of rabbits, and Kate saw that a thin supermarket bag was tucked down the bottom of the pram. When she opened it to look inside the smell of roast ham rose from it.

Ham. Maggie. Suppose Maggie had, in spite of her confusion, remembered that ham should have featured in her lunch hour and gone into the shop to get some for herself. Suppose the mother had been careless enough of her child's safety to leave the pram outside the shop? There was a slim chance that that could be where Maggie had walked off with it.

She went back into the sitting-room. Maggie was still sitting where she had been put, but now her eyes were shut.

'You can't sleep now,' Kate said, holding out the packet. 'Did you buy this?'

Maggie's eyes flew open. 'What is it?' She looked at the packet as though it would bite her.

'Did you go into the supermarket? Come on, wake up and think, Maggie.'

'I was going to have ham for lunch. . . .'

'I know you were. I was getting it. It's in your fridge. I was late. The point is, did you think I'd forgotten and got some yourself?'

Maggie's lip began to tremble and her hands plucked at her coat. It was clear that she didn't have much idea what she had done in the vital time between leaving home and finding herself standing near the pool.

'Your purse!' Kate said, suddenly realizing that Maggie must have had one with her if she had indeed bought the ham. 'Feel

29

in your pocket.' Then, as Maggie went on staring at her bemusedly, 'Oh – let me!'

The purse was there. Inside it was an itemized supermarket
receipt with the day's date on it.

Kate went over to the phone and began to dial the number
on the till receipt.

'What are you doing?' Maggie asked fearfully.

'Ringing the shop to see if that's where you found the baby.
I've got to do it, Maggie '

'I know that.' It was the nearest to normal she had sounded,
but she was alarmingly pale.

'They'll know you were ill. They'll know you'd never have
done anything like that if you hadn't been mixed up after taking
those tablets.' Kate suddenly realized as she spoke that she had
given Maggie brandy on top of a triple dose of tranquillizers.
She dropped the phone and darted over to remove the glass,
thankful to see that it was still almost as full as when she had
put it in Maggie's shaking hands. 'Better not drink this now
you're feeling better,' she said, hoping she sounded less alarmed
than she felt. 'You don't want to make yourself any more mixed
up than you already are.'

Maggie's eyes swam with sudden tears. 'Am I going mad,
Kate?'

Kate had a frantic urge to shout *No, but you're tipping me
over the edge.* 'No. Not mad at all. Just more poorly than any of
us realized.' Then, as Maggie attempted to grab her hand, she
pulled away. 'I'm sorry, Maggie. I've just got to sort this out
before I deal with you.'

She dialled the number again, and it was answered immediately by a male voice stating the shop's name, then adding, 'Can
I help you?'

'This might seem an odd thing to ask,' she began hesitantly,
'But has anything worrying happened in the store this afternoon?'

The line went dead for a second, then a different voice,
calm and yet distinctly authoritative, said, 'Who is speaking?'

Kate knew she had been put on to the police, even as she
asked, 'Are you the manager?'

'He's out of the office at the moment. What can I do for you?'

Maggie's eyes were on her, full of fear and pleading. Kate turned half-away so that she didn't have to look at her. 'You're the police, aren't you?'

'Have you some reason to expect the police to be answering this phone? Is there something you want to tell me, dear?' She could picture what kind of man he was from the voice in her ear. Plumpish, with his uniform buttons straining, a bit of a chauvinist with his patronizing 'dear', the kind who had seen it all before.

He was humouring her. 'How about beginning with your name?' he was saying persuasively. 'That seems a sensible place to start.'

'Callender. Kate Callender,' she said obediently.

'Like the place in Scotland?' She murmured assent. 'I took my dog to a vet called Callender the other day. There's a coincidence. Not a relative, I suppose?'

'My husband.' Kate swallowed. Now Fergus was in the picture too. If this man had been to the surgery, he most likely knew Fergus's Christian name or at least the initial. His colleague would be looking it up in a telephone directory right now, but they weren't in the directory, yet, so he wasn't being as clever as he thought.

'And you are?' she asked briefly, beginning to come round from her nervous paralysis.

'You can call me Bill.'

She hadn't the least desire to call him Bill.

'Now, there's absolutely no reason to be frightened,' he went on, professionally reassuring. 'Just tell me why you're calling, Kate. I know from what you said that you think something worrying may have happened here, and you think it may involve the police. But I can't help you unless you tell me what you have to do with all this, can I? Suppose you let me give you a bit of a start? Are you calling to say you've found something? Something very precious? I do hope you are. We all hope you are.'

'Yes.' Her mouth was dry and her voice came in a whisper. Then more loudly, 'Yes I am. The baby. She's here. She's safe.

Perfectly safe.' How garbled she must sound.

'That's very good. Exactly what all of us wanted to hear. Now, if you just tell me where you are, we can come round straight away and collect her. Put things right again.' Kate pictured the word being passed to the baby's mother. Oh, how she envied that mother, who could have things put right for her. 'We'll be there in no time at all if you just tell us where you're ringing from,' the persuasive voice was saying in her ear.

Kate had a momentary picture of the white car with its red and blue stripe, its flashing light and siren shattering the quietness of Gaia Lane. Then there would be questions. Endless questions, once the child was back with her mother and they had nothing more to gain by patience and tolerance. She swallowed hard.

'There was a reason for what happened,' she said defensively. 'I want you to realize that. It wasn't a deliberately criminal act. My mother-in-law is not a criminal.'

'Your mother-in-law?' His voice registered the involvement of someone else, but he didn't pursue it. 'I'm sure she isn't. And neither are you, dear. You're returning a child who was lost. Nothing criminal about that. Quite the reverse.'

'Please don't patronize me,' she said sharply. 'I'm not an idiot. I know this is a serious matter. I just want to be sure that you realize there was a reason for it.'

'Of course there was. If you just give me your address. . . ?'

He was right to be single-minded about tracking them down, she acknowledged. And even if he'd wanted her to, she doubted whether she could have embarked on a detailed explanation of their recent family history and its effect on all of them over the phone.

She told him where she was, and when he attempted to keep her talking while, no doubt, someone was dispatched at once to the address, she put the phone down on him.

'They're coming. And now I'm going to ring Fergus,' she told Maggie. Maggie gave a little squawking moan. Tears were sliding down her cheeks. Kate ignored her with a callousness born of her own desperation.

'Get me Fergus, please,' she said baldly when Zoe, the receptionist Kate had never taken to, picked up the phone.

'Ooh, Kate,' Zoe answered in a mock-worried voice, 'I don't know whether that's such a good idea. He's not in the best of moods, and he's got a man-eating moggy in the surgery.'

'Please get him out of the surgery – and at once!' Kate said loudly. Her sharpness had the desired effect, because the phone clattered down on the counter at the other end of the line, and after the briefest of pauses Fergus's voice said, 'What's up, Kate? Make it snappy. I've got an animal on the table.'

She could have screamed at him. The effort to stop the sound fighting its way up her throat was superhuman.

'You've got to come home,' she said. 'Your mother's in trouble.'

'So what's new about that?' Fergus said dismissively. 'Surely it's nothing that I can't deal with this evening in my leisure time.' The emphasis he put on 'leisure' was the last excruciating straw.

'She's stolen somebody's baby, and the police are coming any minute now. Probably to arrest her,' she said harshly.

'She's *what*?' Now she had his full attention. 'What are you trying to—'

'Fergus!' She cut ruthlessly into his questioning. 'Come home. Now!' And she slammed the phone down.

She was at the end of her tether. How much more was she going to be expected to deal with? There was a limit, and she had reached hers. She paced up and down so distractedly that Maggie emerged tentatively from her own little world of terror to ask if she was all right.

Kate gave a shrill laugh at the ridiculous question.

'Oh yes,' she said with hysterical sarcasm. 'I'm fine. Everything's lovely. My daughter's dead, you've stolen somebody else's, my husband thinks I'm for the funny farm, and God knows what the police have in store for us. But everything's fine.'

They stared at each other, both shocked by what she had said. 'You must hate me,' Maggie said shakily at last.

There was no time to answer. What answer would she have given, in any case? She didn't hate Maggie, but she certainly hated these happenings Maggie had triggered. A police car was drawing up in the drive outside the sitting-room window. No flashing light. No siren. But there, its threat implicit in the blue uniforms it contained. Kate shrank back, afraid that the baby's mother would be there too, and unable to bear seeing the result of Maggie's act on her face.

She felt resentment such as she had never experienced surge up in her as she went past the pram in the hall. The baby, as though infected by her anger started into wakefulness with an outraged cry. The sound seemed to magnify Kate's feelings.

She raged inside herself at a deity who was supposed to care for the least of his creations, but was so sublimely indifferent to the catastrophic tumbling into tragedy of her own life. She raged against the police who would come in with their notebooks and their questions and their laborious unknown proceedings. And she raged blindingly against Fergus whose answer to the insuperable problems in their lives from now on, if last night was anything to go by, was to solve them between the sheets.

Her anger was so violent that she was literally shaking as the doorbell rang. It was so hugely, crassly unfair that there should be this to cope with on top of everything else.

She heard the squeal of the Land-Rover's brakes, heard the door slam, heard Fergus's voice as he spoke to the policeman on the doorstep. And suddenly the solution leapt into her mind.

Walk out. Leave them to deal with the questions and answers now that she had brought them all together. It was simple, selfish, and supremely desirable, and she acted upon it instantly.

She grabbed her coat and went through to the kitchen at the rear of the house, waited a moment with the back door open, and when she heard Fergus's key in the front door lock, she silently let herself out.

The house had been built in the days of gracious living and there was a service path screened by a thick cotoneaster hedge from the main drive and anyone who might have waited in the police car.

Kate made her escape down the path and headed for town. Let them sort it out. Let someone else cope. She had had enough.

Chapter Three

Evensong was drawing to a close when Kate walked into the Cathedral. She sat at the back of the nave, waiting until the end of the service when she could go to the point near the Lady Chapel that drew her like a magnet each time she entered the building. The choir was singing Purcell's *Hear My Prayer*, the boys' pure voices floating up to the vaulted roof, ethereal and heartbreaking. High up there at the intersection of the nave and transepts, there were two powerful spotlights, piercing in the shadowy remoteness. They always seemed to Kate like the eyes of God staring down at her, weighing her in the balance, forcing her to judge herself.

She often came in here since Lucy's death. She had the commonly-held feeling – more of a hope than a conviction – that there might be 'something' beyond the concrete and visible. She supposed she must believe in God because she talked to him when she was here. It wasn't praying, though. More often than not, she didn't even speak politely. Since the monologue was in her head and he never did her the courtesy of making it a dialogue, her desperate accusations didn't offend anyone else. Here, as nowhere else, she was free to say what she wanted.

Now she stared up at the eyes and told them wearily that she had had enough. If the intention was to break her, then success was perilously close. She didn't think she could take much more.

Yes, I ran away, she directed defiantly upwards. And I don't care. I don't care how bad a time Fergus is having. I don't care how confused and upset Maggie is. I'm just relieved to be out of it all. There's nothing left in me to give to anyone else. It's all gone.

You care for lilies of the field and falling sparrows, but what about us? Where were you when Lucy needed watching? And when Maggie saw that baby outside the supermarket? Is the famous compassion only poured out on wildlife? If you really are pulling our strings, then its a *danse macabre* that we're being made to perform. And I'm so utterly weary of it.

The end of Evensong brought a general clearing of throats and gathering-up of shopping bags. An elderly lady two seats away caught Kate's eye and smiled. 'I always feel better for coming, however much I feel disinclined to turn out, don't you?' she said. Then she must have read Kate's expression, because she hurriedly added, 'Not always at once, of course, and sometimes in the most unconnected way.' Kate managed a smile, then hurried off down towards the transept and along into the south aisle to the Sleeping Children memorial.

She had always thought how lovely the sculpture of the two sleeping girls was, but since Lucy's death, the memorial had taken on special significance. Paradoxically it was easier to remember Lucy here than anywhere more closely connected with her brief life. Kate pictured her now in the hollow of the older girl's arm, turned inwards as was the child on the other side of her sister. She imagined Lucy's tender, translucent fingers reaching to touch the hand of the younger child. Perhaps it was a sense of Lucy not being alone that came to her when she was here. She was just grateful for any comfort, and gave herself up to it now, closing her eyes to the two children, replacing them with her mental image of three.

A hand cupped her elbow. 'Excuse me, but are you all right?' The verger was at her side, looking into her face with a mixture of diffidence and concern.

'Fine', she said, with false cheerfulness. 'Just daydreaming.'

'Sorry to disturb you, then, but I'm afraid the Cathedral is about to close.' He smiled and moved slowly on to round up a party of Japanese in the Lady Chapel. Kate took a few hesitant steps in the direction of the South Door, and then stopped, gripped by a feeling of utter hopelessness. She didn't know what to do next. It would be getting dark now, and trailing round town in the dark didn't appeal. But she didn't want to go back home. She had no idea how long it would take for the police to ask all their questions.

She felt in her pocket for a handkerchief. A crumpled piece of paper, pulled out at the same time, fell on the floor. Kate picked it up and smoothed it out. The name and telephone number on it were information for which she had searched high and low a couple of weeks ago. So that was where it had been, stuffed in her coat pocket. She had turned every drawer and cupboard in the office inside out, sure that she had put it somewhere safe.

She joined the huddle of people near the door, remembering the woman whose number it was. Jan Hambleton had come up to her when she was having a coffee in town one day, recognizing her as someone who worked in the Information Office. Jan wanted to explore the ways of advertising somewhere to let, she said, either on a long-term lodger basis or as part of the visitors' accommodation scheme. Kate had promised to let her have useful information, warning her that there were special requirements for official bed-and-breakfast hostesses.

'Requirements?' Jan had said with mock horror. 'I don't know that Brocklebank Farm is the sort of place that meets requirements. Mine, maybe, but official ones . . . hell's bells! I thought they would just say thanks very much and bung us in the brochure. Maybe I'll have second thoughts about that half of the idea.'

'I'll send you the details, anyway,' Kate told her. The fact that she hadn't been able to do so had plagued her conscience since then.

She had liked Jan Hambleton, and could still picture her – a cheerful, open-looking redhead with the rebellious kind of curly hair that springs from the scalp as though from an explosion. Jan had tried to tame it by tying a folded batik scarf round her head, twenties style. Her clothes – a long black skirt with an embroidered hem under a purple cape – owed nothing to fashion but a lot to originality. She had told Kate that she was 'an arty-farty type, always throwing pots or painting daubs and then stuck with the job of selling them, or drowning under a sea of clutter.' She said she travelled around quite a lot to different craft fairs. Since the house was isolated and her absence meant the hassle of getting someone to feed the various animal hangers-on, as she put it, she had begun to wonder if a willing lodger whose services were written into the tenancy agreement might be a good idea.

The verger who had spoken to Kate was standing holding the South door open, seeing people out. He gave her a special smile.

'Come again, and finish that daydream!'

'I expect I shall,' Kate told him. Outside in the Close a breeze was getting up. She turned up the collar of her coat, and headed towards the road, taking the long way round and still thinking of Jan Hambleton. She knew roughly where the woman's house was, because she and Fergus had looked at a property in that particular part of Hints when they were house-hunting, and been very tempted by it. Only the steep, difficult nature of the lane down from the A5 had put them off. Fergus had thought of being snowed in for winter night call-outs, of the impossibility of the area from Maggie's point of view with buses not exactly frequent and the hill an obstacle as time went on, and they had opted for the safer area behind the Cathedral.

It was lovely where Jan lived, though, Kate thought. Going down that lane was like entering another world, a quiet, safe, tucked-away world, with woods and grassy hills all round and the Bourne Brook bubbling away over the ford down in the valley. Unbidden, the voice of the elderly lady who had spoken to her at the close of Evensong floated into Kate's mind. 'Not always at once . . . and sometimes in the most unexpected way.' Kate found herself gripping the paper in her pocket.

No! She was being crazy. She had walked out of the house to get away from a particular situation that she found unbearable.

That situation must be well on its way to being resolved by now. She couldn't possibly be beginning to contemplate something so much more extreme than that brief act of protest, could she?

She walked on. The old lady's words, the paper in her pocket, and her deep sense of having reached the end of her tether worked remorselessly. Almost against her will, an idea was beginning to shape itself in her mind. Before she let it grow any more, there was something she had to find out. She could do that without committing herself. After that, she would see. When she came to a public telephone box she didn't hesitate. She went straight in and dialled the number on the scrap of paper.

When Fergus came back downstairs after going through every room in an attempt to find Kate, the police doctor was just finishing his examination of the baby in the hall.

'She's fine,' he said briefly. 'Better get her back to the station for her mother to check she's the right one.'

The policewoman who had been hovering in the sitting-room doorway took the child and put her back in the pram.

'Can't take her without this.'

'Then I hope you can collapse the thing. Damned if I can. All these levers. . . .'

'Men!' she said, reducing the pram to a carrycot and separate wheels in no time, and disappearing through the front door.

Fergus felt bemused and useless as he followed the doctor into the sitting-room where two plain-clothes officers were questioning Maggie. His life seemed to be getting completely out of hand. There were uniformed police outside the front and back doors, and two police cars as well as the doctor's car on the drive. The house didn't feel like home any more.

The older officer broke off and raised his eyebrows at Fergus. 'Any luck?'

'No. No sign of her anywhere. I can't think what she's up to. He sat down beside Maggie and put his hand on hers. 'I'm sorry, Mum. Kate had no right to leave you like this.'

'Can you blame her?' Maggie pulled her hand free from his and turned to the doctor. 'I suppose you all think I'm absolutely mad.'

'She's not!' Fergus jumped to his feet again. 'She's distressed. We all are at present.'

'Yes, we know about your daughter, Mr Callender,' the officer said calmly. 'It must have been a terrible time for all of you. We understand that. But the taking of a child, whatever the trigger, is a serious business and has to be fully investigated.'

Fergus subsided as far as the arm of the settee.

'What made you take this baby?' the detective asked Maggie.

'I wasn't meaning to take someone else's baby. The pram . . . it's just like Lucy's.'

'I can show you – it's in the loft,' Fergus interjected anxiously.

'Mr Callender – we'll be a lot quicker if you just let us get on without interruption. All right?' The officer turned patiently to Maggie again.

'But the baby in the pram, surely she can't have looked like Lucy?'

Maggie shook her head tiredly. 'No. But I didn't realize that at first. I was in a muddle, you see. I'd got the doctor's tablets – tranquillizers – mixed up with my aspirins. I'd felt really bad earlier in the day.'

'Perhaps your son could collect all your medication for the doctor to look at? You know where it is?' the officer asked Fergus.

Fergus nodded and left the room. When he came back the three men were looking with some sympathy at Maggie, whose head had fallen back against the settee. Her eyes were closed and she looked very pale.

The doctor looked at the two bottles then handed the aspirins back to Fergus. 'Mrs Callender—' He touched Maggie gently on the shoulder and she startled awake again. 'Can you remember how many of the doctor's tablets you took this morning?'

She rubbed her eyes. 'One when I got up like I always do.'

She looked embarrassed. 'Then another one mid-morning on purpose because I felt so bad. Then when the headache didn't stop, I thought I was taking aspirins, but I made another stupid mistake and took two of those.' She pointed to the bottle in his hand.

'So you'd had four of these things before going out?' The doctor turned to the officer. 'I'm surprised she was still on her feet. This is high-strength medication.'

The officer nodded. 'Mrs Callender, there was quite a gap between the child going missing and your daughter-in-law getting in touch with the shop the baby was taken from. Can you remember what you did in that time?'

'It's all so confused . . . I walked round Minster Pool. I can remember doing that. I used to take Lucy round there. I thought I was still pushing Lucy in her pram. . . .' Her voice dried in her throat, and it was obviously an effort for her to go on. 'I think I sat on a seat for a while. Maybe I had a little sleep.' Her face became very distressed at the picture she had created of the defenceless child in the pram, the nearby water, and her sleeping, heedless self. 'Oh, God knows what might have happened!'

'Let's stick to what actually did happen,' Mrs Callender. No point in distressing yourself with what might have been. The child's safely back with its mother by now.' He turned to Fergus. 'I think we can leave it there for the moment, Mr Callender. We shall need to speak to your wife when she turns up, then we'll be in touch when the reports are completed.'

'What's going to happen?' Fergus asked.

'All the circumstances will be taken into account. I should get your own GP to have a look at your mother. And we shall need a psychiatrist's report. Proper medical supervision will obviously be important.'

Fergus saw them out, then came back in and dialled her own doctor who promised to come straight round.

'Don't worry,' Fergus told his mother. 'I got the distinct impression that nothing bad would happen to you.'

Maggie startled him by saying passionately, 'I hope he sends me away. Locks me up somewhere. I couldn't bear anything else.'

The unaccustomed feeling of helplessness welled up in Fergus again. 'I'll – I'll make you some tea,' he said inadequately.

Kate let herself into the dark, empty house. She was chilled to the bone after sitting on a seat by Stowe Pool for the past couple of hours, trying to work out what she should do. She turned up the heating and dragged a chair close to the radiator, too numb even to turn the lights on.

Time passed, her head full of milling thoughts.

At last she heard his car coming up the drive. She got to her feet, and stood staring towards the hall, waiting as the car door slammed, then his key turned in the lock.

He was furious, not surprisingly, she saw when he came to a halt in the open doorway.

'Fergus,' she said, 'We've got to talk.'

'I've been saying that for weeks, with precious little response from you.'

'I know you have. But it's only now that I know what I want to say.'

He was in no mood to listen. 'Well it can wait. I haven't eaten since midday. I don't suppose your glooming around in the dark has produced anything as useful as a meal?' Full of aggressive indignation, he stalked off in the direction of the kitchen.

Kate followed him, removing her coat and dropping it on the hall chest on the way. She found him standing helplessly beside the table, the momentum that had brought him into the kitchen spent. She could see that he was absolutely exhausted.

'Sit down,' she said, pulling a chair out. For the first time in months she felt stronger than Fergus, and the feeling was good. 'I'll do us soup and an omelette. There's apple pie left from last night. It won't take long.' She put rolls in the oven to crisp, opened tins, cracked eggs into a bowl, then sat down opposite him.

'Only a few minutes now. Do you want to tell me what happened?' His hand was clutching the edge of the table as though he needed to hang on to something. She reached out towards it, but he drew it away sharply.

'Do you really want to know? I thought you couldn't get away from it all quickly enough.' The anger in his eyes accused her, but she refused to be made the guilty one.

'Of course I want to know. I felt then like I imagine you feel now, Fergus. It wasn't that I didn't care. I just couldn't take any more.'

The soup was bubbling up in the pan. She got up, filled his bowl and put it on the table, then hesitated. 'I'd better take some round for Maggie. She must be as exhausted as you are.'

Fergus had started to eat at once. He paused long enough to say baldly, 'She isn't there.'

Kate sat down slowly, staring at him. 'Are you saying the police took her into custody? Surely not.'

He shook his head. 'The police were decent enough. They were concerned that she didn't seem to have anybody looking after her, of course. Finding her alone and distressed under the circumstances didn't help.'

Kate went over to light the gas for their omelette.

'I didn't leave Maggie alone,' she said, her back towards him. 'I waited until your key was in the lock, then I went out the back way.'

'They weren't to know that, were they?'

'I can't change what happened, Fergus.' She turned the gas off again, realizing that eating and this kind of talking didn't go together. 'I realize that I should have stayed and explained what I'd managed to drag out of Maggie. But she wasn't the only one to be distressed. She'd brought a pram just like Lucy's to the door, damn it! And a baby. . . .' There was a moment's silence while Kate swallowed hard to steady her voice. 'Where is she, if she's not with the police?'

'She's in hospital.'

'Hospital? Because of the pills?'

'No. She's gone into Ashfield.'

43

Kate's voice rose in shock. 'But that's for—'

'Head cases, largely. I know.'

'But Maggie isn't mad. She was mega-confused today, yes, but only because she'd taken too many pills. Why did they make her go there?'

'They didn't. She wanted to go. And it's run as a sort of convalescent place as well as somewhere for the treatment of nervous illnesses. In any case, she was adamant about it. She couldn't get there quickly enough.' Fergus pushed his soup bowl away, still half-full. 'They checked the baby first, of course.'

'They didn't bring the mother with them, then? I couldn't bear the thought of that.'

'No, thank God. It was bad enough feeling like a child molester in front of the police, never mind the poor kid's mother. Once the baby'd gone, the doctor started on Maggie. He got her to tell him as much as she could remember. There was a chunk of the day that she'd lost completely.'

'Did she tell him about her tablets? She took too many. That was why the whole business happened.'

'She did. I had to go and get everything she's taking. The police said she'd have to be assessed by a psychiatrist.' Fergus looked despairingly at Kate. 'Imagine my mother, my sane, sensible mother, being turned inside out by some shrink who doesn't know her from Adam. I just can't believe all this is happening. I got her own doctor out to have a look at her as soon as the police had gone. She was the one who was adamant that she wanted to go away. Nothing Bill Terry or I could say would dissuade her. He said that what she had done with a cocktail of mind-blowing pills inside her wasn't anything to rejoice about, but neither was it anything that called for instant locking-up. He didn't pull any punches on the financial side, either. He told her his practice wouldn't fund unnecessary hospital care. She'd have to go into a private clinic if she wanted to escape from the world, and she'd have to pay her own fees.'

'How on earth can she afford that?'

'Apparently Dad took out some kind of insurance thing for her in the days when the fees were manageable and they'd kept it up ever since. I had no idea. What do I know about anything these days? What really gets me, you know' – he tossed the end of roll he had been turning over as he spoke into his rejected soup, and swore as splashes leapt on to the table – 'What really gets me is that after all we've done, all the running to and fro and consoling when we damn well needed consoling ourselves – after all that, my mother should have been so eager to get away from us. I can't for the life of me understand that. Can you?'

'Oh yes,' Kate said with conviction. 'Yes. I can understand it.'

'Then explain it to me.'

Carefully, her mind told her. Carefully, he's so hurt. And you're going to hurt him even more. Keep to Maggie. Explain Maggie first.

'I think she's been so sad for us that she hasn't been able to cope with her own sadness. It's as though she hadn't the right to cry when she wanted to cry, because we were always around watching her, and treading carefully so that we didn't upset her. We've all been damping down our own feelings because of each other, Fergus. Only the feelings don't go away, do they? They turn on us, each one of us individually. Maggie's have been putting chains round her. Being with us has kept them there. She must have realized that.'

He shifted irritably in his chair. 'You sound like a ruddy psychiatrist yourself.'

'You did ask.'

'Sorry. I know I did.' Elbows on the table, he propped his chin on cupped hands and blew out a sigh of frustration. 'If you've understood so clearly, why didn't you try to make my mother understand before she got into such a mess?'

'But it wasn't clear to me. I was in too much of a mess myself. It wasn't until I walked out this afternoon and went along and sat in the cathedral that I began to see what the answer might be.'

'You really think she'll get better away from us?'

Knowing what else she wanted to go on and say, Kate chose her words carefully. 'I don't think she had much chance of improving as long as we struggled on as we were.'

He was silent for a moment, gazing into space, then his eyes focused on her. 'And if we turn all that round, does it mean that without her, we'll stand more of a chance too?'

She looked steadily back at him, calling on all her resolve. 'No, Fergus. I don't think it does.'

He questioned the logic of her words, their real meaning not quite sinking in. 'I don't see why not. If we've been affected by the same stifling thing as Mum, surely we'll be better away from her just as she's likely to be better away from us, according to you.'

'But we wouldn't be away from each other, would we?'

He stared at her, still not understanding. 'Why should we want to be? We've got the same problem. We've no need to hide anything from each other.'

'The same problem, yes. But not the same way of dealing with it, the same rate of coming to terms with it.'

'I know that. You can't accuse me of not understanding that.'

'I don't. But the fact that I'm continually aware of needing your understanding doesn't help me to deal with what's inside me. I'm too conscious of what I'm doing to you to get to grips with what's wrong with me.'

Fergus gave an explosive sigh. 'You're losing me, Kate. All this psychobabble goes through my head like a puff of smoke. I'm not clear just what it is you're saying to me.'

Kate took a quivering gulp of air. 'All right, Fergus, I'm saying that I need to get away for a while.'

'A holiday?' His race brightened. 'Why didn't you say so? There's no reason why we shouldn't get away now that Mum's being taken care of. And I've got another ten days to take before the year ends. We could go skiing . . . or we could go to the other extreme and fly off to the sun somewhere. Yes . . . I think that's a really good idea. Got anything in mind? It seems so long since we looked forward to anything.'

Kate looked at him desperately. 'I wasn't meaning a holiday, Fergus.' There was no easy way to put it. It had to come straight and hard. 'I didn't mean that I wanted us to go away. I – I meant that I needed to get away. By myself.' Then, to make cruelly sure that this time he understood, 'I need to get away from you.'

He had looked tired before, but now she watched the little colour he had drain from his face.

'You can't be serious.'

'I am.'

'You can't mean you want to leave me?'

'I'm sorry, but I do. For a little while.' Tension tugged at every nerve. She blindly picked up a tea towel and started drying the already dry dishes that had been standing in the drainer by the sink since breakfast time, hardly realizing what she was doing.

Fergus leapt to his feet and snatched the tea towel from her, pulling the plate she was wiping out of her hand so that it smashed on the tiles at their feet.

'Leave it!' he shouted. 'At least have the decency to tell me that you want to walk out on me without half your mind on the bloody washing-up.'

'I didn't say I wanted to walk out for good.'

'People never do, do they? But how many trial separations do you know that end in someone coming back?'

'I'm not even thinking of it as a trial separation. I can't explain it any better than I've already tried to do, Fergus. I just feel I need to deal with myself before I can deal with us. That's all.'

He kicked a chair out of his way and went to lean on the wall by the door, staring at her with burning hostility.

'What is it with you? There's nothing unique about you. Lucy was my baby too. Do you think you're the only one to feel completely gutted that she's gone? Why should your feelings be the ones to put us in this hell of a mess?'

'I don't know. I just don't know. But nothing's right, and I've got to give myself – no, give us – the chance to find out why.

We've reached rock bottom, Fergus. We've got to find some way up.'

'And what if your way up isn't my way? What if these fictitious heights you're aiming for don't happen to be the ones I'm standing on?'

'We're not really together now, are we, Fergus? Not as we ought to be. You know that.'

'But how can you imagine that putting distance between us will bring us closer?' He strode across the kitchen, shards of broken plate crunching under his feet, and gripped her shoulders, his face urgent with need to make her take back her threat of leaving. 'Don't do it, Kate! Please don't do it.' His voice broke on the last words, and he pulled her to him, rubbing his face into her hair as though he could change her mind by the strength of his physical hold on her.

For a moment Kate let herself sag into the familiar arms, her head against his chest, his heart thudding in her ear. She felt the pain she was inflicting on him, felt too the pain in herself, but if her heart might be softening, her mind was firm.

'I've got to do it,' she said. 'It's the one thing I feel certain about.' She reached up and touched his face. 'I do love you, Fergus. It's just that I can't cope with loving you at present. I wish you could understand.'

He drew furiously away from her. 'Do you know what you make me feel like? People who bring their animals to me to be put down do just what you've done – sign the death warrant and tell Rex they love him. That's what you make me feel like. A dog on the point of being put down.'

'A touch over-dramatic, Fergus,' she said drily. 'Let's keep a grip on reality. All I want to do is have a bit of time on my own to sort myself out. I don't have any lethal injection for you in mind.'

He got out the dustpan and brush and crouched down to sweep up the broken plate. Kate stood looking down on his wiry dark head, infinitely sorry for him, but just as sorry for herself.

'Shall I do that omelette?' she asked tentatively.

'Stuff your omelette,' Fergus said ungraciously.

He tipped the bits of china in the bin and then stood looking at her, his eyes cold now, the threat of tears gone. 'Might I ask where you plan to look for somewhere to stay during this retreat you fancy?'

'I've already got somewhere.'

'Before you even discussed it with me? Where?'

She put the bowl of eggs away in the fridge. 'I'd rather not say. I'm sorry, Fergus. I just want to be sure I really do get time on my own. I don't want you storming over every two minutes. I'll keep in touch, and if there's an emergency you can always get me at the Information Centre. I shall obviously still be coming in to do my job there.'

He was white with anger. 'You've worked it all out, haven't you.'

'No further than that.'

'I don't suppose you've given a thought to how I'm going to manage. Who's going to take messages?'

'You can leave the answerphone on.'

'And am I expected to cook and clean and wash in my spare time?'

'You're not exactly helpless. You didn't allow yourself to starve as a student. In any case, you can get Jean to come over and see to the house. She's already mentioned that she could do with a bit more cleaning work than the hours she does at the surgery.'

'Anything else you've worked out? What about a stand-in for sex? Given any thought to that?'

Kate didn't look at him. 'That's your province, Fergus.' Then she turned and left the kitchen to go upstairs.

Before she had reached the top, Fergus was racing after her.

'That was a rotten thing to say. I'm sorry.' He snatched at her arm and pulled her round to face him. 'Don't do this. Please don't do it. I can't bear to be walked out on like this. What have I done?'

'Absolutely nothing but your level best. But even your best's not working. The fault's in me, Fergus. Not you. I love you, but

I can't – I simply can't bear the thought of making love with you. How do you think I feel about that? It hurts being with you – in our house, in our bed, and feeling like I do.'

She gently detached herself and went on into the bedroom. Her case, packed as soon as she came in from the cathedral, was lying on the bed.

Fergus rushed past her to go and stand in front of it. 'I'm begging you,' he said.

Hearts can break, Kate thought desperately. Her heart felt to be so full of conflicting emotions that it must surely burst. 'There's no point in going on like this, tearing at each other,' she said shakily. 'I had meant to leave in the morning, but I think it would be better for both of us if I went tonight.'

Fergus snatched the case up and backed against the wall trapping it behind him. 'I won't let you. I can't let you do this.'

'I'll just go without the case, Fergus.'

At the end of her strength, Kate turned and walked downstairs. She was buttoning her coat in the hall when Fergus came down, carrying the case.

'I'm wasting my time, aren't I?' he said, his voice drained of all passion.

'Yes.'

'If I could just know where you'll be? I'm begging you, Kate.' She couldn't bear to look at what she was doing to him, but she couldn't change her mind.

'I'm not going far, but it has to be my place. I told you, I shall be at the Information Centre,' she repeated wearily. 'I'm not disappearing off the face of the earth.'

'You're disappearing from my earth. That's what matters.'

He refused to let her take her case, following her out to the car, throwing trivial questions at her until the very last minute as though he could bind her to him with a chain of words.

'What are we going to tell people?'

'Nothing. Why should we? What need can there be to talk to anyone about it? We haven't had a social life for months.'

'Jean will talk.'

'Get her to come on my Information Centre days. That'll

take care of my absence. Now, leave it, Fergus.'

She switched on the car engine, and as she began to reverse round the Land-Rover, she heard his last agonized shout of reproach: 'You're the one doing the leaving. . . .'

All the way through town she felt to be straining to get away from the painful bonds of home, but once on the main road she lowered her window and let the night breeze dry the tears on her face. She was almost ashamed to find after a while that it was also bringing her the first faint dawning of a sense of freedom.

Chapter Four

Maggie wondered if she would manage to sleep at all. Added to the mess of a life that had sent her to Ashfield, there was the uneasiness of being in a strange place, and the dehumanizing sensation of having nothing she really wanted in the way of personal possessions. Fergus had done his best to assemble the things he thought she would need but it was an odd collection he had put together. She was wearing a horrible nightdress she never wore but couldn't quite bring herself to throw away, a present once from her mother-in-law, and the clean flannel Fergus had got out of the linen cupboard was an old one that had last been used by her husband. It was rather comforting, though, to think that it had washed Donald's face. The sad thing was that she couldn't always bring into her mind a picture of the face she had loved so much, but the feel of him stayed clear.

They had been very kind to her here. When they found she had not even had lunch, they had made sure that instead of the light sandwich supper chosen by most of the patients, she was brought plaice and duchesse potatoes, with green beans, nicely cooked, and a trifle to follow that had fresh – well, frozen, she supposed – raspberries in it.

Later, a doctor had come to speak to her. She presumed that he was a psychiatrist, because he had asked her several non-medical type questions that had offended her a little. Did she know what day it was? Who was the current Prime Minister? What was her date of birth? Then he had read her expression, and smiled, saying that she was obviously in no difficulty with that type of question. He would leave the more specific ones until tomorrow when she had had a night's rest.

He told her that he was unwilling for her to have anything to help her to sleep in view of the uncertain amount of medication she had taken earlier in the day, but he would make sure that a milk drink was brought in to her before she was ready to settle down.

She had had her milk drink now, and the nice little nurse had tucked her up in a way that made it seem their ages were reversed.

Light filtered into her room through the reeded glass in the half-moon pane over the top of the door. It was a pleasant room in an impersonal kind of way. Everything had been chosen to match everything else. Even the flower prints could have been taken straight off the curtain material. She had her own bathroom, which was a relief. So far she hadn't needed to set a foot outside her door.

She had heard the woman next door crying earlier on, great racking sobs, punctuated by a placating male voice, probably her husband, who was obviously trying his best to make her feel better. Maggie wondered what the tears were about. Was it something worse than having a precious grandchild die when she was in your care? Was it something that made you feel more guilty than taking someone else's baby? And yet she couldn't cry. She had never cried since Lucy's death. All the tears seemed to have seeped into her chest and frozen into a solid, painful mass there. Perhaps the ice had spread into her head, and was partly responsible for today.

She would have to talk about it tomorrow, she supposed, when that quite nice doctor said he would be seeing her again. But talking wouldn't change anything. Lucy would still have gone. They would all still feel devastated by her loss. And she would still feel herself in danger of going mad.

If only she didn't have to talk to anyone ever again. It would be lovely if she could just stay here, in this room, and not see anyone except the motherly little nurse, who spoke in kind clichés with no undertones.

There had been trouble in the room on the other side of her too. Female shouting, and male aggrieved responses. Not that she could make out the words – or had any desire to do so. But the tone was quite enough to indicate the type of conversation. She would have to be careful at visiting times. She didn't want her business reaching the ears of other people in the corridor. She didn't like the thought of visitors at all, come to that. How shameful not to want to see your own son and daughter-in-law. But she didn't. Kate, obviously sick to the back teeth of her, had walked out on her, so perhaps she wouldn't even consider coming to visit. But Fergus would turn up, she supposed.

She felt disturbed at having yet another thing to feel guilty about, and sat up restlessly. She turned round to switch on the bed light, and saw that there was a framed notice of some kind over her head. She reached for her glasses and knelt up on the pillow to read it.

It wasn't a notice, it was a poem by Susan Coolidge, whose name rang a bell. She frowned, then suddenly remembered. *What Katy Did*. Surely someone called Coolidge had written that. It had been one of her favourite girls' books, years ago. She read the poem.

It was brief, only seven lines. She read it twice, and its last line several times more. It was the kind of poem that would be described as 'uplifting' – the kind of poem Marmee from another of her old favourites, *Little Women*, might have favoured. Maggie wondered how many people had read it under stress, and in what different circumstances it had been seen as applicable or trashed as pious rubbish.

She took off her glasses and settled herself down again. She found the last words of the poem going round and round in her mind trying to brainwash her into believing them. 'Take heart with the day and begin again,' the poem ended bracingly. Good in theory. Not so easy in practice. All the same, she clung to the last two words and repeated them thoughtfully inside her head. You never knew. Beginning again might still be far off, but at least tonight she had put an end to a situation that was slowly driving her out of her mind.

The little nurse, on the first of her night-time rounds, opened the door carefully and shone a torch on the bed, then nodded with satisfaction and quietly went out again.

By the time Kate turned into the lane leading down to Jan Hambleton's house, her brief sensation of relief to be actually taking action had faded again. What if Jan couldn't take her in tonight? She had deliberately not stopped to ring her again, thinking that once she was on the doorstep it would be more difficult for Jan to turn her away. But now it was beginning to seem such an awful cheek to arrive out of the blue like this. What if Jan were out? She couldn't go back home with her tail between her legs and face Fergus again after such a show of determination. She would just have to find another bolthole for tonight.

She drove into a paved courtyard which had obviously once been a farmyard judging by the surrounding buildings illuminated by the sweep of the headlights. There was an outside light on in a porch, and light showed too round the curtains at the windows on either side of it. So Jan was either in, or out and pretending to be in.

Kate switched off the engine and went over to the door. Nobody had looked out when her car turned into the yard, but as she drew near she heard country and western music loud enough to drown any car engine, and someone enthusiastically singing along with it, slightly off key. The singing stopped when she knocked and the volume of the music was turned down.

'Who is it?' a voice, recognizably Jan's, called.

Kate's legs almost gave way with relief. 'Kate Callender. I phoned you earlier.'

'Good Lord! Hang on a minute.' There were sounds of a chain being struggled with and a reluctant key turned, then the door was flung open and Jan was smiling on the doorstep.

'Well! Now you've surprised me twice in one day. Come on in. Sorry about the stink in here. It's food for the hens cooking. Sit down while I take it off the Aga and put it outside the door. That'll get rid of the worst of the pong.'

Kate sat down at the scrubbed-top table, glad of a few moments to pull herself together. She watched Jan manoeuvre the huge pan outside the door. She was wearing blue dungarees over a navy and white striped shirt, and her fiery hair was held back by a rubber band.

'Now, let me pour us both a cup of coffee – it's just made,' she said, coming back inside 'Then you can tell me what brings you out here at this ungodly hour.'

'I know it's late. I hope I didn't alarm you, turning up like this after you'd locked up for the night.'

'You mean the chain and barricades? They're just my anti-burglar device.' She put a mug in front of Kate. 'Sugar? No? Have a shortbread, then. For once I didn't burn them.'

'Just the coffee, thanks.' Kate sipped her coffee, feeling unutterably tired, then realized that Jan was looking at her quizzically, and now, as their eyes met, raising her eyebrows even further. 'Sorry,' she said. 'You want to know why I'm here. Well, I wondered if you could let me move in tonight instead of tomorrow morning. Things have got a bit complicated.'

'You look as though they have. In fact, you look as though "complicated" is a bit of an understatement. What is it? Husband been playing away?'

'No, nothing like that.'

'You, then? Been caught out?' Then, seeing that her direct-ness was taking Kate's breath away, Jan grinned. 'Sorry. If you don't want to talk about it, you don't have to. Take no notice of me. I was born nosy. My friends tell me that if I were a cat I wouldn't last five minutes. I'm quite used to being told to shut up.'

'You deserve an explanation, having me turn up at this time of night, but I'd rather not try to give it just now, if you'll forgive me. I'm absolutely whacked. It's been like ten bad days rolled into one. I just want to blot it out.'

'That bad, eh? Right. No more questions. Let's get down to basics. It's fine for you to take over the house tonight. It's presentable. Just the bed to make up, and that won't take a minute.'

'Oh! I'm so grateful!' Hot on the heels of the flood of relief that went through Kate came a delayed reaction to what Jan had said. 'House? Did you say "house"? I thought it was a room in this house that was on offer.'

'No, it's a separate building. This place used to be a dairy farm and we kept all the properties that went with it. The fields we rent out to a chap across the river for his sheep. Does it matter that you're not going to be in with us? You're not nervous about being in a place on your own?'

'I can't think of anything I'd like more at the moment,' Kate said with feeling. 'No, I just hadn't understood that it was a whole house I'd be moving into.'

'Not exactly a palace! It's part of a barn conversion. One up, one down plus kitchen and bathroom.'

'You're not asking enough rent, you know. Separate accommodation's worth much more than an en suite bedroom.'

'Wait until you find out all the jobs I'm going to lumber you with before you say that. I told you when we first talked that services rendered would be involved, didn't I? But I won't let you in for details of all that tonight.'

A grey and white cat pushed through the cat flap, tensed and inspected Kate, then jumped up on the chair next to her and sat staring at her.

'Meet Quaker,' Jan said. 'Brainless, but harmless. Loves anyone who feeds him. I hope you're not allergic, because feeding him from time to time when I'm away could be one of the jobs I wasn't going to mention.'

'Not at all. I like cats.' Kate reached out and tickled Quaker under the chin. Quaker allowed the liberty, eyes blissfully closed. Kate drew back her hand, remembering Middy, her own cat, to whom she had not given a thought until now. Fergus would feed him, wouldn't he? He was a vet. He wasn't going to neglect an animal under his own roof. She drove thoughts of Middy out of her mind. 'Whereabouts is the cottage – or whatever you call it – in relation to here?'

'Barn Crest . . . and it's just one field away. There's a track leading to it just after the big group of trees I told you to look out for before our place. In fact, you can see the lights in the houses from this doorway.'

'Houses? There's more than one, then?'

'Yes. Three actually. The other half of the conversion, Barn Close, belongs to my brother. He's only here odd weekends. A girl's living in the separate cottage at present. Rather a mistake of mine. I was a bit of a mutt to take her in, I think. She's a one-off type, doesn't seem to live in the real world. It was the baby that persuaded me. I keep telling myself that the not-so-fond mother isn't the kind to hang around for long. There's no need to be alarmed about her. She's just hippy, not malevolent. More coffee?'

Kate smothered a yawn. 'Sorry. Your lovely Aga's making me sleepy. No more coffee, thanks.'

Jan got up suddenly. 'You look exhausted. I'll take you over. Have you much luggage?'

'Just an overnight bag. I'll collect my stuff tomorrow.'

'Good. I saw you came by car, but it'll be better to walk over now and leave driving down the track until daylight. There are bags of potholes, I'm afraid. I'll just get the torch. She paused. 'I don't suppose you brought any supplies – food, I mean?'

Kate shook her head. 'No time to think of anything. It doesn't matter. I can shop tomorrow.'

'Then just come over here for breakfast in the morning. Any time after seven, and it doesn't matter how late. I'm not out until afternoon.'

Kate felt a surge of emotion rise up in her. 'You're so kind . . .' she managed to say.

'Bollocks!' Jan said cheerfully. 'The devil's concubine, my brother calls me. And my husband walked out after ten years. Let's be having you!' She gave Kate's arm a squeeze as she propelled her out into the yard.

Fergus surfaced to the buzz of the alarm clock from the half-night's sleep he had eventually fallen into. He turned his head slowly, hoping to see that Kate had changed her mind and crept back into their bed, but there was only a hurtful empty expanse. He thumped her pillow, then buried his head in it, smelling the faint sweetness of the shampoo she used on the cold cotton.

He couldn't believe this was happening. Maybe Kate was having some sort of breakdown. He didn't wish that on her, but it would at least be a more satisfactory explanation of this hellish situation than her calm insistence last night that leaving him was for the best.

He felt knackered. And he was on early surgery this morning. The thought of a sequence of difficult animals and their sometimes more difficult owners had never had less appeal.

Where the hell was Kate? He couldn't bear the fact that she had not only gone off, but off into the blue. How could she do it? What had happened to that warm sense of excitement and sheer privilege they had once shared? How could she inflict on him the torture of not knowing where she was in the world?

Mechanically, he went and showered then dressed and headed for the kitchen, leaving the bed unmade and the bathroom awash. To hell with it.

Last night's attempt at a meal was still around in the kitchen, soup plates streaked with congealed cream of tomato, bread gone hard as nails, butter looking suspiciously as though the bloody cat had been at it. It was Kate's cat, that black fiend leering at him from its basket.

'She's dumped you, too, sneak thief!' Fergus said, giving the basket a vicious shove with his foot, then instantly regretting it and tipping half of a tin of Middy's favourite cat food into the empty dish on the floor. Middy squatted tight in his basket, resentment in both ears, refusing to be bought with anything as mundane as tinned food.

There was only one crusty slice of toasting wholewheat in the bread bin, a reminder to Fergus that there would be shopping to see to as well as everything else. He hated shopping. And when on earth was he going to have time to do it? He didn't want people seeing him trailing round the supermarket getting meals for one. He would have to give up an afternoon off and go over to Tamworth or somewhere where there wasn't likely to be anyone he knew snooping.

Then there would be the washing. He had noticed that there was only one pair of clean pants in the drawer. A fat lot Kate cared about whether he could dress decently. You'd think if she had thought about this business as seriously as she claimed to have done, she would have managed to fit in a bit of washing and stocking up of the kitchen cupboards.

His one piece of toast was quietly going up in smoke, he realized. It was beyond redemption. He felt sick with hopelessness, but the hopelessness came from his inability to cope with the turn his life had taken. It had nothing to do with the loss of a piece of toast. He didn't want anything to eat, anyway. Zoe would make him a coffee when he got to the surgery. He looked in the mirror in the hall as he shrugged his duffel coat on and tried to arrange his face into a more normal, non-devastated expression. It didn't work.

Kate had spent a restless early part of the night, the momentous nature of what she had done in leaving Fergus reaching out of the darkness and whipping her into fits of panic. What had seemed at the time so necessary and right took on quite different proportions in the small hours. Could she really have walked out of her home and away from the husband she loved? She did love Fergus. That was what made her behaviour so hard to justify in the dead of night. She tossed and turned in the strange bed, wondering if Fergus was sleeping or if he was lying awake cursing her for what she had done.

There were strange sounds from the valley below. The hoot of an owl from time to time and the cry of a vixen – she could put a name to those. But there were also sudden outbursts of something that sounded like fear or pain from night-roving creatures she couldn't identify. It seemed to her over-heated mind that death and destruction were all around her in the darkness.

She fell asleep eventually, having last looked at her watch at a quarter to three. When she surfaced again sunlight was reaching into her bedroom round the edges of the curtains. It was almost nine o'clock.

She felt calmer after her sleep. Everything seemed more possible in daylight. She threw back the duvet and, putting on her dressing gown, went on a tour of this house she had landed herself with, and which she had just not taken in at all last night.

The bedroom was quite spacious, and light and cheerful with its limed oak furniture and green and white colour scheme. The stairs came up into the corner of the bedroom, and a door opposite the top of them led into the bathroom. She went in to use the loo, and looked around. There was both bath and shower, and plenty of room to do more than swing a cat.

Middy. Had Frergus fed him? Guilt stabbed, then was followed by exasperation. Could she really be worrying about leaving a cat when she had at the same time left a husband? Determinedly putting both out of her mind, Kate went down the stairs and looked around at her living-room. It was quite a stylish room, with two comfortable looking settees; one at right-angles to the stone fireplace, the other facing the hearth. There was a wood-burning stove, not lit, but the room was warm, so Jan must have switched on the central heating last night.

Kate went through into the kitchen at the back of the house. Since it was shining in at the front of the house now, the sun would finish the day at the window over the sink, but even without it, the room was cheerful with its yellow walls. She unlocked the door and opened it, going out in bare feet past the pile of logs against the house wall on to the sloping lawn, startling a rabbit which scuttled back into the trees beyond the fence. From somewhere further down there was the sound of a water fowl beating its wings against the water, and if she listened hard, Kate could hear the quiet burbling of the river itself.

She stood there for a few moments, curling her toes in the grass, smelling the greenery all around, too numb to fully believe that this, for the time being, was her place. Then her bare feet began to protest. It was, after all, late October, not the height of summer. She went indoors and perched on a stool in the kitchen, making a list of what she needed to pick up from home – there was another stab of guilt at the word – before turning up for her afternoon shift at the Information Centre.

The house already looked like a thing deserted. Kate surveyed the kitchen, remembering last night and picturing, from the depressing evidence before her eyes, Fergus's morning. From habit, she cleared the table and put the dirty dishes to soak in the sink before going upstairs. The bedroom reproached her in the same way as the kitchen had. She looked at the bed . . . their bed, now Fergus's bed, and for the millionth time wondered how it was that a place of such closeness and love should have become for her a chasm across which Fergus was no longer able to reach her. She straightened her drooping shoulders. That was what she was giving herself time to find out, wasn't it?

The phone rang and she first stretched out a hand towards it, then told herself that it was no longer her place to do that. It rang on and on. So Fergus hadn't remembered to switch the answerphone on. There was a lot that Fergus was going to have to remember to do, she thought, as she went into the wreck of the bathroom and began to tidy up in there. She stopped half-way through the job, realizing that he was perhaps going to resent what she was doing, see it as a criticism of him instead of the helpful gesture she had intended it to be. Suddenly the house seemed an alien place, and herself a trespasser. She flung the things she had come to collect into a case and hurried out to the car with it.

Last night, at the time of leaving, she had really not looked beyond the need to get away. She was beginning to realize now that it was much more complicated than that. Home changed with rejection. It was no longer hers to do as she pleased in. Perhaps Fergus, soured by resentment of her behaviour, would become a different Fergus. Maybe she herself would change, and not in the way she wanted to. The change could be in some unknown direction instead of turning her back into the Kate she had once been. What if there should be no going back?

Thoroughly depressed by her line of thought, Kate forced herself to drive to the supermarket and concentrate on less complicated matters. Whatever the outcome of this impulsive move she had made, she was going to have to eat and wash dishes, clothes and herself. She must hang on to the little things until she was more able to face the big ones.

'Isn't that your husband?' Marianne, Kate's fellow worker at the Information Centre asked towards the end of the after-noon. No one had been into the Centre in the past half hour, and Marianne was looking idly out of the window. With a sinking feeling in the pit of her stomach, Kate went over to join her, and saw that it was indeed Fergus.

He was standing opposite the Centre, staring blankly across the street, but as soon as he saw her he came to life with a jolt and beckoned agitatedly.

'Go on,' Marianne said with a grin. 'The master calls. Don't keep him waiting. We're not exactly rushed off our feet in here.' She looked at her watch. 'About break time, actually. I'll nip upstairs and put the kettle on. You could even invite him in for a cup of tea.'

'Can't think why he didn't just come in,' Kate said untruthfully. 'I won't be a minute, Marianne. I'll be back straight away if I see a rush of customers.'

She hurried across the street, shivering in the cold air. It had been a deliberate decision not to put her coat on. She didn't want to look as though she was willing to spend much time with Fergus.

'Why are you doing this?' she asked abruptly when she was face to face with him, stiff with awkwardness at the situation, and aware that Marianne was probably still casting an eye in their direction.

'Don't be angry. I had an idea.' He opened the carrier bag he was holding, revealing a box containing a mobile phone. 'Please take it, Kate. I can't bear for it not to be possible to get in touch with you. I've programmed its number into the phone at home, and into my own mobile. That way you don't have to tell me a number that you're afraid I might be able to trace. Please, Kate.'

Kate swallowed hard. Under the circumstances, it seemed such a humble, generous gesture. And yet she resented it. But how could she refuse? She took the bag.

'All right. I'll take it. But I'd rather you—'

He cut in. 'You'd rather I didn't ring you at all. I know that. I'll try not to. I just want to feel that I could reach you if I really needed to.'

'All right. All right.' She touched his arm briefly, not knowing whether she wanted to weep at his self-abasement, or turn away resentfully from what she sensed was a way of intruding on her need for separateness. But even as she made the gesture, his tone changed.

'I expect you're thinking what a spineless sod I am.' His face was flushing an angry red, and Kate wondered if he had been drinking.

'Have you had some lunch?' she asked.

'Yes. Most of it liquid, before the interrogation starts.' He seized her wrist and pushed his face towards hers. 'And do you want to know why? It's because I've been thinking all morning that if I'd filled myself with a bit of dutch courage the night before last I'd have forced you to go on with what we started in bed and you'd be coming home where you belong tonight.'

A woman passing by, fortunately a complete stranger, who had been looking absently at them as she passed suddenly averted her eyes and Kate knew that she had heard enough to be intrigued. 'You're shouting, Fergus. And you're talking nonsense. Calm down. You can't force someone to make love. Whatever you might have achieved, it wouldn't have been love.'

'Damned if I'd care!' He flung her wrist away from him, then with another swift change of mood he said, 'I hurt, Kate. That's what makes me talk like this. Not just the couple of pints I've had.'

'I know,' she said. They looked at each other for a moment, beyond words. A gust of wind swirled past them, and Kate shivered and rubbed her arms.

'Go in. You'll catch cold,' Fergus told her tiredly. 'Just . . . just don't get lost.'

Kate shook her head, unable to speak, then turned and hurried back into the Centre.

'All right?' Marianne called from the back room, emerging with a mug of tea for Kate.

'Yes. He just wanted me to see the mobile phone he's bought me.' It was a true, if incomplete explanation. She hoped it would satisfy Marianne.

'And he couldn't wait until you came home! Sweet!' Marianne said.

Kate had been wondering all afternoon how to get round the difficulty of the occasions when Marianne needed to ring her at home, either for information, or to let her know about a change of working shift. The phone solved the problem for her.

'Actually, I'm not going to be at home much for a few days,' she said, blending invention with truth. 'That's why Fergus has got the mobile for me. An elderly friend has just come out of hospital after a hip replacement, so I said I would stay with her until she was more able to care for herself. She's not on the phone, so you'd better have the number of this mobile thing in case you need to get in touch.'

They just had time to sort out the number for Marianne to put in the staff book before a small cluster of visitors came straggling in, and Kate was thankfully able to spend the rest of the afternoon on business that made demands neither on her emotions nor on her powers of invention.

Chapter Five

Maggie sat in the waiting area outside Dr Lawson's consulting-room, thankful that no one else was around. She felt apprehensive about this third meeting with him. The second, two days ago, on the morning after she arrived at Ashfield, had left her exhausted by a storm of weeping that had incapacitated her by its violence and unexpectedness. After the months of arid, aching grief when she would have given anything to be able to shout and weep out the pain she felt, she was humili-ated to have gone to pieces in front of a stranger. He had been very kind, passing her tissues, sitting quietly waiting for her to compose herself, then, when it became obvious that this wasn't going to happen, leaving her to cry herself out alone in his office, and make her way back to her own room when she felt able. She hoped that a pattern for future meetings had not been established, and felt embarrassed as well as nervous.

The door opened and Dr Lawson invited her in. Maggie thought again how young everyone seemed. He was not much older than Fergus, a tall, rangy man with a craggy face and the most penetrating blue eyes she had ever seen, eyes that were looking assessingly at her across his desk.

'How are you, Mrs Callender?'

'More in control of myself, I hope. I must apologize for last time, Dr Lawson. I'm not like that as a rule. I never cry.'

He smiled, brushing away her apology. 'You obviously needed to do so then. Tears have a purpose. Don't underestimate it. How's the tremor? Hold your hands out for me.'

66

Maggie's outstretched hands quivered under his gaze.

'Better than they were, I think,' he went on. 'How do you feel to be settling down here?'

'Very well, thank you.' How little that meant. It was like the meaningless courtesy of the head waiter's check on meal satisfaction in a restaurant.

'How are the new tablets suiting you? Any unwanted side effects?'

Maggie grimaced. 'It would be hard to sort out which were side effects and which the weirdnesses of my general behaviour at the moment – but no, I haven't noticed anything in particular. I still hate having to take mind-blowing drugs.'

'Would you resent having a plaster cast on a broken arm?'

'Of course not, but—'

'Well, then. QED.' He leaned back in his chair, hands clasped on the desk, eyes never leaving her own. 'Today I want to talk about the time before you moved here. When exactly did you come down to Lichfield?'

'Almost a year ago. My husband had died a year before that, and Fergus and Kate were moving south. They suggested that I should move with them. The house they wanted had a separate place that would do for me.'

'And were you happy to exchange the house you had presumably chosen to live in for something that "would do for you"?'

Maggie's colour heightened. 'I thought hard about it. Donald had gone. Fergus was going. And he and Kate were expecting the baby. Lucy.' She had had to steel herself to say the name. 'It didn't seem that there was much left for me up in the north.'

'No other children? No close relatives in the area?'

'We only had Fergus. And I had no brothers and sisters, so my family's gone now. Donald's family is up in Scotland. They are all farming folk, too, so we couldn't see much of them.'

'What kind of marriage would you say you had?'

'The best kind,' Maggie said firmly. 'Donald was a lovely man. I couldn't have asked for better.'

'And Fergus?'

'Never gave us cause for worry. Quite the opposite. All the

way through school and university we had every reason to be proud of him. And he never grew too smart for his parents.'

Dr Lawson raised his eyebrows. 'That's quite an idyllic picture you paint.' He paused, tapping his fingers together thoughtfully. 'And yet I understand that you don't wish to see this son of whom you are so proud. Why do you think that is?'

Maggie stiffened. 'Is nothing thought of as my own private business?'

'Everything you do has a bearing on my assessment of your particular case,' he answered, unruffled. 'You asked your son to bring in some personal possessions that you required, and when he handed them over at Reception and was asked if he wished to go along and see you, he told the receptionist that you had specifically said that he should not visit at present. I am interested to know why you should have felt you had to do that.'

'I can't think why you need to ask. Things are not easy between us after what happened. I can imagine how Fergus feels about me after what I did, and as for me, I can hardly bear to look him in the eye.'

'Why do you say "after what I did"? Fergus's child was a victim of cot death. Nothing you did makes you responsible for that, nor would anyone else – had they been in your place that night – have been held responsible.'

Maggie's hands flew out in a wild gesture. 'I know. I know what I am supposed to think. But that has no bearing on the way I feel, Dr Lawson.'

'Very well. Let's move on to your daughter-in-law. Kate. You and your husband and Fergus – all getting on so well together. Did you feel in any way that she was responsible for breaking up such a happy family unit?'

'Not for a moment!' There was no mistaking the sincerity of Maggie's answer. 'Douglas and I would have loved more children. When Kate came along we couldn't have loved her more if she had been our own daughter.'

There was a pause. 'And have you heard from her since you came to Ashfield?' Dr Lawson asked, the question, so gently put, piercing Maggie's mind with all the deadliness of a rapier.

'No, as I suppose you well know.' Her voice shook ominously.

'And if she had tried to contact you, would you have told Kate to stay away from you too?'

'I think so.'

'But would it have been more satisfactory to have had the opportunity of taking the initiative yourself?'

'How can you talk of "satisfactory" in circumstances like these?'

'Perhaps the word was badly chosen. So . . . let's review the situation. Here we have a family, rich in mutual love and respect, further enhanced by the addition of a daughter-in-law who could not be better chosen. A happy, integrated family. Why should such a family when faced with a situation which admittedly is one of the most painful possible, be split apart by the tragedy instead of finding mutual support and comfort in each other? Why should such a thing happen?'

Maggie leapt to her feet. 'And why should you be ferreting around in a perfectly normal family to find some nasty behind-the-scenes cause for what has happened? I thought you were here to provide the answers, not ask endless offensive questions.'

She stormed out of his office, ignoring the secretary's kindly 'Are you all right, Mrs Callender?' and headed blindly for the door that opened into the gardens. Outside, she kept going until she was as far away from the hospital building as possible, at the extreme limit of the grounds. Fortunately, because her legs felt as though they would give way, there was a seat, hidden in a recess of the boundary hedge, and Maggie sat down, heedless of the chill in the air.

What was happening to her? She never cried, and the last time she saw Dr Lawson she had practically set the man awash with her tears. She never lost her temper, and today she had shouted at him, and – worse – walked out on him. She had always prided herself on her patience and ability to cope. Where was either of those qualities now? The next meeting didn't bear thinking about. She had thought Ashfield would solve all her problems, but instead it seemed to be bringing them to the boil.

Fergus aimed a vicious kick at the washing machine. Through its glass eye he could see the load of pants, shirts and towels which had been assorted colours when he put it in last night. On his way to bed, while the infernal machine was only part-way through its cycle, his eye had been caught by swirling garments of a uniform rose pink. He had yanked the plug out of its socket, thinking that he might be able to remove the load and attempt to find out what was happening to it, but the door of the machine remained as firmly sealed as if it were the vault of the Bank of England.

Once the initial bewilderment had worn off, he had realized that it might have been wiser to wash the brightly coloured items separately. His fury was increased by the realization that it was the red T-shirt of Kate's that had ruined practically every item of washable clothing he possessed. When he did his first load of washing – successfully – he had left things belonging to Kate in the laundry basket. Why should he clear away any mess she had left behind her? But then, in the depths of his misery, he had caught himself pulling out her nightdress to bury his face in the scent of her, and her silk blouse to feel its softness against his skin, and he had told himself not to be so pitiful. Get the reminders of her wiped out and hidden away before he went completely to pieces. A fat lot of good that had done him. He was either going to have to go around dressed like a pervert, or spend a fortune replacing what had gone into the wash as perfectly good clothes.

This morning brought no solution to the problem of getting into the washing machine. The poncey-looking load, topped by pink water and a layer of disgusting pink foam, huddled dankly in the bottom of the drum. Somewhere in the house there must be an instruction book, but Fergus hadn't the least idea where to start looking for it. He would have to ask one of the women at work, he supposed, but that meant having to explain Kate's absence. How on earth he could do that, he hadn't the faintest idea. He couldn't say she had gone away for a bit of a break, because she was going to be there in the Information Centre for everyone to see three half-days a week. Life seemed to be becoming one long series of problems.

Then he remembered the mobile phone. If Kate had the thing switched on, there would be no need to let anyone else know that he was clueless with washing machines or – infinitely worse – that his marriage was teetering on the edge.

Kate answered at the first ring. 'Hello?' Her voice sounded cautious.

'I hardly dared hope you would have the thing switched on,' Fergus said.

'I arranged with Marianne to be available from eight to half past each morning in case she needs me to fill in for her. What do you want, Fergus?'

'You needn't sound so ungracious. I'm not ringing up just to say hello.'

'Then please say what you want to say.'

Fergus stifled the urge to shout 'Come home!' with all his might. 'I've got a problem with the washing machine.'

Kate made a disgusted sound. 'Then get a man in.'

'Not that kind of problem. It hasn't broken down. I stopped it in mid-programme to get something out, but I can't open the door.'

'Just as well. What on earth do you think would happen to all the water if you did?'

Fergus had started the conversation very much on the wrong foot, but now he felt even more of a fool. It had never occurred to him that if he had had his way, he would have dyed the kitchen floor pink as well as most of his wardrobe.

'Why did you suddenly want to get something out of the machine anyway?' Kate asked.

'If you must know, because I'd put something the wrong colour in and I wanted to stop it doing too much damage. It was something of yours, actually,' he added, trying to shift the blame.

'The red T-shirt. And now everything's ruined.'

Fergus could remember the time when something like this –

man against domesticity – would have sent Kate into fits of laughter, but now she sounded midway between angry and depressed.

'How was I to know?' he said belligerently.

'If you'd done your own washing at university instead of running home to mother every weekend you'd have more of an idea how to toss a few clothes into the machine.'

'Just put it on the list under "hopeless in bed" and feel even more justified in settling into your bolthole, then,' he said coldly.

Kate sighed. 'I wasn't implying anything like that.'

'You don't need to. It's there between us, like a ruddy brick wall.'

'Which I want to be able to knock down. You know that.'

'Do I? Would you know it if our positions were reversed and I'd left you?'

There was silence for a moment.

'There's nothing to be gained by starting that sort of discussion,' Kate said at last. 'This is what you have to do as far as the washing machine's concerned: plug it in, then push in the knob with all the programme letters on it and turn it round until the 'I' is opposite the mark, then pull it out again. That will empty the tub and spin the washing. When the spin's finished, you'll be able to take out the load. Have you got that?'

'Yes. Then what? Is there anything I can do to turn things white again?'

'You can try bleach – read the instructions on the bottle. But it won't work with everything.'

'Thank you. Sorry to have troubled you,' Fergus said stiffly. 'I would have asked someone else, but that would have meant explaining your being away, and how could I do that when you're still working in town?'

'As far as that goes, I've told Marianne that I'm staying with a friend who's had a hip operation until she's more sure of herself.'

'How ingenious. I hadn't been clever enough to think up something as credible as that, either.'

'Fergus' – Kate paused for a long moment. 'I do love you, you know.'

'Do you? Somehow that sounds as much like an insult as anything.' Fergus said, and put the phone down.

Mid-morning, Kate was still unsettled by Fergus's phone call. If today had been one of her work days, she would have put the spiky conversation behind her, but a whole day of no fixed activity stretched ahead of her. All the time in the world to brood.

She had done all there was to be done in the way of house-work, and since it was impossible to wander round the shops in the centre of Lichfield without being constantly on the alert for Fergus, shopping held no appeal. She decided to try and walk off her frustration. So far she had only driven to and fro along the bumpy track leading to her temporary home, but there was a 'public footpath' sign pointing in this direction where the track left the road, so presumably the right of way went further than the three properties.

She opened the door and went out into a brilliant Indian Summer day.

No one had as yet put in an appearance in the adjoining half of the converted barn, and Kate had not yet seen the third cottage. It was hidden by a screen of elder and hawthorn further along the track.

It turned out to be a straightforward farm worker's cottage with no trace of old-world prettiness about it. The hippy type Jan had talked about obviously had very little interest in where she lived. The curtain at one window drooped messily, coming adrift from its rail. There were unwashed empty milk bottles outside the door, and a brimming dustbin bag spilled its contents near the gate, with lazy end-of-season wasps hovering around it.

Noisy music was coming from somewhere, Radio One by the sound of it. The current piece came to an end as Kate drew level with the end of the cottage, and in the momentary silence before the forced matiness of the DJ took over, she realized that the music had been masking another sound, the crying of a baby.

It stopped Kate in her tracks. She hadn't really heard a baby crying for so long. Feelings she thought she had got under control welled up, their attack as ferocious as the crying that prompted them. With an effort, she controlled herself and began walking again until she saw the pram. It was pushed over against the hedge at the side of the cottage, an old-fashioned hard-bodied type of pram, the kind you never see nowadays, that looked as though it had served a succession of families. It was rocking to and fro with the force of the baby's anger, and furiously pedalling legs in a blue babygrow pummelled the air. A cover lay on the ground, presumably kicked off. Kate hesitated, instinct telling her to go and pick up the cover, inclination urging her to distance herself from this child whose cry aroused memories she couldn't bear. She told herself that it was nothing to do with her, that the day was warm and the child would come to no harm without its blanket, that the mother would be sure to hear her child now the music had stopped.

She walked on, and the sound gradually faded away, muffled by the trees and eventually cut off completely by the contours of the land.

The crying baby had taken the glow out of the day. What was she doing, Kate asked herself, hiding in the outskirts of Lichfield, away from Fergus, but not far enough away, pretending to be doing something about herself and her problems, but in reality just marking time, achieving nothing. She had kidded herself that she was taking a dramatic step to resolve the situation between her and Fergus, but if she were honest, all she was doing was turning her back on it.

The path came to a halt at the water's edge. She could see it continuing on the far side, but the stepping stones that would take her over were below water after the heavy rain there had been for the past two days, and her trainers were not the sort of thing to get her over with dry feet.

She sat on the stump of a tree, staring into the water. Turning her back was getting to be quite a way of life. She had done it again just now with the baby at the cottage. What was happening to her? She of all people should be the first to rush to protect a child. Her own experience over the past months ought to have made her sensitive to signs of danger. And yet she had looked at the neglected state of the cottage, heard the ignored distress of a child, and walked away.

Shame and anger fought in her. Shame for her own feeble avoiding of a situation she would rather not be involved in, and anger that circumstances had dropped her squarely into it. It was anger that got the upper hold as she made her way back, walking first into earshot of the still-crying child, then through the gate past the stinking bin bags to bang on the cottage door.

The radio was at full volume, but her hammering was loud enough and different enough a sound to be heard by anyone who was in or around the cottage. Suppose the child's mother had left it alone, though, while she went along to the farm, or even further?

Kate tried the handle, but the door didn't give. She braced her knee against it and shoved hard in case it was merely sticking, but this time she could feel the grip of the old-fashioned lock.

She shaded her eyes and peered through the window. The inside of the cottage was not much better than the outside had suggested. The sink was full of dirty dishes. The lid of the pedal bin was held upright by the rubbish piled in it, which seemed to consist largely of used nappies. Baby clothes waiting to be washed spilled over from the table to the floor, and a blowfly was buzzing round a half-full tin of minced beef with a spoon in it.

Kate thought of the tender care that had surrounded Lucy for every moment of her brief life. The baby alarm alerting them to her slightest murmur, the mysteries of bottle sterilizing they had religiously mastered, the wipes, the creams, the lotions that had taken over the bathroom, the way her own day had centred on Lucy's needs. And yet Lucy was dead, while this child survived apparent neglect and obvious lack of hygiene. Where was the fairness, the justice in that?

She went over to the pram and looked down on the child, a girl of around ten months at a guess, with dark curly hair damp with tears or sweat from the fury of her crying. Her eyes were screwed tight in a contorted red face, and the crying had reached the stage when involuntary shudders punctuated every sob.

Kate reached into the pram and touched the hot cheek. 'Hey . . .' she said softly. 'What's all this about?'

Eyes that were vivid blue flew open and the shock of seeing a strange face momentarily stopped the sobbing, but not the distressed intakes of breath that made the child's lips quiver against the pearly white of four front teeth.

'Don't cry. I'm here.' Kate lifted the child, and as her arms cradled the little body, it was as though every particle of herself was imprinted with the sense of Lucy, who leapt from her memory and became warm, living flesh again. 'I'm here, I'm here . . .' she repeated, not knowing if it was to the living or the dead child that she spoke. Her hand of its own accord eased the hot little head into the hollow of her neck, and still murmuring soft reassurance she walked round to the back of the cottage, hardly knowing what she was doing.

She was brought to an abrupt halt as she rounded the corner of the cottage.

A girl was sprawled on a piece of carpet in the long unmown grass, her skirt pulled up to her crotch, her shirt unbuttoned so that the sun played on tanned flesh and grubby underwear. Her eyes were closed, but she was not asleep. One hand held a half smoked cigarette, the other tapped on her midriff in time to the blaring of the radio that sat just inside the open window.

The child in Kate's arms writhed and reached for her mother, becoming in that instant herself and not a ghost child.

'Your baby was crying,' Kate said harshly, anger once again ousting any tenderness the child had aroused in her.

'So what's new?' the girl said, barely opening her eyes.

'She's been crying hard for the past half-hour.'

The girl sat up slowly. 'You been timing her or what?' Her

gaze sharpened. 'You from the Social?'

'No. Passing by. Here. She wants to go to you.' Kate lowered the wriggling baby on to the girl's lap. The girl didn't even put her cigarette down, just held the baby with one arm and took a slow, insolent drag, then puffed a cloud of smoke towards Kate's face.

'It's something they do, you know, babies,' she said. 'Cry. You get used to it. This one cried non-stop for the first three months. At least I get a good night's sleep now.'

Kate controlled herself with difficulty. 'There's crying and crying. This sounded like the kind you do something about.'

The girl snorted. 'There speaks one of the nannied class. If you're stuck on your own with a kid you take every break you can get.' The baby began to whimper again, and the girl stubbed out her cigarette on the grass with a rough, 'Oh, shut it, Rosie!' Then she balanced the baby on her knees while she undid her bra and latched the child on to a breast that was as brown as the rest of her. For the first time she grinned up at Kate. 'Can't get her to drop this. She gags at everything else. Saves on the milk bill, I suppose.'

Kate thought of the foul milk bottles. The child probably had an instinct for survival. 'How old is she?'

'Nine months. Four more years to when she's at school – roll on the day.'

A sweeping sense of unfairness overwhelmed Kate again. 'You're lucky to have her.'

The girl gave a snort of scepticism. 'More like I'd have been lucky if I'd not had her. Or lucky if her beloved father had pitched in and done his bit instead of swanning off the minute he knew I was up the spout. Men! You can keep 'em.'

'He can be made to help financially.'

'Made to help financially!' the girl mocked. 'The bugger hasn't got any finance. He was sponging off me while we were together. He's probably doing the same with some other dumb woman. You can't take nothing from nothing.' She smoothed Rosie's hair back with a hand that was not ungentle. 'You from around here or what?'

'Next door. I'm renting the far half of the barn.'

'That mean you'll be poking your nose in regularly, then?'

'What a pity there's no one else around to teach Rosie some manners,' Kate said, turning on her heel.

The girl jumped up and darted round in front of her, the baby still determinedly anchored. 'Don't go off in a strop. It's only my way of speaking. It's lonely out here. Not the place to fall out with the neighbours. Besides, I could do to borrow a bit of bread. I've run out. It's more for Rosie than me,' she added craftily.

'Does that mean you'll be on the scrounge all the time?' Kate asked with deliberate mocking sarcasm.

The girl yelped with laughter. 'You'll do! You're not as stuffy as you try to make out. What's your name?'

'Kate. And yours?'

'Lynne. How about the bread, now we're introduced? I can walk on with you.'

Kate eyed the still feeding Rosie. 'Not like that, you can't. I'll bring you half a loaf back. Wholemeal. It's all I've got.' Her eyes rested on the baby. 'She's lovely. Make the most of her.'

'What other option have I? Thanks for the bread, anyway.' Kate couldn't suppress a smile at the girl's in-your-face attitude. There was something almost refreshing about it after so many months with people who tripped over their own tactfulness.

Maggie had a crystal-clear idea of how she intended this next session with Dr Lawson to go. No more tears. No more disgraceful loss of temper. She would show him how wrong he was to imply that there was some hidden agenda in the family. She would be her calm, normal, steady self. She breathed deeply as she walked through the door into his room. Calm. She was calm.

Dr Lawson was finishing off his notes on the last patient. He smiled briefly. 'Give me a moment, Mrs Callender. Do sit down.'

Maggie looked at the crown of his lowered head as he added

a few more words. Thick, fair hair, with no sign of thinning or greying. Hair that sat smoothly and neatly, unlike Fergus's. Fergus had an awkward double crown and his wiry dark hair fought a constant battle of direction. She could almost feel it under her hand. Smoothing his unruly head had always been the last laughing exchange between them when he left for his daily cycle ride to school.

'What are you thinking?' Dr Lawson asked. He was looking at her with a quizzical expression. The last patient's file was in the tray and her own was open before him. She must have been in a bit of a trance.

'I was thinking that you couldn't be much older than my son.'

'Does that worry you?'

Maggie felt her calm begin to flutter. 'Why do you turn the most harmless observation into a significant statement?'

Her grinned at her. 'Comes with the job. You'll get used to it when you know me better.'

Maggie grimaced. 'Do you really think so? Back where I come from we don't ferret around in our feelings much. Too many real issues to deal with, I suppose. In a howling blizzard you have to dig the sheep out of the snowdrift, not go in for self-analysis.' There was a brief silence. Dr Lawson sat back in his chair, looking down at his hands. The tips of his fingers were spread, touching each other precisely, tapping rhythmically.

'I can see that . . .' he said slowly. 'But what also occurs to me is the incongruity between what you describe as natural behaviour to you, and your present situation.'

'Where's the difference? There's been the greatest of tragedies in our lives. We're coping with it as best we can.'

'That's what you really think?'

Maggie gripped the handkerchief she hadn't needed so far.

'What are you trying to get me to say?'

'Compare the two situations. Sheep need help. Despite the difficulties, the dangers, the appalling discomfort, you struggle through impossible weather to save them. Is that what you said?'

Maggie shifted impatiently in her chair. 'You know perfectly well that it is.'

'Very well. Now take your present situation. Your beloved grandchild dies. But you are here at Ashfield. You won't see your son. And it looks as though your daughter-in-law is apparently not showing the least desire to come and see you. Not exactly a strict parallel with the shepherd and his sheep, is it?'

Maggie could feel her face beginning to grow red. But she would not lose her cool this time. She would not let this overgrown schoolboy with his penetrating questions trigger off any more of the embarrassing behaviour he had so far managed to push her into. She would remain silent. Breathe deeply.

He leaned forward and repositioned his pen on her open file. 'The shepherd didn't stay put by his good coal fire, did he? And even worse, he didn't get into his four-track vehicle and disappear in a puff of smoke in the opposite direction.'

Maggie looked at him. 'Are you accusing me of running away?'

He shrugged. 'It's not my job to accuse.'

'But you think I've done just that. Run away?'

'Mrs Callender . . . I don't tell you what I think. I don't try to tell you what you are to think. I put different aspects of your situation to you as I see them, and I ask you to consider them and come to your own conclusions.'

'At the drop of a hat?'

'In your own good time.'

'Then I'll go and do just that.' Maggie half rose from her chair, but he made her subside again with a wave of his hand.

'I haven't quite finished. There's one more point I'd like to talk around this session. Is that all right?'

'Do I have any choice in the matter?'

He grinned. 'You seem to have got yourself out of my room fast enough on other occasions.'

She refused to smile back at him and just sat staring steadily at him.

'I'll take that as agreement,' he said equably. 'What I would like you to consider is exactly why you came to Ashfield.'

'Because I took someone else's baby.' She spaced the words out syllable by syllable as though speaking to an idiot.

'Mrs Callender, your own doctor told you that you were not mad – not even unbalanced enough for his practice to think it necessary to fund the shortest time in care.'

'I needed space to pull myself together.'

'You could have had space in a hotel or guest house. But you chose to come to Ashfield at considerable expense to yourself. I imagine you are normally thrifty, Mrs Callender. Why Ashfield?'

Maggie was silent.

'Could it be that deep down you know that something is not right in your life? Did you want to get away from the pain of the immediate situation? Or was it a little further back that you began to feel the need to escape – perhaps when you burned the boats of your previous life on the Borders? Or is it even further back than that? Did you perhaps begin to feel trapped in that idyllic marriage of yours?'

Maggie's hands were trembling violently. She could hardly force her voice from her throat and her cheeks were burning.

'That is the most ludicrously outrageous suggestion,' she said.

Dr Lawson sat back in his chair. 'Then why aren't you laughing at it?' he said.

Chapter Six

I'd defy anyone, Zoe thought, miracle worker or not, to keep their mind on clients' bills with this racket coming from Fergus's consulting-room. Fergus was responsible for most of the noise, with Mrs Stillman's feeble protests and the occasional pathetic yelp from her Peke providing a Greek Chorus effect.

'But she's such an appealing little face—' Mrs Stillman's apologetic voice was cut off by a muffled yelp from Su Lei and a bellow from Fergus. 'Don't hurt her!' Mrs Stillman's voice pleaded, an octave higher up the panic scale. 'It's so hard not to—'

' "Hard" is what this mess is that I'm having to hook out of Su Lei's rear,' Fergus said unpleasantly. Zoe blinked at the picture conjured up by his words. 'If you didn't persist in stuffing chocolate and God knows what rubbish in at the other end, it wouldn't be necessary to go through this pantomime every few weeks.'

Mrs Stillman now sounded to be dissolving into tears. 'I don't think you have any right to speak to me in that rude way. I'm a client, and a human being.'

'Then how about behaving like one to this overblown creature? She's twice the weight she should be. She's two, but she breathes like a decrepit twelve-year-old with a heart condition. I've told you the harm you're doing her until I'm blue in the face.'

Zoe had been scribbling on a message slip, and now she

walked purposefully over to the consulting-room door, rapped briskly on it and went in at once.

Mrs Stillman was hidden behind a tissue. Sue Lei, looking desperately unhappy, crouched panting on the examination table. Fergus turned his angry glare from Mrs Stillman to Zoe.

'Sorry to interrupt, Fergus,' she said brightly before he could snarl at her to get out, 'but there's an urgent telephone message you ought to see straight away. I'll hold it for you, shall I?' She angled the paper so that Mrs Stillman couldn't possibly see it.

'Go easy, Fergus,' she had written. 'The woman might have a heart condition.'

'I thought I'd better let you know straight away,' she said brightly. 'Anything you want me to do?' She was thankful to see that the wild look in Fergus's eyes, though still there, had at least not intensified – might have even faded a bit.

'No need for you to interrupt your own work,' he said curtly. 'I've just about finished here.' He was peeling off his disgusting gloves as he spoke. 'Anyone in the dispensary?' He dropped them in the bin, then turned towards the sink to wash his hands.

'No. I told Joan. she could go.'

'Then there is something you could do.' He dried his hands quickly and scribbled on a prescription pad. 'Get these for me, would you?' He glanced at Mrs Stillman. 'Something to help Su Lei over this current problem. And some ointment for you to apply.'

Zoe was relieved as she took the prescription and left the room to see Mrs Stillman managing a shaky smile.

When she came back from the dispensary with the ointment and envelope of pills for Sue Lei, Fergus was standing in the open doorway of the consulting-room speaking quite normally to Mrs Stillman.

'Thanks, Zoe' he said, taking the pills. 'Now, give her one of these every morning for the next five days, and *please*—'

'I know,' Mrs Stillman said, her chins wobbling as she firmed her mouth. 'No more chocolates. I won't buy any.' She blushed. 'It won't hurt me to be a little more restrained either. I'm sorry,

Mr Callender. I'm afraid I'm a foolish person.'

Fergus smiled his normal sweet smile. 'And I'm a bad-tempered one. Restraint all round is what's called for, eh, Mrs Stillman?'

The door safely closed and locked behind her, he gave a mock puff of relief, running both hands through his hair so that it stood on end.

'Well . . . the cavalry galloped up in the nick of time, Zoe.'

Zoe was not in the mood for joking. 'I've never heard you losing it to that extent, Fergus. What if there'd been a waiting-room full of people? You have no idea how unpleasant you sounded.'

'It was a singularly unpleasant job!' Fergus said quickly.

'They often are, aren't they? But so far you've managed not to be so absolutely foul while you're doing them. I was beginning to be afraid that we'd have an official complaint on our hands.'

'We still might, once she's missing her chocolates.'

'I don't think so. She might be silly but she's not vicious.'

'And I suppose you think the reverse applies to me? Can't drum up much of a defence for myself.' He straightened up. 'Ah, well . . . another day gone. At least that's something to be thankful for.'

He was going to walk through to collect his things from the cloakroom, but Zoe came out from behind her desk and barred his way.

'What is the matter with you these days, Fergus?'

He stared defensively at her. 'What? Just because I was pissed off with having my advice perpetually ignored? That animal's health is being ruined by stupid treatment. You saw the size of it.'

'No. Not just that. You're not yourself any of the time.'

He made a dismissive gesture. 'I'm not clockwork. I have good days and bad days. I don't know what you're talking about.'

He made to walk past her, but Zoe put a hand flat on his chest and stopped him. 'And you've worn this shirt for three days. You needn't deny it – not with those distinctive pink streaks.'

'So I'm behind with the washing. Big deal!'

'*You're* behind with the washing? Not Kate? Since when did you go all new man on us?'

Fergus brushed her hand aside angrily. 'Mind your own bloody business!'

Zoe stared after him as he went into the cloakroom. So that was it, was it? He'd got into a long-distance spat with Kate, and everyone else was suffering because of it. She tried to imagine Kate, whom she'd always found a bit snooty, scrapping like a fishwife with Fergus and then going on strike. Did he have to cook his own meals as well? And sleep in the spare room? She shook her head tolerantly. Well, the sooner they sorted themselves out the better for everyone. But they'd been through a lot, and she supposed that they deserved allowances to be made.

She tidied up her work station and when she was ready to leave she called a cheerful goodnight in the direction of the cloakroom. Fergus didn't answer.

Suit yourself, Zoe thought, closing the main door behind herself. Tomorrow's another day.

'You're getting quite fond of our garden, Mrs Callender,' the girl on the desk said as Maggie told her she was going out for a few minutes.

'Nice to get some fresh air,' Maggie smiled, pulling on her gloves. 'This place is very warm – not that I'm objecting too much. It would be worse to be cold.'

It was a bright but crisp November day. Ashfield's grounds were well kept, and extensive enough to give a decent walk. Maggie liked the way the garden was divided up into separate 'rooms'. You could usually get away from others who were outside, not that the other people were unpleasant. At first she had been wary of any contact, unsure of just what flawed personalities were hidden behind unrevealing outward appearances. But she had slowly learned that there was nothing to be afraid of. Just people working out problems.

Perhaps that is why we are here, Maggie thought. We are too good at covering up what we feel . . . and in the end we erupt like volcanoes and threaten to damage others as well as ourselves.

'You are so reluctant to talk about the matters that really concern you,' Dr Lawson had told her only that morning.

'How can you say that? We have done nothing but talk about things of the deepest concern to me ever since I came here.'

'I have questioned and encouraged you. You have given only as little as you could get away with. Come on, admit it.'

She had been bound to smile at his straight talking. 'I told you – I've lived most of my life in a community where practical matters were the prime concern. In any case, the thing that pains me most is something only my immediate family can fully understand.'

'And at the moment you are not even discussing the weather with either Fergus or Kate, are you?'

She had looked down at her hands, twisting her wedding ring round and round on her finger. 'Fergus has rung every day to ask how I am. I realize that I can't go on not speaking to him.'

'Good. But that's still rather a negative approach. Couldn't you notch the enthusiasm up a bit and go so far as to say that you're getting round to wanting to speak to him?' His steady, open smile was gently persuasive.

'It would be a step back, a move closer to the atmosphere I wanted to get away from.'

'But it's only by going into the dark places, confronting our greatest fears, that we learn how to deal with them.'

She sighed. 'All right. I shall ring my son this evening.'

'Well done!' He had got up, signifying the end of the session.

'So soon?'

'Always leave on a winning high. I shall look forward to hearing next time that you were actually glad to be back in contact with your family.'

'I hope you are right.'

'Trust me. I'm a doctor!' And they had parted for once on laughter.

But I shall have to keep my promise, Maggie thought now, reaching the top of the garden where she had her favourite seat, one set in a recess in the boundary hedge. At this time of year the forsythia hedge was thin, and Maggie could see into the adjoining garden of the private house next to Ashfield.

It was the vegetable garden that she loved to look at. There were rows of cabbages, sprouts, leeks, and even lettuces covered by old-fashioned bell cloches. It made Maggie think of the productive garden she and her husband had once had. She had always loved growing things to eat, more than flowers in fact.

She was alone and hadn't seen a soul on her walk through the grounds, so she gave in to the urge to see more of the garden next door and climbed carefully up on her bench. She leaned on a thick branch of the forsythia and craned forward to look down the garden. She could see strawberry beds and rows of raspberry canes now, and an orchard, with windfalls left on the grass for the birds.

She turned to look in the other direction towards the top end of the garden, and nearly fell off her bench with shock. A man of around her own age was kneeling on a rubber mat, a trowel in his hand, working in a stretch of newly raked soil. He was looking up at her, his weathered face full of amusement.

'Well, good afternoon!' he said. 'You must be either incredibly tall, or living dangerously.'

'I'm so sorry!' Maggie said, practically incoherent with confusion. 'I thought – I mean, I didn't know there was anyone there. Please excuse me. You must think me dreadfully rude.' She tottered wildly as she attempted to turn and get down.

'Please don't move!' he urged her. 'Not while you're still suffering totally unnecessarily from shock. I should hate to see you spread-eagled on the ground because of me.'

He had scrambled to his feet and was coming towards the hedge, and Maggie saw that he was wearing the kind of decrepit cords that Donald used to favour, with a navy-blue polo-necked sweater on top of which he had a quilted sleeveless jacket. He had a shock of silvery hair. When he was standing below her, looking up, she saw that there were laughter lines around his light blue eyes.

'There's absolutely no need to be alarmed. I truly am flattered that you should want to look at my vegetables,' he said disarmingly. 'In fact, if you are visiting, I'll cut you a cabbage to take home with you. If you're staying at Ashfield a while there isn't much point. I hear the food's good.'

'I'm staying, for the moment,' Maggie said. 'No doubt you're thinking that my behaviour is well suited to my status as resident.'

'The contrary, in fact. Most people I see through the hedge are too preoccupied with their own problems to look at anything. If you're looking out at the world, you must be going home soon.'

'You're very kind. And you have the most beautiful vegetable garden.' Although still feeling rather silly, perched on her bench like a dunce in the corner of the classroom, Maggie was gradually regaining control of herself.

'I do, don't I?' he said, grinning at his own smugness. 'It's my pride and joy. Can't keep up with eating the produce these days, but fortunately I've got family and friends who help me out.'

'I always liked growing things to eat,' Maggie said. 'Peas fresh from the pod – nothing to beat them.'

'Raspberries with the warmth of the sun still in them. Sheer poetry!'

'Of course, there are greenfly, and slugs!'

'And things that bolt and things that wilt or don't put in an appearance at all. That's gardening for you!'

They laughed.

'If you can spare a hand, I'd like to introduce myself,' he said, reaching up towards her. 'Gordon Hart. And I truly am delighted to meet you.'

Still holding on to her steadying branch, Maggie put her hand in his. 'Maggie Callender.'

'From somewhere much further north, by the sound of things.'

'The Borders. A hill farm.'

'And you could bear to leave it?'

'I had no choice. When Donald died I couldn't have stayed there. I moved down here to be near my son and his wife.'

Uncomfortable with the direction the conversation was taking, Maggie asked, 'What were you planting?'

'Next season's broad beans. Look – why don't you get carefully down off that bench and come round for the full conducted tour? I usually put the kettle on round about this time. Careful, now.'

Maggie had at once scrambled down from the bench, not from eagerness to fall in with his suggestion, but because the invitation had suddenly jolted her over the threshold separating the normal Maggie from the agoraphobic wreck of herself. The thought of walking the length of the Ashfield garden, going out into the main road, and then step by step covering an equal distance of strange territory appalled her. Her composure, so briefly regained, splintered and left her breathless and panicking.

'Thank you, but I must go in. They like to know – they'll wonder where on earth I've got to. It was only for a short – I was only getting a breath of fresh air. Thank you for being so understanding about my stupid behaviour.' She was backing away from the hedge as she spoke, but she could see him looking quizzically at her through it, his good humour unruffled.

'Another time, then, if you feel like it.' The fact that he seemed unperturbed by her peculiar behaviour made her feel worse.

'Goodbye,' she said abruptly, and hurried back towards the house, cheeks burning, heart pounding. 'Fool!' she berated herself. 'Utter fool. For once you were enjoying talking to someone but you couldn't let it last, could you? You had to behave like a prime idiot. Kidding yourself that you were feeling better, were you? Don't you believe it. You're still halfway to being certifiable.'

The thought of ringing Fergus lay ahead, and she found that afternoon tea had been cleared away. It seemed no more than she deserved.

Kate drove into the farmyard in the last of the afternoon's watery sunshine, glad to be back after her Friday stint in the Information Centre. These days her part-time job had turned into an endurance test. She spent every minute there hoping Fergus wasn't going to turn up. So far he hadn't, though there had been further accusing phone calls.

Jan was away for the weekend at one of her Craft Fairs, so Quaker was to be fed, and after Quaker the hens.

Kate rummaged in her bag for the key to the house. It wouldn't turn at her first attempt, so she tried the opposite direction. That worked, but the door was still locked. Jan must have driven off and left the house open, she realized.

Quaker wasn't around but he'd been in as his breakfast dish was empty. Kate put it in the sink and filled a clean dish with a mixture of biscuits and the current favourite tinned food. Jan must have left in a hurry. Her coffee mug and plate with a couple of toast crusts were still on the table. Kate washed the things up, and had just gone over to put the mug and plate back on the dresser when out of the corner of her eye she became aware that someone had appeared in the doorway leading through to the rest of the house.

She was so startled that the mug crashed to the ground and she shot back, banging her hip painfully against the corner of the table.

'I'm so sorry to startle you,' the intruder said, sounding and looking nothing like the burglar she had initially thought him to be. 'Did you hurt yourself? I'll clear that up. Just leave it.'

He was tall and broad shouldered, his build suggesting that he could do an impressive amount of damage if he felt so inclined, but his long dark overcoat and blue scarf, fashionably threaded through itself in the neck of his coat, were reassuring. Even more reassuring was the thick, rebellious red hair, so like Jan's own.

'You must be Jan's brother!' Kate said thankfully.

'Spot on. Nat Hambleton.' His handshake was almost as painful as her collision with the table. 'And you must be Kate. Jan told me you'd taken the other half of the barn.' He moved over to get a dustpan and brush from the cupboard under the sink, proving his familiarity with the house and completing her reassurance.

'I came in to see to Quaker,' she told him.

'Jan's away, then? I didn't know.'

'She's gone to a Craft Fair. In York, I think. I thought she must have gone off and left the door unlocked.'

'And I made you think someone had broken in. Sorry about that. I helped myself to a teatime snack, then crashed out in the sitting-room with Quaker. He's still unconscious through there.' He stood up again, checking the tiled floor. 'That's got all of it, I think.' He tipped the remains of the mug in the bin. 'I don't normally sleep at this time of day, but I've had an abominable drive down. The car hood got itself stuck halfway up. Damned thing!'

'Jan didn't tell me you were coming this weekend,' Kate said.

'She didn't know. I got an unexpected long weekend off. I drove the car into the barn in case it rains tonight. Couldn't leave it outside to fill up like a bucket.'

Mention of the barn reminded Kate of the hens. 'I've to go in there to give the hens their mash.'

'Let me.' He moved swiftly and picked up the heavy pan.

'There's three nights' worth there,' she warned him, following him out into the yard.

His car, a red MG not exactly in the first flush of youth, sat with its hood at forty-five degrees. Nat gave it a vicious, ineffective tug. 'Bastard!' he said, and swept a couple of hens off the bonnet with a wild wave of his arm, adding, 'And you!'

Grinning, Kate scattered handfuls of grain around the mash trough while the hens skittered over her feet in their usual silly way. You couldn't quite start building up a relationship with a hen, she had decided.

When she straightened up and turned round, she saw that

Nat was fishing things out of a zipped holdall in the MG's boot and stuffing them in his overcoat pocket. A packet of corn-flakes and a sliced loaf from a cardboard box of provisions were tucked into a fold of the hood while he closed the boot again. 'That'll do until tomorrow,' he said. 'No point in lugging every-thing down that death trap of a lane tonight.'

'My car's here. Why don't you load all your things into that while I take the pan back.' She handed him her keys. 'Otherwise you'll be sure to find you've something essential missing.'

'Great!' he said, emptying his pockets again and dropping bread and cornflakes back into the box. 'I haven't left anything in the house, so you can lock up when you're ready.'

Kate came out to find him sitting in the passenger seat. 'More room in this than in my flighty Jezebel of a car,' he said, 'and don't bother to tell me I chose it.'

'Why did you? There's a bit of a size discrepancy, isn't there?'

'A daft, boyhood ambition. Had a ride in one belonging to an uncle when I was a kid. Bought this one blinded by the memory, and by the time I'd found out how much I'd grown and what a difference that made, we'd got a relationship going. It's a sad, man thing.'

He pulled his scarf loose and stuffed it in his pocket as they bounced over the potholes on the brief journey down the lane.

'I'm very grateful,' he said as he dumped the holdall on the grass outside the Barns, and lifted the box of provisions off the back seat to join it. 'That's the lot.'

He turned round to smile his thanks, and Kate got her second shock of the evening when she saw the dog collar framed in the dark revers of his coat.

'You didn't know I was *one of those*,' he said, his voice comi-cally distorted.

'How on earth should I? You're hardly my idea of the aver-age priest. You called your car a bastard!'

'Haven't quite completed the transition yet. I was in the army once, until I changed direction. The human being still keeps popping his head over the dog collar.'

'I'm surprised Jan didn't tell me.'

'You make it sound like a necessary plague warning. No reason why she should, really. You wouldn't expect her to say "By the way, my brother's an accountant", would you? Or a plumber. But in any case she tries to believe the church hasn't got its hands on me. Do you know what her first words were after my ordination?'

Kate shook her head. 'I've given up trying to guess what Jan might come out with.'

'She gave me a bear hug, and whispered in my ear right under the bishop's nose "You don't fool me. You're still the little sod who stole my Saturday sweets and dropped me in it by lying about who scratched Dad's car!" '

Kate laughed. 'That sounds about right for Jan.' His next words, though, wiped the smile off her face.

'She did tell me why you were here, though,' he said, 'Just so that we get all the cards on the table since you prefer it that way.'

'Did she?' Kate said coldly. Jan was so easy to talk to that she had told her far more than necessary. Unfortunately it seemed that Jan had not kept it to herself. 'Don't imagine that gives you licence to start preaching at me,' she added rudely.

Nat didn't rise to the offensiveness of her remark. 'Has there been a lot of preaching?' he asked calmly.

'I've made sure there hasn't been.'

'And who have you shot down so far?'

'Nobody. I just haven't taken up the ideas the doctor and latterly Fergus have been putting under my nose.'

'Fergus is your husband?'

'Yes,' she said shortly. 'Look, I don't want to talk about it. Can we get that clear from the start?'

'Occupational hazard. You'll be all right once I've taken my collar off. Calms me down a treat.'

In spite of herself, Kate smiled. 'You are a fool, Nat. However do you manage to carry off funerals?'

'Funerals have never been a problem,' he said. 'They remind me of my wife's. That wipes the smile off my face in no time at all.'

Kate felt as though she had been winded and couldn't speak.

'Sorry,' he said. 'Throwaway lines are the habit of the past five years – a way of deflecting sympathy I couldn't cope with.'

'It certainly works,' Kate said shakily.

'And what about your policy of saying nothing at all to explain scrapping home, husband and mother-in-law? Treat that as a rhetorical question, of course. On that note, I'll leave you,' he added pleasantly. 'Thanks again for the lift.'

He picked up his box and bag, and loped off to Barn Close. Kate unlocked her own door, and thankfully closed it behind her, feeling as though she had been cornered in a field by a mad bull. Was he really a genuine member of the Church of England? Anyone less like a clergyman she had never met, with his unsuitable car and even less appropriate language, not to mention the pair of union jack boxer shorts she had seen him stuffing into his pocket in the barn. Now, as she stood leaning against the front door, she heard the faint sound of music coming through the party wall. Jazz. Good jazz. It would have been too much to expect Evensong.

She shot home the bolts, top and bottom.

The weekend hadn't started well for Fergus.

The phone rang the minute he'd put the last two lamb chops from the freezer under the grill. He had noted that they were the last bit of anything meaty as far as he could see, and as he hurried to the phone he made a mental resolution to do a mammoth supermarket haul the next day. Any other call he'd have dealt with and gone back into the kitchen in plenty of time to save his dinner, but the fact that it was Maggie's voice that greeted him drove everything out of his head.

'If you're not doing anything else tomorrow afternoon, Fergus,' she was saying, 'I could do with a few more clothes and some walking shoes. The ones I'm wearing are not really suitable for the garden. I won't keep you long if you have other arrangements.'

'So it would be convenient for me to drop in, would it?' he was ashamed to hear himself say with coldly unpleasant inflexion. Then he pulled himself together quickly. 'Of course I'll come.' Then, after an awkward pause – there had never been awkwardness between them before – 'I've been ringing every day to ask about you.'

'So they told me. It was very thoughtful of you, Fergus.'

A wave of misery swept over him. She could have been speaking to a stranger, and she was his mother, *his mother*. Until the last few dreadful months, he'd felt loved, safe, the centre of things. Look at it now. First there had been the heart-breaking loss of Lucy. Then his wife and his mother had turned away from him. He felt desolate, emasculated, and there was no one to comfort him.

'How are you?' he asked stiffly.

'Very well. There's no need to worry about me, Fergus.'

Didn't she understand that he wanted to worry about her – wanted her to worry about him for that matter. But Maggie didn't even ask how he was managing. Fergus's throat went dry as he suddenly remembered she had no idea that Kate was not with him.

Anxious now to end the call before he could be asked questions he had no idea how to answer, he said, 'I've got a pen and paper here if you want to give me a list of the things to bring.'

Maggie had to spell out just where he would find the things he wanted, and the exchanging of mundane domestic details about which dress, which cupboard, which drawer, helped to tick the minutes away.

'Someone's just come in with the evening drinks trolley, Fergus,' Maggie said. He could detect the note of thankfulness in her voice. 'Until tomorrow, then. Thank you for seeing to things.'

Fergus hung up the phone and wandered into the sitting-room where he slumped into an easy chair. The conversation had depressed him. He sat weighing every word they had exchanged, trying to read what was behind Maggie's present change of mind. She certainly hadn't felt warm to him, and she had made no mention of wanting to leave Ashfield. He progressed to wondering what on earth he was to do about the

Kate situation. If he was seeing Maggie tomorrow, surely she would be bound to mention Kate at some point. Would it be bad for her mental state if she found that Kate had walked out on him? Would she start imagining that Kate's departure was down to her, just as she imagined she was to blame for Lucy's death?

Kate would have to help him. No point in trying to ring her now, though. She stuck rigidly to putting on her mobile only for the brief time she had told him in the early morning. Resentment built up inside him as he brooded, until he suddenly became aware of the unpleasant smell of burning drifting out of the kitchen and permeating the whole house.

He dashed to the oven to find that his chops, blackened and ruined, had burst into flames. He threw the lot out on to the terrace, and came back indoors thoroughly depressed.

Middy, watching discreetly from the garden border, waited until the smoke died down then went over to investigate. But it was not the standard of food to which she was accustomed, and she went off, tail lashing, to seek better luck at the bottom of the garden on the bank favoured by a tasty line in voles.

Kate answered his call immediately next morning.

'Marianne? Trouble?' Her voice sounded bright. Normal. And she wasn't expecting it to be him.

'Not Marianne,' he said curtly.

'Oh, Fergus. What do you want?' Her tone had changed from friendly to wary.

'Must you sound so hostile? You said I could get in touch at this time.'

'I'm not hostile. It's just that it doesn't help the present situation to have you calling me so often. It brings everything crowding in on me again, Fergus – everything I need to get a distance from, so that I can make sense of it.'

'You make our lives sound like an art appreciation class.'

She sighed. 'Now you're just being silly. You know perfectly well what I mean. Anyway, you haven't phoned just to start an argument. I presume there's more of a reason.'

'There is. My mother called me last night. She wants me to go and see her today.'

'Why haven't you been before now? That's a bit much, Fergus. She's your mother, after all.'

'I haven't been because she told me not to show my face. We haven't spoken since she went into Ashfield, although I've phoned every day. And the point of ringing you is that she has no idea that you've —' he was going to say 'left me', but the awful, permanent sound of that stuck in his throat. 'I miss you like hell, Kate,' he said. 'I wish you'd stop doing this mad thing and come back home.'

She didn't answer that, sticking to the Maggie problem. 'I don't see any problem. If anyone should understand my needing space, Maggie should. Didn't she feel the need to get away too?'

'You make me feel like a bloody leper.'

'That's just you being over-dramatic. If you hadn't been forced to stay put because of the job, you'd probably have felt exactly the same as Maggie does. And as I do.'

There was a silence. Then, 'Are you any nearer sorting out whatever drove you away?' he asked.

Kate sighed. 'Just don't ask me, Fergus. I'm still in limbo. Maybe I needed to draw breath before my brain could start working.'

'I wish I could understand you.'

'And I wish I could make you understand.'

He shifted the phone to his other hand, and forced himself to go back to his original reason for ringing her. 'What shall I do about Mum, then? She's sure to ask about you.'

'Why don't you have a word with her doctor before you see her? He should be the one to advise you about what's likely to be upsetting for her. I honestly don't know what to do about Maggie, Fergus. That was one of the things that was driving me mad. Just hang on a minute, will you?'

She must have put her hand over the mouthpiece. He could hear a conversation going on, but it was muffled and the words were indistinguishable. One thing was shockingly clear, though.

The other voice, the one that wasn't Kate's, was undoubtedly male.

'Fergus?' Kate said, her voice clear again. 'Sorry about that. Where were we? I don't think I can say any more on the subject of Maggie. Except give her my love.'

His mind seething with suspicion, he could hardly manage to answer her. 'Isn't that hypocritical, under the present circumstances?'

'Not at all. It's easier to love her at a distance, without our emotional undercurrents clashing.'

'Kate!' he exploded. 'Cut the small talk. What's going on there? I heard a man's voice. Just what are you playing at?'

Kate actually sounded amused when she answered him.

'Not to worry. It was only the vicar!'

This time Fergus heard the deep male chuckle quite clearly from somewhere in the room she was in. Outraged, he cut off Kate's voice, and the shocking, humiliating picture of the amusement she was sharing with some unknown man at his expense.

The most humiliating part of it all, Fergus thought, was that he had never for one moment considered the possibility that Kate might be involved with someone else. Had he been utterly stupid? Would most men have immediately jumped to the conclusion that her total turn-off from sex meant that she was involved elsewhere? Even now he found the idea hard to accept. Could she really have pretended so convincingly that grief had killed all feeling in her, and at the same time carried on an affair with some other man? That would have been a betrayal of Lucy, not just himself. Surely Kate, his Kate, couldn't have done that?

But the memory of the phone call and the muffled overheard exchanges would not go away. Desperate to do something, Fergus grabbed his mobile phone and drove off, stopping on the various roads out of Lichfield to see if a variation in signal would indicate that he was near to where Kate was staying. But he soon realized that he hadn't a hope in hell of finding her that way. He was more likely to crash his car, careering round the countryside like a maniac. He would be better employed stocking up on food.

He was north of the city, so he decided to shop in Brentwood where chances were that there would be no one who knew him. The supermarket belonged to the chain he was familiar with, but in this unknown branch it took him three times as long as usual to trail round and find what he wanted. He joined the shortest checkout queue, which was still depressingly long, and was trapped in it by an immovable elderly couple with a wheel-chair as well as a trolley before he realized that the person in front of him, turning round and smiling with surprise, was Zoe.

'Hi, Fergus!' she said. 'Why are you in this neck of the woods?'

She was wearing a red tracksuit and her smile was so warm and bright that although he wished her miles away, he couldn't let his annoyance show.

'Just happened to be passing through,' he said. 'Thought it might be less crowded than our usual place. Wrong, wasn't I?'

'Saturday's always murder.' She was looking with undis-guised curiosity into his trolley. 'Well, this is good, isn't it? I can snoop all I want at your shopping, see what the classy Callenders put away.' She drew in a disapproving breath. 'Dear oh dear! You won't get any Brownie points for all these single microwave meals. Didn't your mother teach you that it's cheaper to get the doubles?'

'Perhaps we like different things. How's Rebecca?' Fergus said, hurriedly changing the subject.

'Don't ask. She'll be out until all hours tonight, turning my hair grey. With a past like mine I know only too well what she's likely to be up to, but I'm no more capable of stopping her than my mother was with me.' Her eyes fixed on his chest. 'That shirt's never been ironed, Fergus, surely. What with that and the pink-streaked horror you couldn't bear to part with last week, I'm beginning to think somebody ought to take you in hand.'

The queue edged forward, and Fergus had a moment's reprieve, but Zoe's bright blonde head was soon turning back in his direction.

'I'd never have put you down as the sort to skip shaving at weekends,' she said, head on one side, eyes ranging over his face. 'Quite suits you, though. Makes you look less of the academic and more like a bit of rough.' The woman in front of Zoe turned round enquiringly. Fergus fiddled with his credit cards to avoid meeting her gaze. 'Embarrassing you, am I?' Zoe said unabashed. 'You don't want to take life so seriously, Fergus. Let yourself have a laugh now and then. Do you good, it would.'

He was fingering his jaw. He was, as Zoe had suspected, not the sort to skip shaving. This morning had been exceptional.

'I dashed out early,' he said. His stomach rumbled, reminding him of last night's unsatisfying cheese sandwich.

'Missed your breakfast as well, I expect.' Zoe tutted disapprovingly, missing nothing. 'Growing lad like you needs regular meals. This isn't supposed to be lunch, is it?' She was poking a packet of sandwiches disdainfully. They were plain salad, Fergus realized. 'Not much sustenance in these, is there? Someone your size needs a fat, juicy steak to keep him going.'

'Your turn,' Fergus said thankfully. There was another brief respite while Zoe, who was on first name terms with the girl on the checkout, was brought up to date on yet another slice of private life. He said a dismissive goodbye when she had finally bagged all her shopping and slung the carriers back in her trolley, but he wasn't going to be let off so easily.

'I'll wait for you.' Zoe moved her trolley over to the wall, deaf to his attempt to tell her not to waste her Saturday morning hanging around for him.

When he eventually joined her, she looked at him with a serious face, the laughter gone from her blue eyes.

'Now then, Fergus,' she said firmly. 'You're going to put that trolley in the lock-up here beside mine, then we're going to go into the coffee shop and at least get a cappuccino and a sticky bun inside you. You look like death. And while you're having that, you're going to tell me the real reason you've got meals for one in your trolley. I'm not daft. You haven't been yourself for days now. And it doesn't take the mind of a genius to add up bad temper, clothes that look as though the cat's brought them in, Saturday shopping and single meals and make a bit of an alarming total.'

Somehow she had parked both trolleys and her hand was gripping his arm and marching him to the nearest table in the coffee shop.

'Sit there. I'll be back in a jiffy.' She gave him a pat on the shoulder as he slumped into a chair.

She was as good as her word, and was back in no time to put a chocolate-sprinkled cup of coffee and a fruit bun in front of him.

'I'll butter that for you. There's two sugars in the saucer – I know you like a fair bit. Cheer up, Fergus. I know it's not your sort of place, but the coffee's good, honest!'

Fergus felt himself thawing in the warmth of her ridiculous mothering. Somebody cared about him, even if it was only Zoe.

'There you are.' She pushed the bun towards him. 'Now, don't mess about. Tell me what's going on.'

He drew in a painful breath and met her eyes. 'Kate's walked out,' he said. The relief of letting out the hurtful secret that he had been nursing for two weeks now was like lancing a boil.

'You poor devil!' Zoe's eyes brimmed with sympathy. 'I was afraid it might be that sort of trouble. But you'll sort it out, won't you? Surely she's not gone for good?'

'That's the worst of it. I just don't know. I don't understand her – can't make any sense of what she thinks she's doing. She talks about needing space, and time to herself to think things out. I just want her.'

'Where's she gone?'

'She won't say. I made her take a mobile, or I wouldn't be able to speak to her at all, apart from at the Centre with half the tourists in Lichfield competing. She doesn't like me coming there, in any case.'

'So she's still somewhere around?' Zoe traced an abstract pattern on the table top where he had spilled sugar when he opened the silly little tube it came in.

'Near enough to come in to work. They think she's staying with a friend who's been in hospital. Do you think it's a good sign that she doesn't want them to know?'

'Sounds as though she's keeping her options well and truly open. When I left Ken, the world knew it. And that definitely meant that I wasn't going to change my mind. So keep your chin up, Fergus. She's had a lot to go through. You too, I know. But with her it's more of a physical thing. You've got to remember that. One minute you're feeding a baby, doing everything for it, touching it most of the day. Then it's gone. That must throw you right off balance . . . take a hell of a lot of getting over. It's bound to, Fergus.'

'I know that.' There was so much more crowding his mind, but he wasn't going to lay bare all the details of his life. Perhaps he had been unwise to tell Zoe as much as he had. Only time would tell.

'I haven't told anyone. It's no business of friends or people at the surgery, and in any case if things work out, I'd rather nobody knew that the whole sorry business had happened,' he said.

Zoe looked at him. 'Are you wondering if I'm going to be blabbing to everybody? Don't worry. I can keep my mouth shut about the things that matter. It may not look like it, but it's true. Nobody had a clue about what went on between Ken and me until it was all over – and believe me there was plenty. You can talk a lot without saying the important things, you know, Fergus.'

He drained the last of his coffee and pushed back his chair. 'I must go. My mother's in hospital – needed a rest more than anything and I'm visiting her this afternoon.'

'Never rains but it pours, eh?' Zoe put a hand on his arm. 'If there's anything I can do, Fergus, just speak. And don't worry.' She put a finger on her glossy lips. 'Buttoned tight. I promise.'

'Thanks for everything, Zoe.' He paused, half turned away. 'You've got your car?'

'Yeah.' Her cheeky smile was back in place. 'Totally independent, that's me. Off you go. See you Monday.'

Chapter Seven

Kate switched off her mobile and stood looking down at it, her momentary flash of humour gone. 'Oh dear!' she said helplessly.

Nat watched her from the doorway, the milk he had come to scrounge in his hand. 'Sounds as though your caller was in a hurry.'

'In a rage, more like. It was my husband.'

'Ah!' He nodded his head slowly. 'Perhaps half past seven in the morning isn't the time to speak flippantly about whatever man is in the house with you. Under the circumstances, I mean.'

'If you hadn't come round at such an ungodly hour, it wouldn't have happened, would it?'

'True, but I knew you were up. I saw you go out to the car.'

'To get this thing. I wish I'd left it out there.' Kate slammed the mobile down on the table, and found herself, to her humiliation, on the verge of tears. 'Damn and blast everything!'

'Hardly a wish it's my purpose to promote,' Nat said wryly. 'Why don't I make you a cup of coffee?'

'Out of that as well, are you?' Kate said ungraciously, then, as he slid a box of tissues over towards her, 'Oh, I'm sorry. It's no good blaming everyone else in the world for my own messes.' She scrubbed at her eyes then sat down. 'Coffee's in the cupboard over the mixer. And sugar, if you take it.'

'Black or white?' he called after a moment.

'Black, please. One sugar.'

Moments later when he came back with two mugs she was composed again. 'I don't spend all my time crying,' she said defensively.

'Of course not. What person who had lost a child and thrown away a husband would do that ridiculous thing?' he asked innocently.

'It's nothing to joke about!' Kate said fiercely.

He looked steadily at her. 'Of course it isn't. And I wasn't joking. You'll have to get used to my way of talking. I was only trying to point out that you have every reason to feel wretched.'

'Shouldn't you be telling me that it's all God's will?'

'I wouldn't dream of insulting God to that extent.' He took a long drink of coffee. 'And in case you might think otherwise, I never felt the urge to go in for saintly acceptance and gratitude for what happened to Liz. Quite the reverse in fact.'

Kate's eyes closed in horror. 'I'm sorry. I wasn't thinking . . . Please forgive me.'

'Nothing to forgive. Drink your coffee.'

They sat in silence for a few moments. It wasn't an awkward silence. Perhaps it was because he was Jan's brother that Kate felt she knew him already. There was the same openness about him that she had found in Jan – a direct line between thought and speech that made for complete honesty. The vicar who had been involved with Lucy's funeral had seemed like someone from another planet, speaking from the other side of a glass wall. Kate found herself wondering how it would have been if Nat had been there for her at that awful time. He would probably have cursed as much as she did. The thought was somehow comforting. Her eyes wandered over his un-vicar-like garb of jeans and navy blue polo-necked sweater.

He caught her looking at his neck and grinned. 'Not in uniform today. Mufti's allowed.'

'I can't for the life of me imagine you behaving decorously enough to keep a church congregation happy,' she said.

'Don't try. I'm Chaplain at a Young Offenders' Centre. How's that for a more appropriate background?'

She was surprised into laughter. 'That's certainly easier to picture. It sounds a tough job.'

'Some of them give me a hard time. It's better than it was at first. Sometimes the odd one or two surprise me. I live in hope that maybe I do a bit of something useful. Only time will tell.'

'That's a very guarded answer.'

'Much safer not to kid yourself you're performing miracles. But that's enough about me. What about you? Do you think being here is working?'

'It's easier being here for all sorts of reasons. But I don't think it's solving anything that matters. I've walked out on the things that were bothering me. I haven't sorted them.'

'That sounds like my boys. Whatever went wrong and caused them to get off balance is still there when they go out. They've only been having a breather, marking time. Somehow they've got to get themselves into a state of mind that lets them go forward.'

Kate didn't care for the comparison, but she supposed he had a kind of point.

'I do know there has to be a next step,' she said slowly, 'but the trouble is I haven't a clue what it's got to be. Fergus certainly isn't going to take this situation much longer. Each time I've driven back to Hints this week I've been looking in my rear-view mirror, expecting him to be tracking me back here.'

'Did you ever consider going away somewhere together and trying to talk things through? This is between the two of you after all.'

'Fergus wanted to do that, but I didn't. We were having a weekend away on our own when Lucy died. I think we'd both be remembering that all the time.' She got up with determination. 'And now you are edging into forbidden territory, aren't you?'

He put up his hands in mock surrender and rose to his feet. 'Sorry. What are you doing today? That's an innocent question.'

'I haven't a clue. A few boring chores, then sitting around brooding, I expect.'

'Why not come for a walk?'

The thought of having a shape to her Saturday was tempting. 'How far are you thinking of going?' she asked cautiously.

'Through the fields in Drayton Bassett direction, then circling round to link up with Brockhurst Lane and come home via the ford. No more than six miles at a rough guess.'

'I'd like that, then. What time?'

'Let's say two-ish. That gives me time to deal with that hood, and pop in to see Lynne.'

'Pastoral visiting?'

'A friendly visit, not work. Have you met her?'

'Yes. I wouldn't call it an auspicious meeting, though. I tore her off a strip for letting Rosie cry too long. She gave as good as she got, and ended up cadging half a loaf of bread from me.'

He laughed. 'She's nothing if not a survivor.'

'I was seriously concerned about Rosie, though. The cottage doesn't exactly look a model of hygiene.'

'Hygiene's more of a danger than a bit of dirt, these days, haven't you heard? Lynne's finding her way little by little.'

'Thanks to an exceptionally kind landlady, and a neighbour who can provide anything she doesn't have in the cupboard.'

'I think she probably wants contact with another human being as much as the bits and bobs she scrounges. This isn't the easiest of places to live when you've no transport and a pram to push.'

Kate sighed resignedly. 'I hope you're not going to put me in the wrong like this every step of this afternoon's walk.'

'No. Not at all.' He grinned at her. 'But now that I know your attitude, I'll make sure I let you have your milk back.'

'Oh, go away,' Kate said with spirit.

'See you at two.' With a mock salute, he was off. The house seemed quiet and several degrees colder.

The visit did not get off to a good start.

The girl on reception told Fergus that Maggie was in the Green Sitting Room, and told him how to find it.

It was ridiculous to feel apprehensive like this, Fergus told himself as he made his way along the corridors. He had done nothing wrong. He hadn't wanted Maggie to take off into this place. He hadn't refused to come and see her. The choices had all been on her side. So why should he feel like a misbehaving schoolboy?

Outside the green room he juggled the suitcase and zipped hanging case of dresses and blouses Maggie had asked him to bring in, finally managing to free a hand to tap on the door and open it.

Maggie was chatting to someone over by the window, and wasn't aware Fergus was there until he was halfway across the room.

'Fergus!' She broke off mid-sentence and stood up to kiss him. Her greeting and the warm hug she gave him were reassuring, but she looked different and Fergus couldn't think why. 'Don't feel you have to rush away, Gordon,' she turned to say to the person half rising from his chair opposite hers. 'This is my son, Fergus Callender. Gordon Hart, Fergus.'

Fergus shook hands warily with the elderly, white-haired man. What was wrong with this one, he wondered. He didn't know what to expect from the people here. The man seemed pleasant enough, though.

'How are things?' Fergus said, 'You're looking well, mother.'

'And so I should with all this good food, and a complete rest and change of scenery.'

'I'm glad that you can look at being here in that way.'

Maggie smiled 'And why ever should I look at it otherwise? Everyone has been very kind to me.' She turned to Gordon Hart. 'My son didn't altogether approve of my coming here, Gordon,' she said.

The man answered diplomatically. 'The place has an excellent reputation.' He began to show signs of getting to his feet again.

'There's absolutely no need to leave us,' Maggie said firmly, then turned to look hard at Fergus.

'I can't say you are looking on top of the world yourself, Fergus. Have you been working too hard?'

'Pretty much as usual. This week has had its moments.'
Maggie began telling the Hart man how her son had always
wanted to be a vet. Fergus was annoyed by her obvious desire
not to be left alone with him. He could come up with a few
shockers of conversational gambits if he chose, he thought.
How about giving Mr Gordon Hart a frank and revealing
account of life back at home since Maggie chose to leave. His
mother wouldn't be smiling so brightly if she heard that he
hadn't a clue where his wife was living nor what she was getting
up to. And she might soft-pedal the good food here if he told
her that he was eating rubbish at the end of each working day,
and his house was rapidly turning into a tip.

The Hart fellow had got up at last.

'No, Maggie,' he said with determination, silencing another
protest. 'You'll want time with your son, he hasn't come here
to see me.' He patted Maggie on the shoulder. 'Remember
what I said. I'll be in touch.'

'If you must,' Maggie said reluctantly. 'Go, I mean. Thanks
for your company, Gordon. And I'll let you know.'

What was going on, Fergus wondered. All this remembering
and letting know. But Maggie was speaking to him now. 'I see
you brought my things, Fergus. It would be better to take them
to my room. Gordon will point it out to you.'

Fergus followed Gordon Hart across to the door, not liking the
fact that this stranger should be showing him his mother's room.
It was all wrong. The whole of life was wrong. But there was no
point in being boorish. 'Have you been here long?' he asked.

'About twenty years,' the man answered calmly, then as
Fergus turned to look at him in astonishment he burst out
laughing. 'In Lichfield, not here. Don't worry. The turnover at
Ashfield is much quicker than that! I had the impression you
thought I was one of the patients – but I'm not. I live next door.
I got talking to your mother through the hedge. We have a joint
interest in gardening, we discovered. I thought she might enjoy
some of the late grapes from my conservatory. Here we are.'

Fergus was feeling rather ridiculous. 'Very kind of you.
Thanks. I'll get rid of this stuff of mother's now.'

Gordon Hart nodded pleasantly. 'See you again some time,' he said as he went on his way.

Frowning at the man's assumption of ongoing acquaintance, Fergus went into Maggie's room and disposed of her things while questions buzzed in his head.

When he rejoined Maggie, he realized why she looked different.

'You've had your hair cut!' he said. All his life, Maggie had knotted her long hair on the crown of her head. Now it was short, giving her face a strangely elfin look in spite of her years as it curled softly against brow and cheek.

'There's a visiting hairdresser. I suddenly thought a change would be a good thing. What do you think?'

'I had no idea it was so curly. It looks nice. Different, but pretty.'

'Thank you, Fergus. Let's hope the inner me can change too.'

He looked round anxiously. 'Are we likely to be invaded by hordes of people? I want to be able to talk properly, not be permanently editing what I say for possible listeners.'

'We can always go along to my room if necessary. But nobody will disturb us. All having their forty winks, I expect.'

'Well, then. Down to the nitty gritty. How are you?'

'I'm calmer. But that's not surprising since I'm on stronger medication. And I am pleased to see you, Fergus.'

Her eyes filled as she said this, and Fergus put his hand over hers and gripped it hard. 'And I'm pleased to see you. It's been lonely without you.'

'More like missing toothache, I think. I've turned into a great trial to you both.' A flicker of pain disturbed her face. 'How is Kate?' she asked.

The million dollar question. His mind was suddenly made up. He couldn't tell his vulnerable mother what had really happened and see her slump under the weight of the knowledge. From nowhere the cover story Kate had told Marianne at the Centre flashed in his mind.

'She's away at the moment, looking after a friend who's just had a hip replacement.'

109

'Which friend is that?' Maggie asked, and Fergus realized that the story was too sketchy by far.

'One of the choir members,' he said on sudden inspiration.

Maggie nodded. 'That's good of Kate. Does that explain why you're less than at your best, Fergus?'

He shrugged. 'I suppose so. I've been too well looked after all my life. Looking after myself comes as a bit of a shock.'

Maggie looked at him with affection. 'It won't hurt you to find out how much goes on behind the scenes.'

Fergus brought her back to a safer subject, not wanting to have to go into any details about his housekeeping capabilities. 'You haven't said anything about this doctor fellow. Is he helping you?'

Maggie grimaced. 'Who can help me but myself when it comes to the point? He's a nice enough young man. Asks a lot of irrelevant questions. I get very angry with him, but he doesn't turn a hair. It's like trying to make a steam roller change course.'

'What sort of irrelevant questions?'

'If I think they're irrelevant there's no point in talking about them,' Maggie said sharply.

'Only asking. What about this Gordon Hart, then? Or is he a forbidden subject as well?'

'Hardly. You've met him, after all.'

'Is it all right for any Tom, Dick or Harry to come walking in to see patients here?'

Maggie stiffened. 'I'm not a prisoner here, Fergus. I can have anyone I choose to visit me.'

'Of course – but don't be surprised that I find that hard to accept, having for two weeks been excluded from the favoured number.'

She sighed. 'I'm sorry. I needed time to sort my tired mind out. And it was as much for you and Kate that I made the break. Don't hold it against me. You know fine what painful process has brought us all to this point.' She closed her eyes and Fergus realized that she wasn't looking as well as when he arrived.

'Just be careful, that's all. And let Dr Lawson know what's going on.' He stood up and leaned over to kiss her. 'I think I've tired you out. I'm sorry. I'll go now, but I take it the ban is lifted and I can come again?'

'Oh, away with you, you silly boy, of course you can!' Maggie said, sounding more like her old self than at any other time. 'Let me send you away on a happier note. I'm to try to get myself next door to Gordon's for tea tomorrow afternoon. How's that for a sign of progress? And he checked with Dr Lawson before he asked me. They know each other well. I wasn't sure about it, but he says he'll come and walk me round. It might be a first step, Fergus, mightn't it?'

But towards what, exactly, Fergus thought, finding that he was suddenly resentful for his father's sake as he left Ashfield.

There was something about walking through the rolling, wooded countryside on such an unseasonally lovely day that made the self-imposed barriers Kate had built around herself seem silly.

Nat had been telling her about his childhood, making her laugh with tales of the escapades he and Jan had been involved in. They were children of the vicarage themselves, she learned with some surprise, and had led their mild, bewildered father a merry dance in each of the parishes in his charge until they were old enough to leave home and commit their indiscretions elsewhere. The wild streak in them both, he claimed, had come from their mother, an actress in provincial rep until her marriage.

'But her starring role was as Mrs Vicar,' he said. 'Dad retires next year, and she's made every cold and draughty vicarage they've lived in absolutely hum with life and colour. Injected a lot of go into more than one church drama group, too. Good old Mum!'

'I envy you of all that. I never knew my mother. She died soon after I was born.'

'That's tough.' There was genuine compassion in the look he gave her. 'One-parent families are no picnic.'

111

'Mine was barely a one-parent set-up. Dad worked on the rigs. He was away more than he was around.'

'So who looked after you?'

'We had a next-door neighbour – a widow with no family – who was glad of a job. Alice Beattie. She moved into our house when Dad was away, and back into her own place when he came back. It worked. At least, it worked while Dad was away. When he was home, the house seemed different. I remember telling Auntie Alice once that it was a different colour when Dad was there.' She glanced at Nat. 'Not a bad way of describing living with someone who's depressed. I spent more time round with Auntie Alice than at home with him. Looking back, I don't think he ever got over losing my mother.'

'Sounds as though he could have done with medical help.'

'He had no time for doctors. They hadn't saved my mother. Why should he think they could do anything for him?'

'Ah! I see!'

Kate stopped. 'What do you see?'

'Doesn't that explain a lot about your own attitude to outside help of any kind? Sorry. That just slipped out. Consider it unsaid. I'll endeavour to button up.'

Kate marched off again. 'You never switch off, do you? Everybody joins the ranks of the young offenders to be analysed, or the church flock needing a dose of the dratted fellowship!'

His laugh rang out. 'I've never heard it called that before.'

'Well, you know what I mean. Professional understanding. Duty friendship. I need to understand myself – like myself, for that matter. Not have other people do it for me.'

'But wouldn't you agree that attitudes picked up in childhood influence later thinking, either positively or negatively?'

She walked on in silence for a moment or two, then stopped and turned to face him. 'I suppose so.'

'Then just file that thought and take it out as and when you want for private use. OK? And don't stop telling me about young Kate. Please? Fancy a bit of a breather here after that climb? This is pretty well the highest point of the walk. We've done a bit of a detour, but it's worth it for the view.'

The surprisingly warm November sunshine was full on them as they stood near Roundhill Wood, looking down over the fields and farms below. The still air was suddenly disturbed by a raucous chorus from a distant rookery, carried clearly on the still air.

'A foretaste of what we'll hear when we're much closer on the route back,' Nat said. 'Noisy beggars, aren't they?'

'Back home it was the gulls. It takes a lot to outdo them.'

'Where was home?'

'Whitehaven. I haven't been back for ages. Dad died in my first term at Edinburgh – an accident on the rig. Everyone else was all right. It was almost as though he wanted it to happen.'

'Poor, sad man. And poor you.' They began walking downhill.

'What about this Alice Beattie?' Nat said after a moment or two. 'Isn't she still there?'

'I suppose so. I used to write to her. She never had the phone. Once I got to university, I'm afraid I didn't have much time for anyone else. It was like a different world.'

'Was that where you met Fergus?'

'Yes. We were both at Edinburgh. He was part way through his veterinary course when I started Fine Art. It had been touch and go whether I got there. I had an argument with a bus – fortunately after the exams were over. It was a pretty bad accident, and I only just managed to get fit again by the time term started. Meeting Fergus changed my life. We used to go to his parents for weekends, and they were so warm, so comfortable to be with. They genuinely made me feel that they couldn't have enough of me. When you've seemed all your life to be the kind of person who creates problems, you have no idea how wonderful it was to be welcomed with open arms into a family. Aunt Alice had been good to me, but it was a job for her, when all's said and done. And I think I made her life difficult the last year I was in Whitehaven. I expect she was glad to be free of the responsibility of keeping a rebellious sixth-former on the rails. I don't suppose she pictured having to do that when she took me on as a baby. She came to our wedding, but after that

113

contact faded away. There were Christmas and birthday cards but that was all. I never told her that I was expecting Lucy. Then I was busy with the move to Lichfield and learning how to cope with a new baby. After that. . . .' She drew in a shaky breath. 'Well, what was the point of contacting her then?' She looked quickly at Nat. 'I'm doing far too much talking.'

They walked along in silence. After a while Kate said, 'I've filled you with disapproval, haven't I?'

'No. Just filled me with questions.'

'At least you don't keep trying to force God down my throat. I appreciate that, given your profession.'

'I think he prefers the heart to the gullet,' Nat said drily. 'But in any case, I've always favoured the surreptitious approach. So be warned. Now – as far as what you've been saying, shall I tell you a funny thing that's struck me?'

'I don't expect I stand a chance of stopping you,' Kate answered warily.

'Of course. This is it. All the time you were talking about Edinburgh, getting married, the wonder of joining a functional family, the transformation in your life . . . you hardly mentioned Fergus. It was as though you wanted in-laws more than a husband.'

It just isn't true, Kate told herself for the umpteenth time at the end of Monday afternoon. All through the night and at the back of her mind all day Nat's shocking comment on her marriage had flashed like a warning light.

'Are you all right?' Marianne asked in a quiet period in the early afternoon. 'You look washed out. Are you sure you're not doing too much at the moment? If you could do with a bit of a break from here, I know Julia would be happy to do extra time for a while. She's got unexpected repair bills coming up. Just let me know.'

'You're kind to think of that, but I honestly would rather have more to do than hang around with time on my hands.' Kate was glad to see a group of people coming through the door. The afternoon turned out to be reasonably busy for

November, and she was able to leave at a quarter to five without any further questioning from Marianne.

The sense of escape was short lived. Fergus was waiting outside.

'We need to talk,' he said, and his expression made it clear that he was not going to take a refusal.

Kate knew that after Saturday morning she owed him this. 'Where?' she asked.

'Where are you parked?'

'Opposite The Friary.'

'That'll do. I'm in no mood for chatting over the teacups.'

'Evidently.'

They walked in silence to the car park, and once in the car Kate switched on the engine and put the heater on at full blast.

'I'm sorry about Saturday morning,' she began.

'I bet you are! Sorry to be caught out.'

'Don't be so ridiculous, Fergus.'

He was electric with anger. The space in the car seemed very small and inadequate. 'If you're involved with someone else, I want to know.' She could see the pulse in his temple throbbing violently.

'How can you sit there after the past months and imagine me capable of finding the "go" to start an affair? You of all people should know what a crazy idea that is.'

'So you expect me to think it's normal for male visitors to be around before breakfast, do you?'

'How do you know I wasn't in some hotel dining-room?'

'Because I've checked every hotel, pub and guest house on the list, and you're not registered at any of them. Who was he, Kate?'

'I told you.'

'You made some facetious remark only one step removed from a bloody actress and bishop joke. You might at least have the decency to be straight with me, Kate. It's bad enough that you're doing this mad living apart thing, but until now I never thought there could be any other reason than the mess our marriage is in. Since Saturday I've been going mad imagining God knows what.'

115

She put every ounce of conviction she could into her voice. 'You've no cause for that, Fergus. Saturday was silly. I would have explained, but you jumped to the wrong conclusion entirely.'

'Can you blame me? And as for saying it was the vicar. . . . What kind of fool do you think I am?'

'But he is a vicar. At least, he's qualified to be one, but at present he's chaplain in some kind of prison. It was just the ludicrousness of you suspecting what you were suspecting, and me having to say a pillar of the church was calling at that time that struck me. I haven't had many laughs recently, Fergus. Don't begrudge me that one.'

She could see that he was torn between wanting to believe her, and fear of being made to look a fool.

'He's staying next door to where I am, but only for the week-end,' she went on. 'He came round to borrow milk. And before you say he'd no business to be borrowing it at that time in the morning, he knew I was up and dressed. I'd been out to the car.'

Suspicion was still lingering in Fergus's eyes. 'Young sort of vicar, is he?'

'For goodness' sake! I haven't asked his age.'

'I bet he's not a grandfatherly type if he gets your sense of humour working at that time in the morning.'

'Oh, Fergus. This is all so unnecessary. You've got to believe me. Between us we might be being less than honest to the world in general at present, but I'm not deceiving you.'

His face creased with pain, then in a convulsive movement he bowed his head to rest it on his clenched fists on the dashboard. 'Come home, Kate,' he said, his voice muffled. 'I can't bear it without you. Everything seems to be slipping away from me. I've been foul at work. And I'm so lonely.'

She ached to be able to say something to comfort him, but what? And he was reaching for her hand now. His touch awoke the familiar wish to recoil. Nothing had changed. Nothing would be gained by going back with her emotions no nearer normality.

116

'Can anywhere be more lonely than our bedroom's been with both of us in it?' she asked him quietly. His hand had stopped reaching for her and came to rest on the seat at his side.

'Yes. Believe me, yes. Our bedroom with you gone from it is far worse.' The silence between them throbbed with sadness. There seemed nothing she could say, nothing she could do.

Fergus straightened up and turned to look at her. It was a defiant look. 'I've spoken to a woman from SIDS. One of us had to.' He gave her time to react, but when she went on staring straight ahead through the windscreen into the darkening car park he went on, 'You're not unique in going off sex. She said it happened to most people in our circumstances. We'll get over that, Kate. But how can we get over anything if we're not together?'

She sighed. 'I'm not stupid, Fergus. I have read things. There are books in the library. None of them came anywhere near explaining how I feel. I have the most appalling sense of unworthiness, Fergus. I know I was a good mother to Lucy. I know I didn't do anything I shouldn't have done, or fail to do anything I should have done. I know what happened was a damnable, inexplicable happening that nobody is to blame for. And yet I have the appalling conviction that I'm totally unfit ever to risk having another child. That's what I feel when I'm near you, when you touch me, when there seems the slightest chance that you want to make love to me.'

Even in the dim interior light she could see that Fergus had gone white. He swallowed, then said, 'Why did you marry me if I repel you so much?'

'Haven't you understood what I was saying? You don't repel me. It's not you. It's something twisted in me.' She was turning her wedding ring round and round on her finger. 'I married you because I loved you. Love you still,' she emphasized. 'Don't you see why it's easier to have space between us until I sort out the mess that's in me? Put those two feelings in conflict, loving you and being utterly unable to make love with you, and believe me it's hell.' Her hands went to the wheel. 'Please go, Fergus. I'm desperately sorry, desperately unhappy.

But there's nothing to be gained by struggling round and round this maze.'

He didn't move. 'Wait a few more minutes. Don't rush off. Let's at least try to part on a less hopeless note.'

He looked so defeated that Kate rested her hands in her lap again. 'Only if you stop trying to force me into something I'm not ready for,' she said shakily.

'Can we talk about Maggie, then? I saw her on Saturday.'

'I should have asked. How did it go?'

Fergus told her about his visit. 'Are you going to see her?' he asked finally.

'Would that be a good idea? A lot of unpleasant memories of our last day together could surface.'

'I just don't know. I don't know about anything.'

'Maybe a card, with a longish message on it?'

'I think she would like that.' His hand went to the door handle. 'I suppose I'd better take myself off.' He looked searchingly at her face. 'I'd like to kiss you, but you might think I had the back seat in mind. If you take any thought away from this miserable meeting, Kate, let it be this: there's more than sex in what I feel for you.'

Kate was crying. Tears were welling from her eyes, sliding down her cheeks and she was doing nothing to brush them away. 'I know there is.' Her broken moan held all the pain in the world.

Fergus let himself out, then stood looking back at her helplessly. There was nothing he could do or say to make her feel better. He closed the car door as quietly and gently as he could, as though closing the bedroom door of an invalid. Which he supposed Kate was. Maybe they both were.

Chapter Eight

Calling in to feed Quaker and the hens on her way home from work on Monday, Kate found a scribbled note from Nat to his sister on Jan's kitchen table, pinned down by an apple from the bowl. Kate read it. It was brief, just saying he was sorry to have missed his sister, he hoped the Craft Weekend had been successful, and he would phone her later that night. Nat's handwriting was like his personality, rushing forward, with dramatic touches in the tails and loops.

The barn seemed a dull place without the red car in it. Kate hung around, watching the hens, brooding about the way the weekend had turned out.

Nat's outspoken comment on her reasons for marrying Fergus had really got under her skin. She'd found herself telling him far more than she would ever believe she could reveal to anyone about the state of her marriage and the way things really were between herself and Fergus. But the man who had jolted her into talking by his ability to get to the heart of a situation, had had nothing to say beyond a useless expression of sympathy once she had finished speaking.

He had disappointed her by disappearing for most of Sunday, just popping round to say a pretty impersonal goodbye on Sunday evening. She had made him coffee, and they'd chatted for a few minutes, but there seemed to be an air of constraint between them. Once she had told him the true nature of the rift in her marriage, he had withdrawn. She had shown him how much she needed help, and he had failed to give it. So much for seeking the counselling everybody urged you to have.

She went back into the house and scribbled a note to tell Jan that the animals were dealt with, then drove down to the Barns. Nat's half of the building looked dark and unfriendly. It had been so good, she realized, to have someone else around. For the first time she felt a wave of nervousness as she got out of the car, but the safety light came on over her own front door, and the shadows withdrew a little.

On a sudden impulse she had picked up one or two goodies for Lynne during her lunch hour. Guilty conscience, she supposed, after Nat's mild reproach. She would have liked him to know that his words had had an effect on her. She decided to take the quiche and fruit down straight away. The fraught encounter with Fergus had exhausted her, and she knew she wouldn't want to turn out again once she had gone through her own front door. She left the car lights on to make the track seem less daunting, but that only made the unlit part close to Lynne's cottage seem darker than ever.

Lynne was a while responding to her knock. The living-room lights were on, and Kate noticed while she was waiting that the curtains were back on track, and at least it hadn't been necessary to circumnavigate a pile of bin bags at the gateway. Maybe Nat was right and Lynne was finding her way. Or more likely, she thought wryly, Nat had brought a bit of order to the cottage himself when he had called in on Saturday morning.

There was the sound of feet galloping down the stairs, then Lynne's voice called, 'Who is it?'

'Only me, Kate.'

The door opened. 'Well! Look who's come slumming!' Lynne said, then laughed. 'Don't stand there looking as though you've been hit in the face with a wet fish. Come in.'

'I thought you might enjoy these,' Kate said, unsure of what the reception would be as she handed over the quiche and bag of clementines.

Unexpectedly, Lynne seemed touched. 'What d'you want to go and do that for?' she said delightedly, peering into the delicatessen bag. 'Looks all right, that does. Might have a bit before

I go out. Thanks, Kate. Real little Lady Bountiful you are, aren't you?'

'I shared one at lunch time with Marianne. They're good. How's Rosie?'

'She's fine. Just put her down. Out like a light.'

'And you're going out? Anywhere nice?'

'Only to the village hall. The women's group have a second-hand sale on. Might get the odd bargain.'

'You look very nice.' Lynne was wearing a long black skirt and a red v-necked jumper. Her long, dark hair looked as though it had been newly washed, and she had gone to town on the make-up.

She grinned knowingly at Kate. 'Don't go reading anything into that. It's still only the women's group's sale. But you never know who might be hanging around.'

Kate asked in all innocence, 'Who's babysitting?'

Lynne laughed. 'Listen to the middle class talking. People like me don't have babysitters, love. We have relatives if we're lucky. If we're not, we manage the best way we can.'

Realization dawned. 'You're not going to leave Rosie alone in the house?' Kate's heart had started to race.

'She never wakes up. She won't know a thing about it.'

'But if she did? Lynne, you can't leave a baby her age on her own. Anything could happen.'

Lynne's good humour was vanishing.

'Never has yet. In any case, if you're so worried, what about babysitting yourself, then?'

She had walked right into that. The past flooded into Kate's mind, carrying on its tide fears, uncertainty, inadequacy. 'I should have thought you could make arrangements with one of the village mothers,' she said. She had been going to add '– babysit for each other', but realized as she spoke that Lynne wasn't in a position to be able to do that. She'd need a babysitter to go babysitting.

'Nobody wants to know,' Lynne said, her voice matter-of-fact. 'I'm the slag who hasn't got two pence to rub together. The one who's got damn all to offer in exchange. The one who might get her hooks into your husband. So I leave Rosie in her cot, safely locked in, and trust to luck nobody's going to shop me. It's that or go mad, cooped up in this place week after week. So . . .' she looked ironically at Kate, 'you're all talk and no action, are you?'

I can't do it, Kate was thinking desperately. I can't stay here with a sleeping child upstairs in a cot. A child anything could happen to – and it would be my responsibility. 'What would be the point of starting to rely on me,' she said inadequately. 'I shan't always be here.'

'Too right, you won't.' Lynne's voice was bitter, full of envy. 'You'll get out, get on, get somewhere. You'll be all right. I'm the one who's going nowhere except downhill. I'll fester away here in the backwoods until I get thrown out. Then what? I sure as hell don't know.' She shook a cigarette out of a packet on the fireplace and struck a match savagely. She saw Kate watching her and read her mind accurately.

'Go on. Find something else to criticize. You're thinking I might whinge about having nothing but I manage to afford fags, aren't you? You'd like to snatch it out of my hand, wouldn't you?' She inhaled deeply, and puffed a cloud of smoke towards Kate. 'Well, sucks to you. Go back to your rented barn conversion and call your friends on your mobile. Go out in your car, why don't you? Me and Rosie can manage just fine. Don't give us a thought.'

'I don't blame you for thinking I'm contemptible,' Kate said quietly. 'No doubt it looks from your point of view as though I have all the luck in the world. But I had a baby too, not so long ago. She died. She went laughing and smiling to bed in her cot, and then, a few short hours later, she was dead. I'm scared to be responsible for anyone else's baby, Lynne.'

Lynne had frozen, her defiant outburst silenced. 'You poor cow,' she said slowly. 'Poor, poor cow. Me and my big mouth.' She sat down beside Kate on the shabby sofa and put an arm round her shoulders. 'That's why you keep trying to put me right about Rosie, isn't it? And there's me thinking you're just another busybody sticking her nose in.' She gave Kate's shoulder a convulsive squeeze, then moved away to drag on her cigarette as though embarrassed by her unaccustomed show of affection. 'How old was she?'

'Fourteen weeks.'

'I'd go mad if that happened to me.'

'Going mad – really barking, raving mad – that would be welcome. It's knowing who you are and what you've lost that's the real torture,' Kate said bitterly. She looked up at Lynne. 'Tell me you're going to change your mind and not leave Rosie, Lynne.'

'Look, I can understand you feeling like you do,' Lynne said. 'But Rosie's well beyond the stage when that sort of thing can happen.'

'But what if something else went wrong? You've got a gas fire and a boiler. They can be lethal. And what if somebody broke in?'

'What if a herd of pigs flew over and one of them dropped on her?' Lynne grinned briefly then thrust a hand impatiently through her hair. 'Don't get me wrong. I talk soft about Rosie, pretend I curse the day I fell for her. It's all just that, though – talk. You've no idea how over the top you're going to feel about a kid until you've got it, have you? But I can't give Rosie everything, Kate. If I don't let myself have a bit of something just for me, I'll have nothing left for her in the end.'

There was a sudden knocking at the door, making both of them jump. 'Someone else come to join the happy hour!' Lynne said ironically, going towards the lobby. Jan's cheerful voice called 'It's only me! Hello, Lynne,' then, as she came into the sitting-room, 'Hi, Kate. Thanks for the animals. Just came down to let you know I was back. You've left your car lights on, did you know? I guessed you were down here when there was no sign of life at your place. What's going on?'

Lynne gave Kate a defiant look behind Jan's back. *Are you going to tell?* she was implying. *See if I care.*

'I brought a bit of shopping in for Lynne,' Kate said lamely. The voice inside her was whispering: *Say it. Say you're going to babysit. Do it. What's your alternative?*

But Jan, unknowingly, provided the solution. 'Lynne – there's a kiddies' clothes sale at the village hall tonight. They're usually good value. I meant to tell you before the weekend but forgot. I could stay here for an hour or two if you want to go along?'

A broad grin spread over Lynne's face. 'I'd seen the notice, and I was just trying to twist Kate's arm and force her into staying here for me, but a volunteer's better than forced labour. Rosie's growing so quickly I really need loads for her. I'll dash off right away. Make yourself a pot of tea if you want it. Cheers, Jan. So long, both.'

Grabbing a coat from behind the door and snatching up a torch from the windowsill, she was off.

Jan looked round. 'Well . . . the place doesn't look bad for Lynne. I think she saves all her housework for winter when it's too much effort to trundle Rosie up the hill. I gather I missed that brother of mine. Did you speak to him?'

'Quite a bit. He's . . . very like you.'

Jan laughed. 'You mean what you see is what you get? We're neither of us gifted in the field of diplomacy. But we mean well.' She looked hard at Kate. 'How are things? Feeling any better?'

'Not much. You walked in on a tricky situation – saved me in the nick of time. Lynne said she was trying to get me to babysit. She wasn't succeeding, I'm afraid. I couldn't face it. Pitiful, isn't it?'

'Not pitiful. Understandable. You've had a tough time. You need to get yourself back on balance. You'll do it in the end.'

'I wish I could feel so confident.' Kate made a determined effort. 'How was York?'

'Lovely, as always. I didn't do badly. Sold a few things, and got orders for the silk cards, so it was well worth going.' She peered through into the kitchen. 'I'm going to put the kettle on. Want a cup of tea?'

'No thanks. I'll get back up to my place and see about food.'

'I feel as though I shan't eat for a week. We stopped and had a slap-up lunch on the strength of our profits. Come to think of it, we probably spent half of them! But who cares! See you later, then.'

*

There was an envelope lying face down on the mat inside the front door. Kate picked it up, and saw Nat's flamboyant writing on it. 'Beware – preaching a bit,' he'd written. The envelope felt quite thick. Her heart suddenly swung upwards. He hadn't gone off without a word that mattered. He had considered what she'd said.

The thought was so utterly comforting that she put the envelope carefully in her skirt pocket to savour its presence and defer the unfolding of the promise of help it might contain. Not until her meal was eaten and coffee prepared did she take a clean knife and carefully slit the envelope open.

Dear Kate, Nat wrote, *I haven't ducked out of offering any response to the confidence you placed in me, but I wanted any comments made to come from consideration, not impulse. I am writing my reply instead of giving it to you face to face. I think you will find this, in the end, more useful and less provocative.*

I have spoken to a friend of mine who has had a fair bit of experience with cases such as yours. He tells me that most people who have lost a child through cot death are desperate to conceive another, despite their increased fears. In being so extremely afraid of having another child you are different. You seem to me to be suffering from both guilt and – this is the important bit – from an overwhelming sense of unworthiness. We have to ask what makes you so different from the large majority of parents like you and Fergus.

Your way of dealing with this present sadness worries me. You have broken all ties not only with Fergus's mother, in charge of your child when she died though as you well know in no way responsible for her death, but also with Fergus himself. When the earlier sadness of the death of Maggie's husband occurred, you all worked together, bringing Maggie south with you, wanting to be together when Lucy was born. Why, after your own personal tragedy, should this total dissolution of the family you wanted all your life have taken place?

But there is something else that has puzzled me, and in a way I wonder if this might not perhaps be the seed from which all the present sadness has grown. You told me of the neighbour who was largely responsible for your upbringing – Alice Beattie, I think her name was – with the utmost affection. You preferred, I think you said, to spend time at her house rather than stay with your father when he was home from the rigs. And yet you seem to have lost contact with her. As the closest to a caring relative that you knew in childhood, I would have expected you to remain in loving touch with her in spite of the fact that you now live at some distance.

I sense in some strange way a pattern. Alice, a stable, loving figure from your past. Maggie, equally loved, welcomed into your family circle in Lichfield just as she had welcomed you into hers. Two figures who were once the focus of your deep affection, but from whom you have cut yourself off.

The difficulty with Maggie is easy to understand. But Alice? Perhaps you should search your heart and your memory of the closing stages of the time when Alice was your nearest and dearest for anything that might lead to understanding of the cooling of your relationship. And there is the (to me) strange matter of your not wanting to tell her of your pregnancy. Most girls just long to tell everyone of the baby-to-be. Were you uncommunicative with everybody, or just with Alice? If you can find no answer to these questions within yourself, then perhaps renewing your contact with Alice might be a profitable place to start your search for healing.

I am not a psychiatrist, Kate, but I do spend my time trying to understand the motives and motivations of the boys in my charge, and I hope that something I have said may point you towards a more profitable path than the by-ways of Hints!

I hope we shall meet again in less taxing circumstances, but in any case I hope you will at least let me know what happens. In the meantime, from the bottom of my heart, God bless. Nat.

Fergus had had a Monday to end all Mondays. A record number of emergency calls had combined with the absence of two of the partners, both down with flu, to put the full weight of the practice on his shoulders. The stressful meeting with Kate, sandwiched between evening surgery and afternoon calls to farms as widely scattered as it was possible for them to be, had added to the exhaustion he felt when finally free to head for home.

But home, with its dark, depressingly unlit windows as he drove up to it, was no longer a welcoming beacon. He stood in the kitchen, cruelly illuminated by strip lights, and looked at the signs of neglect all around. He could scarcely believe how uncared for it had grown in the comparatively short time since Kate had left. He had given the place a perfunctory tidying most days, stuck dishes in the dishwasher at least at the end of the day, but there seemed to be an air of grime building up on floor and kitchen surfaces. He had obviously not been doing enough. The thought of setting to and getting busy with mop and bucket now that he had actually become aware of the mess surrounding him was intolerable.

Getting something to eat was equally daunting. He took a couple of bananas from the fruit dish, both limp and well spotted with dark-brown in spite of only having been bought on Saturday, and helped himself to a glass of milk. That would have to do. He hadn't much appetite in any case. Then he remembered Middy. All the cat dishes were dirty. He emptied half a tin of Whiskas into a soup bowl. So much for hygiene. Perhaps the cat bugs would fight it out with the rest of the bacteria around and leave him be. If not, the way he felt tonight, a day or two in bed would be welcome.

Kate had flung at him the idea of getting one of the cleaners from the surgery to do a bit of extra time for him, but that meant the likelihood of more people seeing through the reason he had cooked up for Kate's absence. How long were people supposed to have someone sleeping in with them after a hip operation, for heaven's sake? That excuse wouldn't hold for much longer.

Biting into the first slimy banana with no relish at all, he made his way upstairs to the room that reminded him only too vividly of Kate's absence. In bed, he wearily turned on his side, away from the empty space that broke his heart. Kate had left the nightdress she had been wearing on her pillow. Fergus pushed his hand into its silky folds, drawing it close and resting his aching head against it. But the feel of Kate that it evoked, and the ever-more faint scent of her, were too painful to be endured. He pushed it back out of reach, and willed himself to go to sleep.

Tuesday morning saw one of the partners back at work, red nosed and full of self pity but at least willing to achieve martyrdom by taking his surgeries. Fergus, for whom Tuesday was his usual free afternoon, was thankful to head for home after lunch with the firm intention of putting the house in order.

When he turned into the drive, there was already a car parked near the front door. Zoe's Vauxhall, he realized with surprise. She had never been to the house before, and since this was one of the days when she only worked mornings, she should have been back in her own home by now. She could quite easily have spoken to him about anything that was bothering her at work. He felt displeased to have his territory invaded.

Zoe got out and came to meet him, unselfconsciously wriggling her skirt down from its ridden-up position.

'What are you doing here?' he said, none too graciously.

'And it's nice to see you too,' she retorted, unabashed. 'You've been taking lessons in friendliness, obviously.'

Reluctantly, he had to grin at her cheeky smile and twinkling eyes. 'All right, I'll rephrase that,' he said. 'What can I do for you?'

She drew in a mock scandalized breath. 'Now there's a question that could get you into trouble. Some girls would be all over you before you'd finished speaking.'

'Cut the crap, Zoe,' he said tiredly. 'Why on earth you couldn't have seen me at work this morning, I can't imagine. For all you know I could have been going anywhere but here after lunch.'

'Wrong! I heard you telling Martin you'd left your mobile at home and you were going straight back there once you'd grabbed a sandwich at the pub. Do I get invited in, or do you want to talk on the doorstep?'

He unlocked the door and stood back to let her go ahead of him into the house. As she passed him, he was suddenly aware of her perfume. Presumably she wore it all the time, but the stronger scents of the surgery stifled it. It was something Kate often wore from the Dior range with its light lily-of-the-valley-notes. It made him long for Kate, then in the same breath hate her for making him so vulnerable.

Zoe was looking round with interest. 'So this is Chateau Callender,' she said.

'Not exactly a chateau at the moment. Go on into the sitting-room.' The hall had muddy wellingtons and an unappealing pair of his trainers lying beside the doormat. His dressing-gown was in a heap at the foot of the stairs, where he had dropped it this morning for some unaccountable reason. The sitting-room curtains hadn't been drawn back. It was a wonder someone didn't come to check if he was dead, Fergus thought, except that probably nobody gave a toss. He yanked the curtains back viciously, and daylight fell on a tray of crusted takeaway dishes from heaven knew when.

'Tell you what,' Zoe said, bending down to scoop up the tray. 'Why don't we go straight into the kitchen, get rid of this lot, and put the kettle on. A cup of coffee would just fit the bill while we talk. I've been doing a bit of shopping – didn't have time for lunch. This way, is it?' She was off, bobbing through the hall like a cheerful waitress. Fergus followed her, resentful of being upstaged in his own home.

'Oh dear!' she said expressively, her eyes taking in the full bin. 'Better get rid of this lot. Dustbin outside at the back, is it?' Before Fergus could answer, she was whisking the bag of rubbish out through the back door, scooping the foil dishes off the tray on her way.

'Do you whiz around at this speed all the time at home?' he asked as she came back in.

'Have to. Becca needs a staff of dozens to clear up after her, and I can't stand mess.' In the time it took him to fill the kettle and get out a couple of mugs, she replaced the kitchen bin bag, somehow guessing exactly where the spares were kept, gave the table and the rest of the units a swipe with a J-cloth, and took off the jacket of her suit to hang it over the back of the chair she subsided into. It was the chair last sat in by Kate when she told Fergus she was going away. The memory stung painfully, as the snatch of perfume had done. Fergus banished it determinedly. Zoe's bright face was staring intently at him.

'Come on, sit down a minute while we wait for the kettle. Have you any news of Kate?'

'Nothing that means anything. I spoke to her yesterday, but the conversation didn't get us anywhere.' Kate's face, tear-stained and desperate, seared his memory.

'I'm sorry. You still don't know where she's staying?'

'Haven't a clue.'

'Nor whether she's getting round to thinking about coming back?'

'Likewise.' The kettle boiled and switched itself off. Fergus got up clumsily, blinded by unhappiness, and made the coffee. 'Sugar?'

'No thanks. Wouldn't mind a biscuit if you've got any.'

He rooted around in the cupboard and found a Kit-Kat behind the empty biscuit barrel. Zoe broke into it eagerly. Her full pink lips as she sucked at the chocolate finger like a child with a lollipop made him think of a much less innocent old TV advert for another chocolate product, which in turn reminded him of things he would do well not to think about.

'So what's this visit all about?' he said.

'I was thinking about you and your washing and everything. It occurred to me that you're a bit of a wimp in the house-keeping area, aren't you?'

'Thanks very much! Flattery will get you everywhere.'

'I mean, I've met your mother when she called in at the surgery a couple of times. She struck me as being the sort who wouldn't let a man lift a finger in what she considered her department. I bet you never did a stroke of washing or cooking for yourself before you were married, did you? And I bet you expected it to go on that way once Kate was on the scene.'

'I never thought of it that way. I was always busy enough. Still am. But I expect you're right, and I've got every opportunity to learn by experience now haven't I?'

Zoe looked slowly and deliberately around. 'I wouldn't say experience was teaching you much at the moment. But that's what I came round for. Listen, Fergus. If you need someone to give the house a once-over and see to the washing and ironing, I could give you a hand on one – or both if you want – of my afternoons off.'

'I should have thought that would be against your principles. Wouldn't it be encouraging a wimp to be a wimp?'

She grinned at him. 'You can't help your upbringing. You're an OK wimp, really.'

He took a long drink of his coffee, warmed by her surprising offer but needing time to think.

'You're a sweet girl, Zoe,' he said at last. 'You're an excellent receptionist, pretty blooming marvellous with the clients, a dab hand at chasing up bills and taming the dratted computer. But you're not a cleaner and you shouldn't be trying to downgrade yourself into one.'

'Every poor cow of a woman's a cleaner!' Zoe countered robustly. 'That's one thing we've not managed to shrug off yet. Suit yourself, Fergus. But I thought I'd make the offer. After all, I know what's going on, don't I? And I don't imagine you want anyone else from the surgery poking their nose inside your front door at the moment.'

Fergus sighed. 'You're right there. But the truth of it is that I don't think I can bring myself to make any arrangements that look as though I'm getting my life to work without Kate in it. It would make this ghastly business seem so much more permanent. And besides, it wouldn't be right for me to put on you.'

Zoe shrugged. 'You wouldn't be. I wasn't thinking just of you, as it happens. And I wasn't talking about charity. Becca wants a computer for Christmas. A bit of extra cash would be pretty useful right now. I wasn't aiming to become one of Fergus's Ministering Angels. Anyway, it's your decision. You know I'm here if you want me.' She drained her coffee and screwed up the Kit-Kat wrapper. 'Well, better be on my way. If you change your mind and want me to come up on Thursday, give me the nod and I'll come prepared with something to change into.' She was slipping her coat on. As she reached back for the second sleeve, her cream jersey shirt was drawn tight against her breast. Fergus, who had been watching her, swallowed and looked down. His instinctive reaction to Zoe's undoubted charms made him feel ashamed. Shame quickly turned into unjustified annoyance, directed at this forceful scrap of a woman with her blonde hair and pert, obtrusive breasts. What was she doing in Kate's kitchen, ordering cups of coffee, trying to organize his life? He got up, scraping his chair back with an ugly sound. He wanted to be rid of her. 'I'm grateful for the offer, Zoe,' he said, 'but kind though you are, I really don't need to make any such arrangement at the moment. I'm sure Kate will be back soon.'

Zoe looked at him with a funny, unreadable expression on her face for a moment. Then she shook her head sadly.

'Determined to manage alone, are you? You're a silly, stubborn man, Fergus. Well, if you do need me any time, I'll be here. Don't look so miserable. What you need is a good, hard hug!'

She was about to launch herself at him, but Fergus sidestepped her and headed for the front door. Even that rebuff didn't flatten Zoe. Her chuckle followed dancing at his heels like a badly behaved puppy

'Not often I get turned down,' she said brightly as she passed him in the doorway. 'Never mind. You can keep that offer on ice as well. See you tomorrow, Fergus.'

There was something irresistible about her unshaken good humour. Fergus stooped down to look at her through the Vauxhall's passenger window.

'Goodbye, you impossible person,' he said.

'That's better!' She blew him a kiss. 'Bye, Fergus.'

*

It was an hour before Fergus got round to checking his mobile. It had no voice mail for him, but it indicated surprisingly that there was a text message waiting. Who on earth was text-messaging him? He thought that was the means of communicating schoolkids overdosed on, not people like him.

The message, when he rolled it up his screen sent him spinning off into a totally unexpected orbit of dismay.

'On way Whitehaven,' it said cryptically. 'Explain later. K.'

What was she doing now? What the hell was she doing now? She'd practically wiped Whitehaven out of her life since their marriage, but now she was heading for it without any word to him of why or where or how long. He'd never done the drive from Lichfield – not once had there been a hint of a suggestion that it might be nice to go there. It must be at least a five to six hour drive, he imagined, and most of it on the M6. Was Kate in sufficiently sound mind to be in charge of a car on the busy M6? He doubted it. He very much doubted it. But what could he do about it? He was as helpless to stop this mad journey as he was to stop anything else Kate took it into her head to do. He pounded the kitchen table with his fists, making the coffee cups dance in their saucers, then buried his face in his hands, feeling new depths of powerlessness engulf him.

Chapter Nine

Kate filtered gingerly into the hurtling traffic on the M6, hugging the inside lane until she adjusted to the change of pace after the green and pleasant A51.

She could hardly believe that she was doing this – heading back on impulse to a place she hadn't had the least desire to visit in the ten years since her father had died in her first year of her fine Art course at Edinburgh.

It had all happened so quickly. She had read and reread Nat's letter, and by the end of the evening, her mind had been made up. She phoned Marianne at ten – too intent on her purpose to be concerned about the time. Marianne was surprised to have her offer of time off taken up so quickly and in such contrast with Kate's initial reaction to the suggestion, but she rang back early on Tuesday morning to say that Julia was happy to fill in for Kate for the rest of the week.

'So your friend is able to cope now?' Marianne said.

Kate had completely forgotten where she was supposed to be.

'Signed off until a three month check-up yesterday,' she improvised, vowing mentally that once this mad period was over, she would never lie again. She wasn't up to it.

'Fergus is a good sort to put up with life without you, isn't he? And quite right to think a complete rest would do you good after all you've been through,' Marianne said, fortunately not waiting for an answer. 'Must rush now or I'll be late opening up. Let me know when you'll be back. Julia won't mind doing another full week if necessary. Have a good rest.'

Kate was incredulous about what she was doing, but at the same time she felt a kind of elation. For the first time since she had walked away from Fergus and Maggie and the sadness of home, she felt to be doing something positive. She had been running away. Now admittedly she was still running, but towards something. Whether Nat's theory had any value or not, something would come of this visit, if only a reawakening of the closeness with Alice that been such a compensating factor throughout all her early years.

She had no clear idea what she was going to do in Whitehaven. The questions raised by Nat in his letter had found no answers in her mind, but at least he had made her think.

She supposed he was right in finding it odd that she had lost touch so completely with Alice. But there didn't seem to be any reason for it – it had just happened. It had not been planned, nor had it been the subject of much thought.

How old would Alice be now? There had been a seventieth birthday, she remembered, before Edinburgh. That was nine years ago now. There had been a card last Christmas, but – she frowned, trying hard to remember – no, no birthday card this year. The thought that Alice could have died – for who would think to let Kate know – caused the steering to wobble sufficiently to make a supermarket lorry about to thunder past her sound his horn.

It wouldn't be a good idea to get herself killed, Kate told herself. She gave her mind to the road and drove steadily on until the Knutsford Service Station where she pulled in for a coffee break. While she was there, she set about finding somewhere to stay in Whitehaven. When she was in the sixth form, she had worked for two consecutive holidays at Lesserby Hall, a Grade I listed hotel just outside the town. She dialled the number Directory Enquiries gave her, and by the time the call ended had a bed for the night and for however long she wished to stay.

Feeling that she had one certainty ahead, Kate resumed her

journey. Roadworks and a lorry that had shed its load of timber caused hold-ups through Lancashire. The traffic thinned out after Lancaster, though, and she was able to get as far as the last Services before the turn-off at Penrith before stopping for a late lunch, glad to think that there were less than twenty more miles of motorway ahead of her.

Mid-afternoon found her driving along past the sparkling waters of Bassenthwaite with Skiddaw's snowy cap dazzling against the blue sky. Why haven't I wanted to come back to this beautiful place, Kate asked herself. She was seeing the Lake District at its best on this dry, bright November day, and its loveliness seemed to fold itself around her like a comforting blanket. Mountains and water . . . she must have subconsciously missed them both.

It was dusk when she reached Lesserby Hall, where she was given a warm welcome. Incredibly, the same manager was there and remembered her, as did several members of staff. Tea was sent up to her room, with scones and shortcake.

Kate felt exhausted, and decided not to attempt to see Alice until the following morning. She was sleepy and the thought of an evening meal after such a generous afternoon tea, didn't appeal. She rang reception and told them that she wouldn't be coming into the dining-room that night, but would look forward to a full English breakfast next morning. She would have a brief walk since she felt to need fresh air after being cooped up in the car all day, but after that she would have a bath and get to bed.

In the end, she was too tired to venture far. She walked round the walled garden of the Hall and called it a day. The hot bath practically had her sleeping in it, and by half past eight she was in bed and dead to the world.

She woke in the small hours and realized that she had not called Fergus. It was too late now. She would have to get in touch in the morning. She lay there awake for a while, thinking of Fergus, and hoping he was not going to give her a hard time in the morning. Maybe she would send him another text message. Yes, that would be best. She would keep all explanations for when she could give them in person. She must have dropped asleep almost at once after that, for she didn't hear another thing until the raucous cries of a gull perched on her windowsill roused her at half past seven next morning.

Maggie had been pleased to know that Fergus was coming to see her again on Wednesday afternoon.

'But how will that fit in with your work?' she asked.

'Work can wait,' he told her. 'I need to talk to you.'

'And I to you,' she told him in a completely different tone of voice from his. She was dying to tell him about her Sunday tea party with Gordon, which she had achieved with pleasure and without problem. True, he had met her at Ashfield's gate and walked her round to his house, but she had done it. She had not been afraid or shaky or felt like fainting. She was proud of her progress, and so was Dr Lawson. Fergus would be too, she was sure.

But Fergus hadn't given her the chance to begin to relate her success.

'I've been keeping something from you, I'm afraid,' he began, pulling the dressing-table stool over to perch opposite her chair. They were in Maggie's room this time, since there had been others in the Green room when she had checked it.

'That sounds ominous,' she said.

'I didn't want to worry you, but things have got to such a pitch that I don't think I can keep it to myself any longer.'

'For goodness sake tell me, Fergus,' Maggie said apprehensively.

'It's about Kate. The day you came to Ashfield, she had some kind of crisis. You remember how she disappeared before I got there? When she came back later that night she told me that she was leaving me. Not for good,' he added hurriedly at Maggie's gasp of dismay. 'At least, she said then that it wasn't for good.'

'A crisis? But you said she was looking after a friend from the choir.' Maggie didn't seem to be able to take in what he was saying.

'That was her idea. Pure invention, to stop people asking questions and finding out what was really going on. Neither of us was particularly proud of the situation.'

'Then where is she?'

'She wouldn't tell me where she was staying. Couldn't bear the thought of me trespassing in her new-found space.' His voice shook with anger.

'Oh, Fergus! The poor girl!'

Fergus felt physical pain in his chest at his mother's words. His wife had walked out on him, and all his mother could find to say about it was 'The poor girl!'

'What about me?' he asked tersely. 'How do you think I feel? I've done my level best to support Kate these past weeks. She wasn't the only one missing Lucy like hell, you know. She was my baby too.'

'I know. Oh, I do know, Fergus. But you had to keep on working. That part of your life was left and had to be carried on. All Kate had been doing for nine months was getting ready for her baby. Then, after a few short weeks of caring for Lucy, suddenly it had all gone. Only a huge emptiness left. I don't think any man can quite realize how devastating that is for a woman.'

'But I was still there. Can any woman realize what it is like for a man to be there, but suddenly to count for nothing?' There was raw pain in his voice, and Maggie reached out and gripped his hand.

There was a silence. Then Maggie said, 'To think that I believed if I got out of the way, it would be so much better for you both.'

'If you hadn't gone, maybe Kate wouldn't have,' Fergus said. All thought of sparing Maggie worry seemed to have vanished. 'It was that awful day that did it. Someone else's baby in the house . . . and the police storming up on top of everything else.'

He withdrew his hand impatiently. Maggie was hurt by his words, but she wasn't, she found, any longer guilty. 'That day grew from everything that had gone before,' she said with dignity. 'And if Kate felt desperate enough to leave, then the desire to get away grew from what had happened before also. Your attitude of blame towards me now has its roots in the past, too. You have always walked on the sunny side, Fergus. You were our golden boy. Everything came easily to you – school, university, your work. People always liked you. Then there was Kate who worshiped you – as was your expectation. It must be hard for you to cope with things going wrong. I can understand your need to find someone to blame.'

Fergus was outraged. 'Are you suggesting that there's a reason in me for everything that has gone wrong?'

'No, of course not. But I am trying to get you to look inside yourself and find out whether you have let Kate see how much you resent the fact that she has been unable to switch off her grief at the drop of a hat. Maybe she can't bear the fact that she simply isn't able to restore your world to its expected state.'

'What Kate can't bear,' Fergus said icily, 'is the thought of ever again having sex with me.' He saw the colour deepen in his mother's cheeks and felt a tiny germ of satisfaction at saying something to shake her. Solve that one with your theories, he wanted to shout at her.

'I'm not in the habit of discussing such private matters,' Maggie said after a moment. 'My generation didn't achieve the freedom of yours. But I can understand that such a devastating blow as the loss of a child will send hurt along every emotional channel. Give her time, Fergus. And don't say things to me now that you will regret when you are feeling more calm. This is something to be healed by you and Kate alone. Nobody else can do it.'

The mild rebuke rankled. 'There's not much that we can do about it with Kate taking herself off to the other end of the country,' Fergus said. 'I haven't told you everything yet. She's gone careering up to Whitehaven now – heaven knows why. She's had no desire to go back there ever since we were married.'

Maggie sighed. 'If she felt the need to do that, then perhaps good will come of it. I always felt sorry that Alice faded so much into the background. She struck me as being a nice, genuine woman, and she'd done a lot for Kate over the years. Just let her be, Fergus. Don't try to force anything. Trying to make reasoned decisions when you're full of grief doesn't always turn out well. I've good cause to know that.'

'What do you mean by that?'

'Look what difficulties my deciding to sell up and come down to Lichfield has caused. That was a hasty decision, not even a year after your father died.'

'Are you saying now that you wish you hadn't decided to come south with us?'

She didn't exactly deny it. 'Nothing as definite as that. I wanted to come with you. I very much didn't want to be alone, miles away from you. But whether I was wise to make myself a part of your new life is a different matter. I have certainly wondered that over the past weeks.'

Fergus stared glumly at the carpet. 'We are hardly what you could call a united family, are we?'

'We've lost our way for the time being. That doesn't mean that we shan't find it one day soon. I presume you are in touch with Kate by some means or other, or you wouldn't know about this present journey of hers?'

'I got her a mobile phone, since she refused to part with an address or telephone number.' His mouth tightened. 'At the moment she seems to be keeping it switched off, but I merit the odd text message now and then – as brief as possible, of course.'

'Try not to be too sorry for yourself, Fergus,' Maggie said quietly.

He jumped to his feet, anger barely controlled. 'I think you have obviously had enough of me and my troubles. No doubt Gordon and his garden produce are more welcome.'

Maggie got up and attempted to hug him. 'Don't be so silly. No one could be more welcome than my son, even if he is not exactly himself at the moment.'

Fergus was beyond appeasement. 'I'm glad that you at least seem to be showing signs of progress,' he said in a tone that held no trace of gladness.

'As you and Kate will, I am sure. Let's part on more hopeful terms. Do you know, Fergus, I actually went round for my tea party with Gordon on Sunday, and there wasn't a trace of nonsense about me. That's good, isn't it?'

'Very. Congratulations.' His voice was tight and unforgiving. 'And now on that happy note, you must excuse me, mother. I'm late for work as it is.'

'Come again, won't you?' she said anxiously.

'I expect so. I seem to be the boring old stable pivot around which everyone else is whirling. I don't have the luxury of doing what fancy dictates.'

'Oh, Fergus!' followed him reproachfully as he closed the door with exaggerated quietness.

All the way back to the surgery he went over their conversation, finding nothing in it to comfort him. A man would think his own mother would side with him in circumstances like these. But no. It was Kate who got all the sympathy, Kate who was at present dishing out all the hurt. He had never felt so alone.

As for his mother suggesting that he could only cope with success, what on earth did she mean by it? Hadn't he taken charge of everything when his father died? Hadn't he damped down his own grief over Lucy to be a tower of strength for Kate? What more could he have done? And if he was 'not quite himself', as Maggie had patronizingly said, well, everyone had a breaking point. How much more was he expected to take without feeling he'd had enough?

Martin, the senior partner, was hanging round in the surgery entrance. 'About time, isn't it, Fergus?' he said, looking ostentatiously at his watch. 'There's a waiting-room full of your clients through there. This isn't good enough.'

'Things haven't been too easy for me in recent weeks,' Fergus said icily, 'I have never cried off work throughout that time. I think one half-hour late – a hospital visit, incidentally – doesn't exactly call for the heavy guns.'

'We make appointments. People expect us to keep them unless there is a good explanation. If you had bothered to phone in, I would have started your surgery for you. As it is we have been expecting you to walk in any minute. A simple phone call, Fergus. Not too much to ask.' Martin, not one to play the senior card normally, was certainly slamming it on the table today.

'Then accept my humble apology. No doubt I shall make up for the time I owe you at the end of the day – or next time you want to go rolling up your trouser leg with your fellow Masons.'

Fergus flung open the waiting-room door. 'I am extremely sorry to have kept you waiting,' he said with exaggerated charm. 'If the first client would like to go along to my room, I will be with you at once.' Shrugging off his Barbour, he darted quickly into the cloakroom to hang it up, then went into his surgery, closing the door on the busy but silently listening staff in Reception.

He worked like a fiend all morning. When the last client had departed, he left the nurse clearing up in the surgery and went to get his coat, needing more than anything a stiff drink.

Martin's voice halted him as he passed the open door of the senior partner's room. 'Have you a minute, Fergus?'

Reluctantly Fergus stepped inside the doorway.

'Close the door, old man.' Martin came round his desk and put a hand on Fergus's shoulder. 'We overstepped the boundary a bit earlier on, didn't we?' He held out a hand 'Best forgotten, eh?'

Fergus relaxed and shook Martin's hand. 'You were absolutely right. I should have let you know or seen my mother at a more convenient time.'

'Everything all right? As all right as it can be, at the moment?'

'The situation's just getting me down a bit. Bad hair day, you could say.' Fergus managed a shaky grin.

'You've coped marvellously. We all think so. I took my own bad temper out on you quite unjustifiably earlier on. I'd had a row with a client. Damned farmers and their tight fists. This one owes us from eighteen months back and still won't fork out.'

They talked shop for a few minutes more, then Fergus left to get his lunch, glad that the unpleasantness had been cleared up.

More often than not he went to The Scales on Market Street. Today the pub was busy and he didn't linger once he had been served and disposed of his pint and Ploughman's. He felt to need fresh air. A quick look at his watch established that he had time for a brisk walk round Stowe Pool before afternoon calls.

The conversation with Maggie still rankled. It was painfully obvious that nobody was going to give much thought to how he was feeling. The sensible thing for him to do, he supposed, was to forget about marking time until Kate came to her senses and get on with organizing his own life so that it ran as smoothly as possible.

There were no boats on the pool, and the water was still and glassy, reflecting the blue sky and fleet of puffy white clouds perfectly. It soothed his spirit.

Back at the practice, he found Zoe alone in reception with her printer rattling merrily.

'Can you come along to my room for a moment?' he asked.

'Sure, Fergus. Be with you in two ticks, once this lot's finished printing.'

He made sure there was nobody in the back room, then stood leaning against the examination table until he heard the tap of Zoe's heels along the corridor.

'All right now?' she asked, coming in and closing the door. 'Don't take Martin too seriously. He'd had a bad time with Maddison first thing. Just wanted to kick something or some-body, and you walked in with perfect timing.'

'I know. We sorted it out. So you can tell all the ear-flappers that they can forget it.'

'All part of life's rich pattern,' Zoe grinned. 'What did you want, then?'

'You offered to help me out at home,' Fergus said.

'And you turned me down.'

'Well, that was yesterday. Today I've changed my mind. I've had a good think, and I'd be grateful if you would go along and wave a magic wand tomorrow. Any hope?'

She smiled her wide, warm smile. 'Of course there is. One afternoon or two?'

Might as well go the whole hog, Fergus thought recklessly. 'Both would solve the washing and ironing problem, and you could split the cleaning between them.'

'Both it is, then. Good for you for coming to your senses. What made you change your mind?'

'A message from Kate. She's left Lichfield. Gone north.'

'Whatever for?'

'That's what I'd like to know.' He straightened up. 'I'm sick of just waiting and dreading. I need somebody. Somebody to help,' he added hurriedly.

Zoe's soft blue eyes seemed to beam warmth and friendship towards him. 'Of course you do,' she said softly.

They looked at each other. The air in the surgery seemed suddenly very quiet and still. Fergus fumbled in his pocket.

'You'd better have a key. Keep it for as long as you're coming and going.' Her hand was soft, her nails delicate almonds, impeccably polished.

'Is that it? Anything more?'

'Just thanks, Zoe.'

'What are friends for?' she said brightly, giving him a wink. Then she was gone.

Fergus stood gazing down at the table, preoccupied. Then he stood to his full height and brushed a hand through his hair.

It was done now. And it was the sensible thing to do. He was sure of it.

Chapter Ten

A leaflet in the hotel told Kate that they had put a memorial on the site of the old William Pit to the men, women and children killed over the years, more than three hundred of them sacrificed to coal. One of those men, killed in the explosion of 1947, was Alice's husband of only twelve months. Alice too had known the joy of love and the pain of loss. How little we appreciate the sadness of others until the same darkness has touched us, Kate thought. On the surface of my mind I have always known about Alice's husband, but only now do I really know.

With an hour to kill before she thought it would be a suitable time to shock Alice by walking back into her life without warning, Kate went down to the old pit site and read the names on the monument until she found Henry's. Her finger traced the letters. Henry, all these others, here briefly, and irrationally taken as Lucy had been. And life goes inexorably on.

How hard it was to make the transition from heartbreak to tender, loving memory. Not to forget, but equally not to allow a shining, much-loved life, now ended, to become something that warped the present.

She straightened up. She was getting maudlin, and she had a meeting ahead that was going to need a positive approach. She would go and have a coffee before heading for Alice's.

She stopped at the first pub she came to, an unrecognizably smart reincarnation of its old self. Lottery money, she supposed, and well used. She went to a table in the window, and sat facing the room. There were few people in the pub at the moment, and no familiar faces, which wasn't surprising after all this time.

It was as she was preparing to go that she saw out of the corner of her eye someone come in from a door at the far end of the bar and speak to the barman. She gave the most casual of glances in that direction as she began to rise to her feet, not even curious, simply attracted by the movement. And at that very moment, the man turned his head and looked in her direction. Suddenly the room spun violently, and Kate sank back into her chair, gripping the edge of the table, waiting for the blackness to recede.

When the faintness passed and she dared to open her eyes again, the man had gone. He obviously hadn't recognized her, or if he had, he hadn't considered it necessary after all this time to come over and speak to her. She ventured gingerly to stand up again. She must have got up too quickly before. There was certainly no reason to have reacted so violently to the sight of a past boyfriend, even one as notorious as Jamie Bragg.

Strange that she should see him now when she was on her way to Alice's. He had caused so many headaches for Alice during those wild, sixth-form months before Kate left Whitehaven. He had been behind the bar himself back then, in one of Whitehaven's other pubs. Now he was still working in the same environment, but judging by his sharp suit he might have reached manager status.

He had gained weight – an occupational hazard, she supposed. To an easily-impressed sixth former he had been exciting back then with his streetwise ways. He had let Kate and her crowd drink under age, risking his own job to do it, and eventually drawing Kate aside from her friends to arrange a meeting with her on her own. As her infatuation with him grew, he had encouraged her to slip out after Alice was in bed to meet him, persuading her back to what he called his 'pad'. The room had had the glamour of the forbidden then, but looking back on it now, she saw it for the seedy scoring ground it had undoubtedly been. She shook her head to banish the picture of a past she was hardly proud of.

Truly relieved to have been spared an awkward, undesired few moments making conversation with him that neither of them wanted, Kate drove towards the street of terraced houses where she had spent the first eighteen years of her life. She parked round the corner, wanting to walk slowly towards Alice, preparing herself.

The street had changed, brightened. Most of the houses were colour washed now, striving for individuality instead of the grey uniformity she remembered. Stone window surrounds were brightened with contrasting colours. Several houses had window boxes.

She walked past her old home, feeling nothing. It had not been a home, really, she supposed. But Alice's house had. She raised the remembered polished brass ship knocker and, catching her breath, rapped a loud tattoo.

After a few moments the door opened slowly, and Alice stood there, her expression enquiring, obviously at first unaware who was on her doorstep.

'Hello, Alice,' Kate said. 'It's been a long time.'

The faded brown eyes sharpened, the glasses were lowered in a familiar gesture to allow Alice to peer over their frames, and the smiling mouth opened in surprise.

'It's never – it is, isn't it? It's Kate! Why, wherever have you sprung from, pet? Come away in!'

Kate followed the old lady into the immaculate cosy sitting-room. There was a coal-effect gas fire now, a fair enough imitation of the real coal fires she remembered from her early childhood.

'What are you doing in this part of the world?' Alice asked delightedly. 'I never thought I'd see you again. Oh, but I'm glad you're here!' She flung her arms round Kate and hugged her hard enough to drive the breath out of her body.

'I've come to see you, Alice.' Kate was made to sit down in a chair by the fire.

'All this way to see me?' A proud smile spread acroas Alice's wrinkled cheeks. 'Aren't I the important one, then!' She reached over and squeezed Kate's hand. 'Oh, love, it's so good to see you.' She peered closely into Kate's face. 'But where's that colour you used to have in your cheeks? You look like a little ghost. Hasn't that husband of yours been looking after you?'

'I've been a bit under the weather,' Kate said, not quite ready yet for explanations. 'No fault of Fergus's. But tell me about you, Alice. You look well.'

'I'm fine apart from a bit of creaking that's only to be expected at my age. Still do a bit, though, you know. There's a young family next door in your old house. They let me baby-sit now and then. Lovely little lad, he is. Just eighteen months old.'

'Still the same old Alice, then! Not happy unless you're looking after somebody.' Kate smiled fondly at the old lady.

Alice was struggling to her feet again. 'But what am I thinking of? You here in my house and I haven't even offered you a cup of tea. I'll go put the kettle on. If I'd known you were coming I'd have baked a cake, as they say. As it is, you'll have to make do with shortbread. There's always some of that on the go.'

Kate reached out to stop her. 'I've had coffee. Sit down. I just want to talk to you. If you'd not been so anti-phone I could have let you know I was coming.'

'Aha! You don't know everything!' Alice reached to pick up a bunched up pinnafore from a small table by her chair, revealing a shiny red telephone. 'What about that, then?' she said proudly. 'Still don't get over-fond of the beggar, though.'

Kate laughed. 'What made you give in after all these years?'

'A small affair called a stroke back in May. I was persuaded that it might be a good idea to be able to ring the quack without walking the streets.'

'You had a stroke? Oh, Alice, and you never told me. Was that the reason I didn't get a birthday card?'

'Oh, you noticed then? I was a bit down at the time. I couldn't have written much at all, and what I wrote wouldn't have been cheerful, so I left well alone. I'm all right now, though. Take my little pills and behave myself. Haven't needed this contraption, really. Nor this, but they made me have it.' She pulled a necklace alarm out of the neck of her blouse. 'Ridiculous object. I was forever setting it off without meaning to at first.'

'Better that than lying on the floor for hours with nobody knowing.' They smiled at each other. 'Oh, it's good to see you,' Kate said with feeling. 'We've drifted apart a bit, haven't we? I didn't mean that to happen.'

'Things do,' Alice said, gazing into the leaping gas flames. 'Beyond our control it seems, sometimes.'

Kate steeled herself. She was going to have to tell Alice about Lucy. It was unthinkable not to. Better get it over with.

'Alice . . .' she said, 'There's a reason for me not looking as fit as I might. I . . . I lost my baby.'

There was a silence. Alice sat as though she had been turned to stone, her eyes fixed on Kate's face. Her mouth opened and closed, then opened again and at last, obviously with the utmost difficulty, she managed to speak.

'You've remembered . . .' she said.

The words didn't make sense. Kate wondered anxiously if the obvious shock her words had given Alice could be enough to cause her to have another stroke.

'How could I forget?' she said, and before she could ask Alice if she was all right, the old woman said something that was even more odd.

'I know I never have.'

'But Alice – you didn't know about the baby.'

'Oh yes I did!' The answer was firmer now, and Alice looked more sure of herself.

'But who could have told you?'

'Why, lassie, you told me yourself. You sat in that very chair, and you told me.'

Alice was clearly not herself. Kate wished she had never spoken. 'I'm sorry, Alice. I've given you too big a shock. I should have led up to it more gently.'

'There was no leading up to it gently back then. It was a case of straight out with it. If we're talking about shocks, that was a

149

shock and a half, I can tell you. Only a week after your birthday it was.'

'But Alice – I wasn't here around my birthday. I was down in Lichfield. As a matter of fact, May this year was when Lucy was born, just ten days after my birthday. So you see I couldn't have been here telling you anything then.'

Alice's hand had gone to her chest and she looked stricken.

'It doesn't matter,' Kate said. 'Anybody can get a little bit mixed up at times.'

'You were talking about this year?' the old lady said, her voice trembling. 'Oh, sweet Mary and Joseph, you haven't remembered at all, have you? What have I done?' She was rocking to and fro in her chair. 'All these years I've kept quiet, worried myself sick about whether I was doing the right thing, and now I've stirred up a hornet's nest, blurting it out like a silly old senile woman.'

Kate left her chair and dropped to her knees near Alice.

'I don't understand what you're saying, but please, don't upset yourself. I couldn't bear it if I made you ill. Can I get you anything? Have you any brandy?'

Alice seized Kate's hand and clung to it. 'Oh, pet, I know you think I'm losing my marbles, but I'm not. We were talking at cross purposes. I'll explain – I'll have to now.' A shudder went through her. 'I don't need brandy. But you must speak first. What was it you were trying to tell me? You've had a baby?'

'A little girl. We called her Lucy. She was beautiful.'

'And something bad happened? Oh, Kate. . . .'

The fear Kate felt for Alice helped her to speak more calmly about Lucy than she would have thought herself capable of. 'She went to bed one night, and never woke up again. No reason for it. It just happened. A nightmare that turned out to be real. I don't seem able to get over it, Alice.'

'Oh, my poor girl ' Alice said softly. 'What a terrible sadness for you. I'm so sorry for you. And that nice Fergus of yours.'

Alice seemed more in control of herself. Kate sat back on her heels.

'Nothing's right between Fergus and me. I feel dead inside.'

Alice squeezed her hand convulsively. 'I know, love. People tell you you'll get over these things, but I don't think it's any use talking about getting over losing somebody you love. But I can tell you that as sure as I sit here, you learn to live with it. In time, pet, the loss will stop filling your mind, and you'll remember the life. It may seem impossible right now, but it will happen.'

'Is that how it was for you with Henry? I never really understood before. But today I went to see his name on the memorial and suddenly, I did.'

Alice nodded. 'I felt like you at first – that I'd never get over it. I hated the mine, the sea, the coal in my bunker, everyone whose man was alive and well. Oh, believe me, Kate. I know how black life can look.'

'But how do you make it change?'

'I haven't any magic recipe, love. I think you just have to slog on, doing the things you know you should do, gritting your teeth and getting on with it. Then one day, you'll find that you're quite enjoying maybe one small bit of what you're doing again. And that's how it grows. You'll see.'

Kate got slowly to her feet. 'I hope you're right.' She picked up a photograph of herself in her eighteenth year from the fireplace. She'd gone to St Bees for the day with her crowd. Jamie must have heard them arranging it, and he'd turned up as well, winkling her away from the others as he always did. Judging by the look on her face, he'd probably taken the picture himself. She was on the beach, leaning against the breakwater with the grassy cliffs in the background and the wind blowing her hair back and snatching the laughter from her mouth.

'I feel a couple of generations older than I was then,' she said to Alice.

'You forgot to take that one with you. I hung on to it. It's been a reproach to me ever since. And now, I've got to talk to you, Kate. You must be wondering what I was blethering about earlier on.'

'You mixed me up with somebody else, I presume. Don't worry Alice. You don't have to go into it if it's going to upset you again.'

'It's been a worry at the back of my mind all these years since you went off to Edinburgh. I've got to tell you now, Kate. I've said too much to keep quiet any longer. You'd only be thinking over what I started saying once you left, and you'd have to know more.'

Kate sat down in her chair again. 'Alice, you're really confusing me. If this is something you really think I ought to know, then you'd better go back to the beginning.'

'I'll say I'm sorry before I start. I've wanted to say it for years now.' She brushed impatiently at her eyes. 'Well, here goes. You don't remember much about that awful accident you had, do you?'

Kate shook her head. 'Only what I was told – that I ran out into the road and nearly got knocked into kingdom come by a bus. But as for actually remembering it myself, it's an absolute blank. The first thing I remember afterwards is Dad being there in the hospital, and asking him what he was doing home. He told me I'd been unconscious for over a week.'

'And before? You don't remember anything just before the accident?' Alice was leaning forward, an expression of intense anxiety on her face.

'What should I remember? Nothing in particular stands out.'

'That's what I was talking about when I said, "You've remembered". I was thinking you were talking about that time.'

'But how could I have been? I was talking about having lost my baby.' Kate suddenly froze as the implication of the words sank in. 'Alice – what are you saying?'

Alice sighed a trembling sigh. 'If you don't remember that time, you perhaps remember that pretty much all that summer we hadn't been getting on as well as we used to?'

'Yes, I remember that.' Kate's eyes were fixed on Alice now. 'And doubtless you remember why? That tearaway you were in with that summer was a bad lot, Kate. And yet you were too old for me to be able to keep tabs on you all the time, however much I tried. That day, the day of the accident, was one of the worst of my life.'

'Go on,' Kate said, still as a statue.

'You came in from a friend's that afternoon, and you sat down where you're sitting now. Then you said—' Alice swallowed and licked her lips nervously. 'I'm sorry, lass. There's no way to say this gently. You said, "Alice, I'm pregnant".'

Kate shifted in her chair. 'But I was mistaken?'

Alice shook her head. 'Oh, no. You'd been scared stiff that you were in trouble for three weeks. You'd done a test at a friend's that morning. You had it in your pocket, you even showed it to me. First time in my life I'd seen one of those things, and it had to be you that showed it to me.'

Kate's head was reeling. How could something so momentous have been blanked out from her mind so completely. Could it really be true? Then she remembered the pub and her sudden inexplicable faintness. Was it possible for a body to remember, even if a mind had been wiped clean?

'You can imagine how I felt,' Alice went on. 'You were in my charge, and I'd let this happen to you. You'd got your place at Edinburgh, practically a dead cert, just waiting for the results of your A levels. Your mocks had been brilliant, so there wasn't much doubt. And now it was all going to be wasted. Your whole life ruined by something I ought to have been able to prevent.'

'But it wasn't ruined. I went to Edinburgh. It might never have happened for all I know about it.'

'We didn't know it was going to turn out that way, that afternoon,' Alice said. 'I was in a total panic. I let rip. I said things I should never have said. You'd come to me for help, and I called you names that should never have crossed my lips. I was so afraid, you see. Afraid for you, afraid for me, terrified what effect it was going to have on your father when he found out. If I could have got my hands on that good-for-nothing Jamie Bragg, I'd have killed him.'

'I saw him,' Kate said bemusedly. 'I saw him this morning – not to speak to. And I hadn't the slightest idea.' She caught her breath. 'Did he know, Alice?'

'You'd gone to his place to try to tell him before you came to me. You were white as a ghost when you were telling me about it. They told you at the pub that he was on his dinner hour. So you went straight over to that place he rented and up to his room, because of course he'd given you a key. He was there, but he was in bed with his latest conquest. So you needn't worry. He never knew. All he knew was that he'd been caught out.' She looked imploringly at Kate. 'I'm sorry to be telling you all this, love. But the fact that I kept quiet about it's bothered me all these years. I never knew whether I was doing the right thing or not.'

'I just can't quite take it all in,' Kate said. 'It's so unbeliev-able that I can't remember anything of it. I feel as though you're talking about someone else, someone entirely different, though I can remember being involved with Jamie Bragg that summer well enough' – her eyes met Alice's – 'and with a guilty enough conscience.'

'Not as guilty as mine. If I'd been driving that damned bus I couldn't have been more responsible for what happened to you.' The old lady's lip trembled.

'You can't say that. It seems clear enough that I got myself into the mess.'

'But you came to me for help. You wanted me to help you get rid of the baby. Me. You know what they say . . . once a Catholic. Well, I might only be a bad Catholic, but the way I reacted to the idea of helping you get fixed up with an abortion, well, the nuns who drummed the fear of God into me would have been proud of the way I let fly at you. You ran out of the house, practically blinded by tears, at your wits end what to do next, I expect, and then just round the corner at the end of the street, that's where it happened. I heard the screech of brakes, and I knew straight away.'

'They told me when I came round at the hospital that it was normal not to remember anything of the time round an accident that results in the sort of trauma I had. It's never really worried me, but now that you tell me all this . . . well, it's different. But they never said anything about my being pregnant.'

'They never knew.' Alice picked up her pinnafore and wiped her face with it. 'At first I was too concerned whether you'd live or not to think of anything else. Then I read your notes one

day and they'd marked "Menstruating" for the nurses' attention. You couldn't take care of yourself, you see. And I thought,
why should they ever know any different at this stage with you
only just finding out yourself. So I didn't say anything to them.
Your father was coming, and I reckoned that I was doing you a
favour by not letting slip to him what had happened, now that
it was obviously over and done with.'

Kate made a valiant attempt at a smile. 'You always were a
canny one, Alice. I'm glad you did that.'

'But I was doing it as much for myself as for you. I don't
deserve an atom of credit. Then when it was clear once you
were getting better that you hadn't a jot of recollection about
what had happened either to you, or between us, you can imagine what a relief it was for me not to be shown up as the
bigoted old failure of a friend I was.'

'Never that, Alice. Never that.' Kate felt completely stunned
with the shock of what Alice had told her. 'Forgive me if I don't
quite know how to react to all this,' she said. 'It's too much of
a shock to find out something like that about the past for me to
know exactly how to handle it. But you were right to tell me.'

'It's a horrible thing to come out with at this time, with your
own bairn only just gone. But for me it's a relief. The mind's a
funny thing. I was never sure whether I was doing you a favour
or not by keeping quiet about what had happened. I've always
wondered if I'd left a time bomb ticking away inside you. That's
why it was easier if I didn't see too much of you over the years.
I was as much to blame as you for the fact that we lost touch.'

'Not any more, though, Alice.' Kate made a big effort to pull
herself together, and got up to go and give Alice a hug.
'Everything's out in the open now, so there's no reason ever to
lose touch again.' She straightened up and deliberately spoke in
as bright a voice as she could summon. 'Now, I don't know
about you, but I think we both need a breathing space. Will you
come and have dinner with me tonight? I'm staying at Lesserby
Hall – you remember the old place, source of summer pocket
money in the past? I'll come and fetch you, and bring you back.
Please say yes.'

Alice's eyes filled with tears. 'You want to take me out for a posh do like that after all I've told you?'

'You didn't invent it. What happened is not your responsibility, Alice.'

'Then as long as you're not too proud to be seen in public with an old woman, I'll look forward to it.'

'Alice Beattie! Wash your mouth out and say a sorry Hail Mary!' The words Alice had so often used in the past, robustly disregarding the fact that Kate did not belong to a Catholic family, set them both laughing, and they parted on memories that were not painful. The others would be digested and dwelt upon later.

Chapter Eleven

Zoe must have left the lights on deliberately, Fergus thought as he drove up to the house on Thursday evening. It was a nice touch.

He let himself in, and picked up the post from the hall table, taking it into the sitting-room. A quick flip through it revealed that there was nothing from Kate. The message he'd had on his mobile hadn't been much better than no message at all – just the news that she had arrived safely, was seeing Alice, and would be in touch. She had ended it with 'love, Kate', but Fergus hadn't been impressed.

The sitting-room smelled of fresh polish and looked more homely than it had done for weeks. Fergus tossed the rest of the post on to the settee and headed towards the stairs for his shower. As he passed the kitchen, he was suddenly aware that there was a more interesting smell coming from behind its closed door. His stomach rumbled appreciatively. He hadn't expected to find Zoe had left a meal in the oven waiting for him. It would be a very quick shower.

Ten minutes later he was running downstairs, hair damply dripping on to his Arran sweater, doing up the zip of his jeans as he hurried towards the tantalizing smell.

'Surprise!' Zoe's voice carolled as he went in, causing him to stop in the doorway with a sudden start. She was over by the sink, draining a pan of vegetables, and beamed at him over her shoulder.

'You can say that again. Where's your car?' he asked.

'Round near the kitchen door – I had a load of stuff to bring in. I thought you'd enjoy having your dinner waiting for a change. Becca's out at a friend's, so if I don't get thrown out, I'll share it with you. Am I on?'

Fergus took in the table, laid for two, the candle waiting to be lit, and the bottle of red wine with its cork already drawn.

'Clocking up overtime already?' he said ironically.

'Just being a mate,' she retorted. 'You get it free, you Scottish tightwad.'

'The wine too?' he asked, grinning.

'Don't push your luck. You pay for that. I did a bit of shopping for you. The rest of it's all non-frivolous. Don't worry, I won't make a habit of this.'

'Who's worrying,' Fergus said, pulling out a chair.

Zoe stopped what she was doing and came closer. 'Just look at you! Did you make any attempt to dry your hair? Come here.' Grabbing the clean kitchen towel from the rail she came round behind him and plonked the towel on his head, rubbing vigorously first at the back, then, pulling his head unceremoniously against her midriff, giving the top and front of his hair the same rough treatment. There was something shockingly intimate in being suddenly assaulted in this way. Enjoyable, though, Fergus thought as he rested his head against the softness of her, closing his eyes. From this close he could smell again the perfume she used . . . the one that Kate used as well. He felt a momentary stab of guilt. Then he banished it. He was having his hair dried, for goodness sake, nothing more exotic than that. His barber did it. His mother used to do it. No big deal.

'There.' Zoe dropped the towel in his lap. 'Wake up, dozy. Give your shoulders a wipe before you catch your death of cold. Then you could make yourself useful and pour us some of that wine.' She went over and opened the oven door to reveal a darkly bubbling casserole. The oven glove had dropped on to the floor, and she reached down to pick it up. Fergus sat watching her, in a relaxed, comfortable daze, his head glowing from her attentions. She was wearing jeans and a white sleeveless turtleneck sweater. Tight jeans, he observed, tight enough to show off any defects. There didn't appear to be any. Enough of that, he told himself, getting up and obeying instruction about the wine. He took a sip from his glass. It was a good Bordeaux.

He sat down again and prepared to enjoy what his nose told him was going to be the best meal he'd eaten for a long time. 'What is it?' he asked, watching with interest as she began spooning out generous helpings on to the dark green plates.

'Braised steak. Nothing fancy. Oh, and I used up the remains of a bottle of red in the fridge in it. Wouldn't want you thinking I'm an alcoholic. Help yourself to vegetables.'

She watched while he added creamy mashed potatoes and carrots and cabbage to his plate, then helped herself, but didn't, he noticed, begin to eat until he had sampled his first mouthful.

'Mmm! So you can cook as well as everything else!' Fergus said appreciatively. 'This is great, Zoe.'

She beamed and relaxed, starting on her own food. 'What sort of afternoon have you had?'

'Nothing too exciting. A few routine farm visits. One sad thing. Old Mrs Hollins called me out to check over that English Blue of hers. He isn't going to survive much longer with a liver condition like he's got. I've tried to bring her round to the idea of considering what's best for him. But he's her life.'

'Isn't he eighteen? It's more than a good age for a cat.'

'Mrs Hollins is a good age for a human. It comes a bit too close to home if you start talking about fair runs. Not the favourite part of my job, persuading owners it's time to let go.' He looked at the casserole dish. 'Any more of that left? It's really good.'

Zoe ladled another generous portion on to his plate. 'I'll give the last bit to this scrounger,' she said, waving the spoon towards Middy, who had magically appeared as soon as the casserole lid was lifted, and was now sitting on top of the boiler, staring fixedly at the object of his desire. He got up, pounding his paws rapturously as Zoe cut up the last of the beef into his dish. 'What's his name?' she asked, putting it down on the floor for him.

'Middy. Short for Midshipman. The white marking round his neck and chest reminded us of a sailor's collar.'

With the word 'us', suddenly Kate was very much there with them causing the conversation to dry up and the easy atmosphere to sharpen.

'Have you heard anything?' Zoe asked.

'Just a message to say she'd arrived safely. Pretty useless, really.'

'Have you any idea what she's intending to do up there?'

'Not the slightest. I thought there might be something in the post now that she's stopped running, but there was nothing. I'm getting pretty fed up, really.'

'Actually the phone rang this evening before you got back. I dithered a bit about whether to answer it, but in the end I just let it ring until whoever it was gave up. What do you want me to do about that while I'm here? I presume Kate doesn't know I'm helping out – and I don't think she's too keen on me in any case. If it had been the surgery, they'd have recognized my voice. So it wants thinking about.'

'I should think the easiest thing is to ignore it and let the answerphone take over. I must have forgotten to set it again today.' Fergus put his knife and fork down, frowning slightly. 'I hate having to be so cloak and dagger about things, but you understand, don't you?'

'Thousands wouldn't, but yes, I do.' She began to clear the table, stacking plates in the dishwasher then bringing cups and saucers over to the table. 'I'll check that the answerphone's on when I get here in future.' The noise of the coffee grinder prevented any more talk for a few moments. Zoe measured the ground coffee into the pot then added boiling water. 'I'll just nip upstairs and get changed while that stands, then once I've had a cup, I'll be off.'

Fergus pottered around in the kitchen, wiping already immaculate surfaces, thinking all the time of Zoe getting changed upstairs. Would she be in his room? – their room, he swiftly corrected, then even more swiftly changed 'their' to 'his and Kate's'. Had he dropped his discarded pants and socks on the floor if that were the case? He'd been taken by surprise tonight, but in future he would have to watch himself.

Zoe came back and poured the coffee. She was restored to her surgery self now in her navy suit and white shirt. 'All right?' she queried. 'Having a bit of a brood, are we?'

Fergus gave a snort of laughter. 'You'd have made a shocker of a dentist with your capacity for putting the drill on the bad spot. Yes, I was having a bit of a brood, as you call it. But at least I can do it on a full stomach. Thanks for all you've done, Zoe. Do you want me to pay as we go along or what?'

Zoe's smile slipped a bit and she sipped her coffee with an air of impatience. 'Do you have to bring everything down to a level of sordid commercialism? I thought we were having a friendly meal.'

'So we were. But before the meal a load of hard work went on that comes under the heading of appreciative, not sordid, commercialism. So come on. Give me an answer.'

'Put it on the slate. It's Becca's Christmas it's meant for. If you pay me as we go along, I'll only be tempted to spend it.'

He went over to the notice board and pinned up a sheet of paper from the pad near the phone, then wrote 'Zoe' in capital letters and added the date plus '4 hours'.

She had come across to read over his shoulder. 'Three, not four.'

He looked round at her face, so close that he could see that the irises of her eyes were not the clear bright blue they seemed to be from a distance, but as varied and complex as the patterns in a kaleidoscope. She gave a horrible frown and repeated 'Three. Don't argue. If I do four next time, I'll tell you, don't worry.'

Fergus turned back and crossed out four, substituting three.

'All right, then. Three, and a very big thank you from me.' She stepped back a bit, then held out her face, pointing to her cheek. 'Three and a bit of appreciation shown in the usual way, never mind your cool thank yous.'

It would have been ridiculously churlish to refuse. Kisses

were tossed around like confetti at the practice for birthdays, anniversaries and Christmases. He leaned forward, aiming at her cheek, but with an impish grin she turned her face at the last minute and it was her soft lips that his mouth touched. Touched, but didn't draw away from.

Instead Fergus closed his eyes and took what was offered, while Zoe leaned into him and slid her arms round his waist, then up inside his sweater.

She was the one who gently withdrew, her cool fingers tracing the path of his rib cage before pulling down his sweater and restoring order with a motherly pat on the hips.

'That's better, Fergus Callender,' she said, looking him in the eyes and giving his cheek a gentle cuff. 'You need to relax more. Life's for living, not just a waiting-room for hanging around in. See you tomorrow. Oh, and by the way, I left my cleaning clothes here in the back bedroom. I hope that's all right. One less thing to remember on Thursday.'

He managed an incoherent reply which brought a cheeky grin and the recommendation to have another coffee to clear his brain, then she was off, her high heels tapping a jaunty retreat across the hall.

It was nothing, he told himself bracingly. A clumsy misplaced casual kiss. Casual? His mouth, recalling the taste of hers, reminded him. Casual? His body echoed, still imprinted with the touch of her fingers.

Yes, casual, he told himself determinedly, going through to the sitting-room and switching on the television. There was a sitcom on – and he watched it, struggling to keep his mind on it. It was Zoe's teasing, affectionate face he kept seeing, superimposed on the girl on the screen.

He had brought some paperwork home with him and that focused his mind much better. But even at the end of the evening, the feel and the taste and the scent of her still lingered. Zoe had always been one for mothering everyone in the practice, he told himself robustly as he went upstairs after sitting through *Newsnight*, not one item of which he could remember. She treated everyone like a lost child.

Mothering? Lost child? The little voice at the back of his mind taunted. Who the hell are you kidding?

Maggie poured the first cup of tea and passed it across the table to Gordon, who liked it weak, then put the teapot down to stand and brew the more businesslike cup she preferred. Her knowledge of Gordon's character and ways increased daily, and she was enjoying the experience of getting to know someone of the opposite sex again.

He caught the little smile on her face and said, 'Now what are you laughing at?'

'You. But I'm not going to tell you why or it will be bad for you,' she told him.

'What an irritating answer that is,' he said, his indulgent expression belying the words. 'I expect you're feeling smug about your afternoon's achievements and you don't want me to get too big-headed for telling you that you'd be fine and being right.'

'I certainly am pleased,' Maggie said, accepting a slice of fruit cake made surprisingly by Gordon himself. Would Donald have made half so good a stab at looking after himself, she wondered. She thought not. There had been a strict demarcation line between male and female duties in their home. She was glad Donald had not needed to find out how ill-equipped he was for solitary retirement.

The cake was incredibly good. Make a cake, build a wall in the garden, iron a shirt immaculately – all jobs were one to Gordon. She rather liked that attitude, new though it was to her.

Today, he had persuaded her to go along to Evensong, and as he predicted, she had thoroughly enjoyed it. Afterwards, he had even talked her into having tea in the café that had been the site of her dreadful panic attack. She had clung on to his arm as they went in, but he had told her the place wasn't a monster, she would be fine. And so she had been. Another ghost had been laid.

Now they were having a second brew in the familiar cheerful and bright conservatory back at his house, surrounded on three sides by garden. Gordon had had the extension built after his wife died, he told her, so that he could feel to be out in his beloved garden even when he was indoors.

He had shown Maggie photographs of Sheila. Photographs in black and white from their student days when they had first met, and colour prints, taken usually in the garden or on the exotic foreign holidays Sheila favoured. Gordon would rather have gone hill walking every summer, he told Maggie, but they had compromised, choosing alternate years' destinations in strictly fair rotation.

There were no photographs of children. 'A big disappointment to us both,' Gordon told Maggie without going into further details

'Did you ever think of adopting?' Maggie asked him now out of the blue.

He had adjusted to this habit of hers of throwing sudden thoughts into the conversation. 'Yes – but not early enough. We kept on hoping, then when we finally faced up to facts and tried to do something about it, we were too old, they told us. You are so lucky to have a son, Maggie.'

'This is not the best time in the world to say that.' Maggie poured her tea, now rich brown and exactly as she liked it. 'But yes, even after all we've been through – and are still going through, I do appreciate that I am lucky.'

'Have you no better news yet?'

'None. I spoke to Fergus this morning and he has heard nothing that throws fresh light on things from Kate.'

'They must heal themselves, Maggie. Nobody can do it for them. You must keep trying to maintain a loving distance. Hard, I know. I'm well aware of how much you want to be able to help.'

Maggie finished the last crumb of cake and pushed her plate away. 'I know you're right. But I'm not going to be able to maintain a physical distance much longer. I shall have to think of moving back to my own place soon.'

Gordon didn't answer for a moment, then he said, 'That isn't strictly necessary. You could always stay here.'

Maggie froze and her face reddened. Gordon smiled reassuringly at her. 'I'm not suggesting we should set up home together.' He stood up and walked over to the window, as though to reassure her by putting more distance between them. 'You've only seen this room, haven't you? Perhaps now is the time to give you a tour of the entire property. This isn't one huge house now, Maggie. I had it divided into two apartments when the builders were in doing the conservatory. The upstairs one is going begging and I think we should shake down very well together as neighbours, don't you?'

'But you hardly know me!' Maggie said.

'That's just not true. I feel as though I've always known you. Don't you feel the same?'

Maggie looked down at her hands, gripping each other in her lap, then up at Gordon. 'Yes, I do. But when I think how little time has passed since we first met with me standing on that ridiculous bench, I can't believe we can be so easy with each other.'

'Well, we are. And I'm glad of it, aren't you?'

'Of course I am.'

'Then come and have a tour of inspection. You need to know what's on offer before you go away and think it over. And if you only want to treat it as a temporary measure, that's all right by me. I know your family is in a state of flux at the moment. We can play it by ear. Don't say anything now. Just come and have a look.'

Maggie got up. Blue eyes twinkling, he nodded his approval, and she smiled back, shaking her head in astonishment at the way the course of her life seemed to be developing a will of its own.

Kate was secretly relieved when Alice rang her early in the evening to call off their arrangement to have dinner together.

'I'm sorry to throw your kindness in your face, love,' she said, her voice pitched twice as loud as it needed to be, 'I'm not being funny or anything, but I feel whacked. It must have taken it out of me, telling you all that this morning.'

'Are you all right?' Kate asked anxiously. 'Shall I come over?'

'No,' Alice shouted. 'I'll be fine. But I've got to know when I need to stay quiet. I've got some home-made soup in the fridge. I'll have a bowl of that, and then get off to my bed. I'll be as right as ninepence in the morning.'

'We'll have lunch tomorrow, then. I'll ring you in the morning – not too early. I don't want to get you out of your bed.'

'You wouldn't. I've got another of these contraptions upstairs. It's only rung once while I was up there. Nearly blew me out of my socks! This time I'll be prepared.'

Alice and her phone obviously had a fragile relationship. Kate smiled, full of affection for her old friend. 'Well, you take care. Have you got a pen and paper there?'

'Right by my side, love.'

'Then take this number down.' Kate dictated her mobile number. 'If you feel bad in the night, give me a ring. I'll leave my mobile switched on.'

'Mobile? Dear Lord! Whatever will that do?'

'It'll ring, then I'll answer. Dead easy.'

'I wasn't meant to be involved with these new-fangled things.'

Kate laughed. 'You're being coaxed into the twenty-first century whether you like it or not. And about time. Now, off you go. See you tomorrow.'

'Night night. Sleep tight. Mind the bugs don't bite,' Alice said, bringing a lifetime of cosy, secure bedtimes crowding back. Kate didn't feel at all secure now, though. The shock of what Alice told her had been growing all day. Nothing could prepare you for a situation like this. How were you expected to react when someone told you that you'd been pregnant, lost your baby, and now knew nothing about the whole life-shattering experience?

Incredulity kept sweeping over her. How could something happen, and leave no trace? But unwillingly, belief crept in. Looking back to the past she could remember, Kate saw that such an outcome of her relationship with Jamie Bragg was only too predictable. It had been exciting to take risks, to feel swept along by passion. Jamie had been scathingly dismissive of anxiety, telling her that he knew what he was doing, he'd be careful, he wasn't wearing L-plates. And she, hotly bewitched as she was, had trusted him to be as good as his word.

His worthless word, as it turned out. What a little fool she had been to fall hook, line and sinker for someone like him. Seen from the viewpoint of her thirty-year-old self, he was completely stripped of the glamour her teenage imagination had endowed him with. At least he never knew she had been pregnant. That was something to be thankful about. He was as ignorant of the result of their careless hours in that back room of his as she had been until this morning. Kate shivered, and with an effort dragged herself back to the present.

It was well past the time when dinner started to be served. She tidied herself up perfunctorily and hurried downstairs to the dining-room, but once there she found she had no appetite. She ate little of her main course and refused one of the trolley's rich deserts. Coffee was the only thing she really wanted . . . hot, strong, and maybe capable of giving her a clearer head. Idiot! she told herself as she was about to pour a third cup. All the coffee was probably going to do was guarantee her a sleepless night. She resisted the third cup she craved, and went back to her room.

Dream followed dream, each one verging on nightmare. In one, her father appeared. She had never dreamed of him before. In the dream he was consumed with grief about her teenage pregnancy. 'What would your mother have thought if she could see you now?' he asked, but with such sadness that Kate woke with tears streaming down her face. She slept again, only to be transported back in time to Lucy's birth. But the midwife who had attended such a joyful occasion, in her dream handed Kate a dead baby instead of the living Lucy. 'It's because of what happened the first time,' she told Kate, her voice cosy and conversational. 'It's only to be expected. Fair's fair after all.'

167

In the end Kate was afraid to let herself sink back into sleep. Her mind focused feverishly on what she would have to face eventually – telling Fergus what she had discovered about her past. She couldn't begin to imagine how he would react. They had both had relationships with other students before they met and been open with each other about their individual pasts. But how innocent that seemed in comparison with the shabby story waiting to be told.

She couldn't see any good coming from what she had found out. Rather the reverse. She had created two potential lives, and both had come to nothing. The fact that she had actually wanted one of them to end was going to double the guilt she felt, rather than banish it. Having so loved and lost Lucy, she shuddered now at the thought of actually choosing to destroy life. The unplanned, unwanted first baby might have been lost through an accident, but she had wanted to end that life, guilty of the intention if not the act.

At seven o'clock with light spreading at last across the sky, she realized what she desperately wanted to do. She rummaged through her bag until she found Nat's card. He had been so right in suspecting that there was something in her past that was casting a deeper shadow over her present sorrow.

His phone rang several times. Kate bit her lip anxiously. If he wasn't in his rented rooms at Mossthorpe where the Detention Centre was, she wouldn't be able to speak to him until tonight, and she was desperate to find a way through the confusion in her mind.

'Hello? Nat Hambleton.' He sounded breathless.

Kate was almost choked with thankfulness that she had reached him. 'It's me,' she said, her voice unsteady. 'Nat, can I possibly come and talk to you?'

He detected the strain at once. 'Kate! What's happened?'

'I can't begin to talk about it on the phone. I did what you suggested – came to Whitehaven. You were right about my needing to go back there. I've got to stay here tomorrow, but is there any chance of seeing you on Friday? I could come back down on the M1 and call in at your place. It wouldn't make all that much of a detour, and it would be such a relief to be able to talk to you.'

'Are things as bad as that?'

'Pretty bad. I shouldn't be making demands like this, I know, but I just have to talk to someone, Nat.'

'You still don't feel like talking to Fergus?'

'Not until I've seen you. I haven't even been talking to him on the phone. We've been reduced to text messages.'

'Oh, Kate! What a sad way for a husband and wife to communicate.' She heard him sigh, but he made no further attempt to question her and got down to seeing what could be arranged. The sound of pages being flicked over came down the line.

'The thing is, Kate, I've got a load of assessment meetings in the next couple of days. They spill over into Saturday. I can't get out of those. There's the Sunday morning service too – but that I can do something about, I think. I'm owed one or two favours. I'm thinking on the hoof at present. Coming here isn't a very good idea. I haven't got a house to myself – there's always someone around here, coming in and out. The best thing I can suggest is for me to get Sunday rearranged, then I can drive down to Lichfield on Saturday once the meetings are over, and see you there where we have more privacy. You sound as though you're at the end of your tether.'

'Absolutely,' Kate said shakily, swallowing hard.

'What do you think? Can you hold on until Saturday?'

Kate steeled herself to answer calmly. 'Yes. Things are always worse at night, aren't they?'

'Why don't you get some rest in during the day if you had such a bad night? You said you had to stay in Whitehaven today?'

'I'm seeing Alice again today. Taking her for lunch.'

'Good. If you're seeing her for a second time it sounds as though getting in touch with her again has been a plus point?'

Kate couldn't answer. Yes, it was good to have seen Alice again and repaired the rift that had been developing between them. But seeing Alice was what had brought the past leaping and snarling into life.

'Kate? Are you still there?'

'Yes. Sorry.'

'Now listen to me,' he said, his voice coming firm and strong down the line. 'You are not to think of trying to drive home tomorrow. Friday's a shocker on the roads. Leave it until Saturday when the motorway will be much less busy. Take advantage of today and tomorrow to do something that will tire you physically. Walk the coastal path. Tackle a hill walk if you feel up to it. Get out in the fresh air anyway – that's the first priority. Go and get something to help you sleep if you think that's necessary – there must be a medical practice where you are still known. Try to shelve your worries. They will be dealt with on Saturday and Sunday. Until then, refuse to let them into your mind. Have you got that?'

'You are such a wonder-worker,' Kate said. 'You've mapped out the next forty-eight hours for me. It's just what I needed – somebody to organize everything.'

'Soon you'll be quite capable of organizing your own life. Just remember that. Are you feeling a bit better now?'

'Much.'

'Let me have a telephone number. And when would be a good time in the evening to check up on you?'

Kate dictated the number. 'I'll be back in my room by half past eight – say nine o'clock.'

'I'll give you a buzz then. Now, if you don't mind, I'd like to get dressed. You fetched me dripping from the shower.'

'Oh, I'm sorry!'

'No harm done, apart from to the carpet. So – I'll speak to you tonight and see you on Saturday, by the end of the afternoon. Drive carefully when it comes to the journey home, won't you?'

'I will. Thank you, Nat. I'm more grateful than I can say.'

'No thanks needed. And now be a good girl and kindly get off the line. Bye, Kate. Bless you.'

'And you,' Kate said softly, meaning it.

Chapter Twelve

Gordon had just given Maggie her first driving lesson. To her surprise she had done reasonably well.

'Why on earth didn't you tackle driving years ago?' he asked as he drew up at Ashfield. 'You're close to a natural.'

'Do you really think so?' Maggie preened herself in the passenger-seat mirror. 'Do you know, I think it's all down to having used an old-fashioned treadle sewing machine years ago. You get the first stages of coordinating hand and foot, doing that.'

He laughed. 'Don't express that theory to your examiner when you're about to take your test. Seriously, though, did you never have the slightest hankering to learn?'

'Donald took me everywhere. The question never came up.'

'The male/female divide again?'

She smiled ruefully. 'I suppose so.'

'What an amenable little woman you have been all your life. There's bags of personality there just waiting to expand, Maggie.'

She patted him on the sleeve. 'You're an old flatterer, but I'm so grateful for the lesson, and I'd really like to go again before I book official lessons when I leave here.'

'Which brings us nicely to my suggestion about where you go after Ashfield. Have you thought about it?'

'I'm still thinking,' Maggie said hesitantly. 'It isn't something I can decide all at once, Gordon. There are a lot of pros and cons to weigh up. And I would have to see what Fergus thought.'

'Does he control your destiny?' Gordon's tone was kind, but his expression when she glanced up at him was challenging.

'You think I'm a hopeless "little woman" type, don't you?'

'I think you have been led along the most pleasant of pathways into assuming that role.' He smiled at her. 'Never mind. You are thinking about my offer. That's all I ask.'

'I must go,' she said, looking at her watch. 'I have an appointment with Dr Lawson in half an hour.'

Gordon got out and came round to open her door. 'Give him my regards. Same time tomorrow for another trip out?'

'Could it possibly be tomorrow morning? It's the art class tomorrow afternoon. That's another thing I never dreamed I'd be any good at. I really enjoy it.'

'You'll have to show me your work. Half past ten, then?'

'Lovely. Goodbye, Gordon, and thank you again.'

'A shared pleasure.' He gave her a little jaunty wave and got back into the car.

Dr Lawson began in his usual way by asking what Maggie would like to say to him. She told him about Gordon's offer of the flat.

'And what do you think about that?' he asked, as always asking questions rather than making comments or suggestions.

'I like Gordon very much. You get out of the habit of making friends as time goes by, and with him no making was necessary.'

'Does the idea of moving away from your family appeal to you?'

'I don't know what they would think about it.'

'That wasn't what I asked. What would you think about it?'

'I just don't know. The thought of being away from all the sadness is appealing. But I don't want to run away.'

'If you did move next door, would you be running away?'

'Not exactly. It would be more a case of thinking a change might be necessary. The idea of my being on the spot to look after any child Fergus and Kate may have in the future might not work. The past will cast a very long shadow. If my home

172

there were available for an au pair, that might be the best solution. For them, anyway.'

'And would Hart's flat be the best solution for you?'

'It's a very nice flat.'

'You're dodging the question again.'

'That's because I can't make up my mind about the answer. I would have to know what Fergus thinks. He's been hurt enough. I don't want to be the one who adds the final straw.'

There was a moment's silence.

'Gordon says, of course,' Maggie reflected, 'that I should concentrate on what I want to do, never mind what Fergus thinks.'

'So Hart is keen for you to move in?'

'He's genuine about the offer of the flat. We get on well. He's teaching me to drive, would you believe it. He says I should have done it long ago. He thinks I've allowed myself to be made into an entirely different person from the one I might have been if I'd allowed myself to form my own ideas instead of accepting what other people thought I should be.'

'And what do you think about that?'

Maggie thought hard, then looked up at Dr Lawson. 'I think that Gordon might just be another of the many people who have tried to mould me into what they wanted me to be.' Her expression betrayed that she was totally surprised by what she had said.

Dr Lawson smiled at her. 'Well done. As an assessment of the situation, that's pretty level-headed. Remember that, and focus firmly on what you want, having weighed up all the pros and cons.'

'Dr Lawson!' Maggie said, smiling. 'Are you actually giving me a piece of advice? That must be a first!'

'Only repeating the advice you have already given yourself. And that's the way it should be.'

'I'm very fond of Gordon and it's lovely to have him as a friend. But I don't want to marry again.'

'Has he indicated that's what he would like eventually?'

'No. But if we're living at close quarters and such an idea

should be mentioned, it could make things awkward, couldn't it?'

'Not if both parties are clear on the position.'

'You make it all sound so easy, Dr Lawson,' she smiled.

'But life isn't easy, is it? And we all have to deal with it in our own way and on our own terms. Well, Mrs Callender, I think you have regained your balance most satisfactorily. I agree with your own GP that you were never in need of hospitalization. You had three of the most disturbing experiences hard on the heels of each other – loss of a partner, moving house, loss of a grandchild. Any one of those would have been enough to disturb anyone's equilibrium. But I'd say you're well on the way to full health now.'

He rose and offered her his hand.

'Thank you,' Maggie said. 'I haven't always reacted appreciatively at the time to what you've had to say. But thinking back, I can see you've always guided me along sensible lines. And being able to stay here and distance myself for a while from all that was upsetting me has been invaluable.'

'I shall look forward to hearing what you decide to do,' Dr Lawson told her. 'Perhaps by next week?'

Perhaps, Maggie thought as she left his room, her mind still approaching the question of her future from many angles. But at least she now felt that she would eventually be capable of coming to a rational decision. And that was progress.

It had been raining for at least half of the long journey down the motorway. Kate stopped off in Lichfield to pick up ready-prepared food. The town was decked in its Christmas finery. She hadn't given thought to Christmas, and now that she was forced to face the idea of it, she could think of nothing she wanted less. It would have been so different if they had been celebrating Lucy's first Christmas. Christmas without her, having known her, seemed impossible. She passed a window full of decorations, and suddenly thought of Rosie. Lynne wouldn't have cash to spare for things like this. The owner was just on the point of closing, but Kate persuaded him to wait while she chose a tree fairy to widen Rosie's eyes. Maybe that was the way through. To think of Christmas this year as something for other people. See it as a spectator, not a participant.

Jan had told her that she would be away for the night, staying with a friend after a concert in Cheltenham. She was going to put her key through Kate's letter box so that Quaker and the hens could be fed on Monday morning. She'd also asked Kate to go and see how Lynne was, saying that she seemed at a very low ebb, depressed by the short days and long nights confined to the house.

What a topsy-turvy world it is, Kate thought. All these sad people. Me, mentally crippled by missing a lost child so desperately. Lynne trapped by a child, however much she loves it. People wanting a baby so that they are almost unable to think of anything else, and yet unable to conceive. Others ill-treating the children they have so easily brought into the world. So much hurting, so much unhappiness.

The lane to the Barns was in a dire state, the headlamps shining on pools of water collected in the ruts. Nat's place was still in darkness. Kate let herself into Barn Crest, picking up Jan's key from the mat. Jan had put the heating on for her, and the house felt warm and welcoming.

Trying to keep her mind focused on what she had to do, Kate dialled Marianne's number to let her know that she would be back at work on Monday, but Marianne was out, so she left a message on the answerphone asking her to ring back.

There was no point in sending any more messages to Fergus. She had told him she was coming back to Lichfield today. Once she had talked to Nat, she hoped she would be able to find the courage to go and speak to Fergus face to face. Enough of text messages.

She picked up the suitcase she had put at the foot of the stairs and went up to unpack and have a quick shower.

She was in the shower when she heard Nat's car coming to a halt in front of the Barns. She had left the door unlocked, and he knocked and let himself in while she was drying herself.

'Kate?' he called from downstairs.

'Down in a minute. Just cleaning myself up a bit,' she answered. As she spoke, her mobile shrilled from the room below.

'Want me to answer this?' Nat called.

'Please. It'll be Marianne. Tell her I'll ring back.'

She hurried into her clothes, half listening to Nat's end of the conversation. Suddenly she froze, realizing that it was Fergus, not Marianne, on the phone. Tiredness had made her forget that leaving the line open left her open to him as well.

Fergus had been trying Kate's mobile since mid-afternoon. He had had enough of bland text messages. Enough of everything, actually. He had been to see Maggie after lunch, and she had calmly broached the subject of moving in with the Hart fellow. Into his house, anyway. Fergus thought she was out of her mind. If she had been unbalanced when she went into Ashfield, she seemed far worse now. Not in her manner, which had been infuriatingly rational in comparison with his own – but in the wildness of the ideas she was coming up with.

After putting her mad suggestion to him and seeing his reaction, she'd told him to go away and think it over when he was feeling less volatile. Volatile was the word she'd used, and a down-putting, patronizing word it had seemed. She'd dismissed him like a queen ending an audience. She'd made him feel totally inadequate. What a mess it all was. His mother made him feel inadequate. His wife made him feel unwanted. And his own self-pity made him feel sick. This whole business felt to be emasculating him.

Now he had at last found Kate's mobile in answering mode, but some chap or other was answering for her.

'Who the hell are you?' Fergus snarled.

'Nat Hambleton. And you are—?'

'Never mind who I am. Why are you answering my wife's mobile?'

'I presume I'm speaking to Fergus?' Nat said unflappably.

'You presume correctly. Where's my wife?'

'She's just having a shower. I'll give her a call.'

176

Kate there with this man. Kate having a shower. Fergus read the worst into the situation. 'And what else have you been giving her?' he shouted, beside himself with undignified rage. 'I suppose you're that pseudo-religious berk who was sniffing around before?'

'Not the way I would have described either myself or my activities,' Nat said mildly, 'but yes, I'm the Reverend Nathaniel Hambleton. And the title's genuine, not pseudo. I really think it would be better if you spoke to Kate.'

'Don't try to tell me what to do. If you're who you say you are, why are you hanging around after my wife?'

'All this is quite unnecessary,' Nat said, his voice taking on a no-nonsense tone. 'I understand you've got problems, but—'

'I don't want your pious understanding. Save it for your job. All I want is to know why, whenever I manage to get through to Kate, which isn't bloody often, you seem to be dancing attendance.'

Kate had appeared in the sitting-room, white-faced, but determined. She held out her hand for the phone.

'Kate's here, Fergus. I'm handing you over to her.' Nat gave her the mobile and gently pushed her down into a chair before going out to the kitchen and closing the door.

'Fergus,' Kate said swallowing hard. 'You have every reason to feel exasperated with me, but not with Nat. He's here because I asked him to come and talk to me. Not because he wanted to travel nearly a hundred miles to listen to a mixed up idiot of a woman.'

'Why him?' Fergus cried. 'Why a total stranger? Why not me? I want to talk to you. What is it about him that makes you want him all the time? I'm the one you ought to be with.'

'How many times have you said I needed to talk to someone, Fergus? I can talk to Nat. He's a purely impartial outsider. He can listen and give an opinion that isn't swayed by emotion.'

'But why him? Why not someone whose job it is to do this sort of thing?'

'I don't know "why him". But he's got a degree in psychology as well as being a qualified clergyman. He's the one who suggested that it might be good for me to go back to Whitehaven, and he was right. Whitehaven was involved in how I am.'

Fergus's voice, though still dangerously unsteady, had calmed down a bit. 'Haven't I got more right to know what's troubling you than a stranger? How would you feel if our positions were reversed and I was hiding out in a secret address with some girl or other just happening to answer the phone when you rang?'

'I'd feel bad.'

'Well, then.' There was a burning silence. Then Fergus said, 'What is this about Whitehaven? Why did you go there? What have you been doing there? Tell me, Kate.'

'I will. But it's too much to begin trying to tell you over the phone. I want to understand more myself before I speak to you. You must trust me, Fergus.'

'You ask a lot of me,' he said bitterly.

'I know I do.'

'I don't know how much more of this I can take.'

'I don't want you to have to take any more. Everything I'm doing is with the intention of trying to find a way through the mess I'm in. I've felt desperate too, Fergus. You're not alone.'

'But I am! Utterly alone. And you're there with this man who seems to answer all your needs, while I can do nothing for you.' She could hear him breathing hard. 'Tell me what you're going to do.'

'Just talk. Have a meal and talk.'

'You're having a meal with him?'

Fergus's voice was rising again. Kate said hurriedly, 'Don't go making a big deal out of that, Fergus. We've both got to eat, and since he's come here to oblige me, it's the least I can do.'

'You're having a meal together,' he repeated. Then, practically deafening her, he shouted, 'How bloody, bloody cosy!' and hung up on her.

Fergus sat on the nursing chair in Lucy's room. He had not been able to bear the thought of that room since the dreadful night when Lucy had been found, so tragically changed from her warm, living self. They had closed the door, waiting to know what to do with the agonizing reminders of the child they had lost.

But after putting the phone down on Kate, he had suddenly realized how much Lucy was getting lost in the aftermath of her death. Her loss seemed to have been pushed into the background by the disintegration of the family that had once focused so lovingly on her. Instead of sorrow, the emotions circulating in the family now were far more violent, emotions like suspicion, jealousy, exasperation, even revenge. For Fergus had wanted to hit out at Kate and this man she seemed to regard as the source of all wisdom, a man who was sharing the meal Fergus should have been having with her.

His feelings towards his mother were explosive too. He resented her upward progress when he felt to be slipping back, and her ability to contemplate changing her life while he couldn't bear the thought of the change to his own that Kate's attitude seemed to threaten.

He looked at the soft toys snuggled together on the shelf, at the exotic bird mobile, gently swaying in the breeze from the open door, at the diminutive wardrobe that contained a row of unbearably poignant reminders of Lucy, dressed in her brightest and best, stealing every show. What joy she had brought, and what turmoil such a bright star passing through their firmament had left behind.

Callender men didn't cry. Since Lucy's death, he had done his best to keep himself rock solid for Kate. That was a need inbred in him, something he understood. But who needed him now? Abandoned by Kate, who seemed hell-bent on seeking her own salvation, and with the contrast between what life had been and what it was today so sharply defined, he felt to be disintegrating, surplus to requirements.

The phone, ringing shrilly, summoned him. He closed Lucy's door behind him, and went into their bedroom to answer it.

'Fergus?' It was not the change-of-heart call from Kate he had briefly hoped for. It was Zoe's voice, but a voice devoid of her usual chirpy brightness. 'Fergus – is that you?'

He dragged himself back into the present with difficulty. 'Yes. What is it, Zoe?'

A sob, quickly smothered, preceded her answer. 'I'm sorry to bother you.' As she spoke, her voice thickened with tears. 'You've got enough on your plate, but I haven't a clue who else to turn to.'

'Zoe, if you've got a problem, then of course you can come to me. What's the matter? I've never heard you sound so upset.'

'It's Becca. She's been caught shoplifting late yesterday afternoon – and not just a one-off. I had the police here. They found that she'd got loads of stuff hidden in her room. All of it with price tags on. I never look in there – there's only suitcases and stuff that's hardly ever used. I had no idea, Fergus.'

'Oh dear! I'm so sorry, Zoe. What's going to happen?'

'She's going to be charged. The security people have been watching her and her friends for some time, apparently. Yesterday was the first time they had concrete evidence. They've contacted her school, so I've had the Head on to me like a ton of bricks as well. It looks as though she's going to be suspended for a time.' Zoe hiccuped to a halt and blew her nose violently. 'I'm so ashamed, Fergus. I know I've not exactly been a saint, but I never got up to anything like this. I've always tried to do my best for Becca. She didn't need to steal. She can't claim to be deprived of much.'

'I'm sure she hasn't been.' He thought of the computer Zoe was saving for and shared her sense of outrage. 'I know it's been a terrible shock for you, Zoe, but try not to get too upset. Kids get up to these inexplicable, crazy things.'

'Other people's kids. Not your own.' Zoe gave a moan of despair. 'I just don't know what to do about it, Fergus. I feel like killing her. How am I ever going to dare let her out of my sight? I couldn't think of anyone but you to talk to about it. I'm sorry. I've no business heaping my troubles on your shoulders.'

Fergus brushed aside her apology again. It was becoming obvious that the state Zoe was in called for more than a quick word of reassurance. 'Where's Becca now?' he asked.

'She's locked herself in her room. She won't speak to me.'

'Then you can't leave the house, obviously. Look, Zoe, I'm going to come over. I can't think over the phone. We'll talk it over more easily face to face. Would you like me to do that?'

Zoe burst into floods of tears again. 'Oh, would you, Fergus?' she sobbed. 'I can't begin to tell you what a difference it would make to have a bit of input from someone like you. I feel so alone.'

'You're not alone. You've got a friend. And more friends at the practice, remember,' Fergus said.

'What on earth are they going to think? It'll be in the paper, won't it?'

'Becca's a minor. She won't be named. But you have nothing to be ashamed of, Zoe. We all know you – straight as a die, and willing to do anything for anyone.'

Zoe snuffled horribly down the phone. 'Don't be too nice to me, Fergus. I'll never stop crying.'

'Yes, you will. Things are never as bad as they seem. Put the kettle on. By the time it's boiled, I'll be nearly there.'

'Thanks a million, really and truly,' Zoe said gruffly. Fergus picked up his car keys and paused only to tip a tin of cat food into Middy's bowl.

Bloody awful though it was for Zoe, he felt almost glad to have proof that other people had troubles too. Suddenly he had been given a focus that was miles away from his own problem. It was like sticking your fingernail hard into your hand at the dentist's to divert your mind from what was going on in your mouth.

But it was more than that, he realized as he sped towards Zoe's house. Somebody needed him. Somebody thought him capable of giving help. Somebody was calling out for him. Deep inside him, his shattered belief in himself began to stir and grow.

Chapter Thirteen

Nat came out from the kitchen once he became aware that the talking had ended.

He gave Kate a consoling hug. 'Not exactly what the doctor ordered,' he said, holding her away from him to look at her face. 'Are you OK?'

If anything she was more white-faced than when she had taken the phone to speak to Fergus, but she answered him calmly.

'More or less. Was he unbearably rude to you?'

'Rude, yes. Unbearably, no. I sympathize with the poor man. You've given him a supremely hard time, you know, Kate.'

'I know I have.' She grimaced. 'And there could be worse to come.'

'I guessed as much from your phone call, but that can wait. Is the stuff on the kitchen table for now?' She nodded and he gently directed her towards the kitchen. 'Then you get busy with the microwave while I fetch the bottle of Spanish plonk I've got in the car. This is recovery time.'

He was firm about it, and refused to listen to anything serious until two mugs of fresh coffee marked the end of the meal.

He pushed his chair back then, stretched out his long legs, and folded his arms. 'Right. Talk,' he said. And she told him everything, not sparing herself in any way.

When she had finished, Kate waited in silence, looking down into her lap, afraid to see what his expression might reveal.

'You really don't remember anything at all of this?' he asked.

'Nothing at all of the time prior to the accident.'

'But you believe Alice?'

'Implicitly. Why should she invent something like that?'

'She's old. It could be a case of dementia, or even spite, if she's sufficiently resentful of being dropped by you.'

Kate shook her head. 'Alice isn't confused. I saw her on four different occasions while I was in Whitehaven. She's sound as a bell. And she hasn't a trace of spite in her. I'm bound to believe her, Nat. The past that I can remember bears out the total credibility of what she says.'

'Did you see any more of this Jamie chap after hospital?'

'No.'

'Why not?'

'I. . . .' She racked her brains, brow furrowed. 'I don't know. There just never seemed to be any question of it. He never came to see me, so perhaps I just accepted that it was over.'

'Or else your subconscious mind, knowing what your conscious self didn't, drew a line under the relationship?' Nat suggested.

Kate looked at him and slowly nodded. 'It fits, doesn't it?' Nat, preoccupied, got up and wandered around the room, picking up random objects and putting them down again, stopping to stare out of the uncurtained window, obviously seeing nothing. Kate watched him in silence. He had made no real comment on what she had told him, merely questioned her on the truth of it. What was he thinking? He wasn't even looking at her. Was he disgusted by her?

'Have I shocked you so much that you don't know what to say, Nat?' she asked him eventually.

He came back to the table and stood shaking his head, his smile reproachful. 'Think again if you imagine a pregnant teenager desperate not to be pregnant is the most heinous crime I've encountered. No. If you want to know the truth, I'm having to acknowledge to myself that I'm out of my depth. Kate – if you remembered this brief, painful pregnancy, then I would say that what you needed to do to get back to normal, is forgive yourself for the past. Your attitude suggests you are being judge, jury, and executioner on your own case – and getting it wrong into the bargain. But it isn't as simple as that. You don't remember either the pregnancy or its ending, and amnesia is not something I can pronounce about with any authority. I think you should see a specialist. It may well be sufficient for you to learn not to allow the past to poison the present. Or it may be necessary for you to have therapy that only a specialist can provide. It would be wrong of me to meddle and jeopardize your health in any way. I'm sorry I can't be of more use, Kate. This must be a disappointment to you.'

She was silent for a moment, then shook her head. 'No. I see the sense in what you say. I did a lot of thinking while I was walking in Cumbria. Without putting it into words, I think I'd already come round to accepting the need for help, much though I've been against it ever since Lucy died. You were the first step towards that.' She smiled. 'The devil I know, if you like.'

Nat sat down opposite her again. 'Good that we agree. You want to get started on this as quickly as possible, I take it?'

'As soon as I know where to go.'

'Can you afford to go privately?'

'Hanging around doesn't make sense after this ghastly time. Yes. We can pay.'

Nat smiled with delight. ' "We"? You realize you said "we"? If anything heralds a break in the clouds, that does, Kate.'

'I know what we're fighting now. It's easier to line up when you know the enemy.'

'Good. So you'll be talking to Fergus – and soon?'

'I've got something to say now. Yes. I'll ring him tonight.'

Nat got up and went over to take his organizer out of the briefcase he'd dropped inside the door. 'At least I can help you with someone to approach. There's a chap in Stafford I have a lot of time for. He's been practising for around twenty years now, and he knows his stuff. Say the word and I'll get in touch with him.'

'At this time on Saturday night?'

'Any time. He won't mind.'

'Then, please Nat, do it'

The appointment was fixed for Wednesday of the following week. Kate felt a mixture of thankfulness and apprehension. But the thankfulness predominated, where before there had only been despair.

Nat had just left to go next door when Kate remembered she had been asked to go and see Lynne. It was not yet half past nine. There was still time. She ran upstairs to get the Kendall Mint Cake she had brought back from Whitehaven for Lynne, and the Christmas fairy for Rosie. She pulled on her wellingtons, remembering the state of the lane, and set off. Nat was unloading his car, but said at once that he would go along with her.

Slipping and sliding on the uneven ruts of the lane, Kate realized just how much of a struggle it must be for Lynne, with no transport and a pram to wrestle along such a surface before tackling the steep hill up to the the main Roman road that Hints straddled. No wonder the poor girl's spirits were low. Summer with birdsong and sunshine was wonderful but winter must be hell for Lynne.

As they were going down the path to the cottage door, they were startled by the sudden shattering of the sitting-room window.

'What on earth was that?' Kate said, directing her torch at the glass on the brick path, while Nat knocked loudly on the door, calling 'Lynne? Are you all right?'

Lynne came to the door, red-faced and aggressive. 'Course I'm not all right,' she snarled 'Damned television's packed up.'

'So you threw it at the window?' Nat said ironically.

'No, just the remote. And you needn't say I shouldn't have done it because I know that well enough. But you try being stuck here in dead silence from the time Rosie goes to bed.' She stood back. 'Well, are you coming in or aren't you?'

Kate noticed the droop of her shoulders as she walked ahead of them into the sitting-room. Lynne looked as though she hadn't brushed her hair since getting out of bed that morning.

When she turned to stare defiantly at them, they could see the dark, bruised shadows under her eyes.

Nat went over to the window to look at the damage.

'I know I'll have to pay for it,' Lynne said bitterly. 'And the TV repair. Not too bright to double the bill, was it? But then, I'm not renowned for being bright.'

'I expect there's a pane of glass lying round somewhere that I can use to replace it,' Nat said. 'But you need that hole stopping up right now, or you'll be frozen as well as fed up.' He gave Lynne's shoulder a squeeze and ran a hand over her head, tousling her hair even more. 'Got anything I can stick over the damage until morning?'

'There's a Pampers box in the kitchen.' Lynne made no move to get it.

'I'll find it,' Kate said. 'You can look at what I've got for you and Rosie while I do that.' She gave Lynne the supermarket bag.

'A couple of new lives?' Lynne said ungraciously, but she began to unwrap the tissue paper around the Christmas fairy, and when Kate came back with the carton, scissors and sellotape, she was looking down at the sparkling white dress and wings of the fairy, touching the net and lace wonderingly. 'Look nice on Rosie's tree, that will, if she ever gets a tree,' she said, her voice downbeat.

Nat was snipping away at the carton, measuring it against the broken window pane. 'How about a cup of coffee for us all?' he said, his eyes indicating the empty beer cans on the floor beside Lynne.

'Good idea!' Kate headed quickly back into the kitchen.

'Yes, you don't have to spell it out. I've had a drink or two,' Lynne said belligerently.

'Or five or six,' Nat corrected, looking owlishly at her.

'It's not exactly a picnic here, you know,' she retorted.

'So what would be the alternative?' Nat cut off a length of sellotape and fought it away from his sleeve where it seemed determined to anchor itself. 'Park bench? Bed and breakfast? Can't say either of those sound much of an improvement.'

'You're so clever!' Lynne had taken the outer wrapping from the box of mint cake and helped herself to a piece without offering any to Nat. 'People get sick of being grateful, you know.'

'Oh – you've tried it then?' he asked innocently.

Lynne threw a piece of mint cake at him. He fielded it easily and tossed it into his mouth. 'Thanks, Lynne, generous of you!'

'Oh – you!' Reluctantly she was forced to smile. 'I can't for the life of me understand why they gave you a dog collar. You're sarky, you're too clever for your own good, and you haven't the first idea how to sympathize with anybody.'

'People are far too good at sympathizing with themselves,' Nat said. 'There. That should stop the wind howling through until morning. I'll fix it more permanently then. In the meantime, try to keep that temper of yours under control. Here comes the coffee.'

He sat next to Lynne on the settee, and when Kate had handed round the mugs, he said, 'Now – what can we do to raise the battered spirits of our friend here? How about this for starters? I'll bring my portable television down for you in the morning when I can see what I'm doing, and you can keep it until I'm next here. But you must promise not to throw things at it.'

Lynne burst into tears. 'Thanks, Nat. I know you think I'm a mess. I think I'm a mess. Sometimes I don't know how I'm going to get through my life. I've made such a dog's dinner of everything.' She looked at Kate. 'People like you with cars and jobs don't know how lucky you are.'

'People like me could have ended up in exactly the same position as you,' Kate said quietly. 'Things are hard for you at present, Lynne, but once Rosie's able to go to nursery and you can get out more, maybe get a job to make things easier, life won't look as black.'

'I know I'm lucky to have this place. But I feel so lonely sometimes. It'd be so much better if I were nearer town.'

'Have you got yourself on any housing lists?' Kate asked.

'I don't seem to have got round to it.'

'Then I'll do some enquiring for you, and if you need to go in to see anyone in town, I'll give you a lift.'

'What's this?' Lynne said, blowing her nose hard. 'Buck up Lynne time?' They went on chatting for a while, until Kate felt she couldn't keep awake another minute.

'I shall have to go and get to bed,' she said, smothering a yawn. 'Today's catching up on me.'

Nat got up as well. 'And I've work to do, so I'll walk up with you. Feeling a bit better now, Lynne?'

'Right as ninepence,' she said with bravado. 'Thanks for the sweets and the fairy, Kate. Rosie'll like it' She looked shame-facedly at Nat. 'Don't tell Jan about the window. I feel bad about it. If you could mend it before she gets back, she needn't know how daft I've been.'

'First thing in the morning, I promise,' he told her again.

'Do you think she'll be all right?' Kate said on the way back.

'She's got to be, hasn't she? I haven't known her drink as much as that before. I hope she hasn't got much more avail-able.'

'I didn't see anything in the kitchen,' Kate said.

'Let's hope the cans we saw were the lot. Lynne doesn't often cry. She's usually pretty tough. Jan's going to have to keep a wary eye on her.'

Kate went to bed with the sober thought that if fate hadn't taken a hand in her own life, she could have been in the same position as Lynne, struggling to cope with a baby and find a way of earning a living for them both. She was learning that having a baby could be painful, just as losing one was. Thankfulness for Fergus flooded through her, and for the first time since the shattering day when she had walked out, she felt a longing to speak to him.

She dialled his number, and was disappointed to find that there was no answer. The answerphone clicked into life, and she had to resort to the familiar process of leaving him a message. This time, though, she didn't hurry to get it over with, ashamed of what she was doing. This time she chose her words

carefully, imagining his delight at last on hearing her voice say
'Fergus, it's Kate. I'd like to come and see you tomorrow. I've
a lot to tell you.'

Fergus sat in Zoe's white and cream sitting-room surrounded by
her plants, drinking a well-earned whisky. The absence of bright
colours had surprised him. When he said as much, Zoe gave a
typical Zoe answer. 'Don't want to be upstaged, do I? I like to
stand out against my background.' Now, she had kicked off her
shoes and curled her legs up beside her on the settee, and was
sipping a modest orange juice, saying that her head was sufficiently done in without the aid of alcohol. Zoe had described
his whisky as well earned. Fergus brushed aside her praise, but
felt deeply satisfied with what he had achieved on her behalf in
the course of a long and taxing evening.

Within a short time of his arrival, he had coaxed Becca out of
her room, and persuaded her to talk to him about what had
happened. It was to him that she disclosed something she had
not breathed a word about, either to her mother, the people at
school or the police.

Her father, she had told him, after keeping his distance for
years, had suddenly reappeared in the area and made himself
known to her. He had played on her guilt for not having
anything to do with him, begging money, badgering her in the
street and even in her own home. When that didn't work, he
threatened to shame her in front of her friends if she didn't pay
up. She had resorted to shoplifting when her own money ran
out. He could flog anything she came up with, he told her.
Craftily, he never let her know where to find him, arranging
each hand-over meeting in a different pub.

Once Zoe knew, Becca begged to go somewhere her father
couldn't find her.

'I don't want to grow up to be like him, Mum,' she sobbed
in Zoe's arms.

'You won't, love. That rat has nothing to do with you apart
from starting you into life,' Zoe stated unshakably. 'You're my
daughter, do you hear? Everything you are comes from me, my

family, and your own kind heart. Do you think that man would have given you a penny if things had been the other way round? Forget him, Becca. Put him in Room 101 like I did years ago.'

'Is there anywhere Becca could stay that he can't possibly know about?' Fergus asked. 'It might be a good idea for her to be out of the way until the police track him down.'

'My mum lives far enough away and she's remarried and changed her name since he left the scene. She'll do anything for Becca.'

Zoe phoned her mother then helped Becca to pack a case. Fergus drove them to the safety of the grandmother's house some thirty miles away, before bringing Zoe back and seeing her safely into the house. She seemed nervous, so he hadn't hurried away.

'You must tell the police everything Becca said,' he told Zoe now, scribbling down the names of all the pubs Becca had mentioned and passing the paper over, 'especially the names of these pubs. They're the only possible lead to tracking her father down. Knowing what he's been up to could make all the difference in the world to how the authorities and school view Becca's case. The police will want to speak to her again, of course, in the light of this new information, but they'll see the sense of her being somewhere out of reach after all she's been through.'

'You bet I'll tell them,' Zoe replied. 'I'll never forgive that creep for what he's done to Becca. I knew he was low, but not that low.' Her eyes filled with tears. 'How could he, Fergus? His own kid . . . I hope they put him inside for this.'

The clock on the fireplace chimed midnight. Zoe shivered. 'Did I lock the door when we came back in?' She sat up in alarm, then subsided against the cushions. 'Yes. I remember pulling the bolts on top and bottom as well. I'll never feel safe here now I know he's been poking around.'

Fergus reached out and gripped her hand. 'Yes you will. You're a fighter, Zoe. This has been a bad weekend for you, but you'll get on top of it. I know. you will.'

She hung on to his hand. 'I can't thank you enough for what

you've done tonight. I was getting nowhere with Becca. If you hadn't got her to talk, I dread to think what might have happened.'

Fergus looked at her face, devoid of make-up for once as she stared into the comforting glow of the gas fire. She looked exhausted, and no wonder. He gave her hand a final squeeze and replaced it gently in her lap, withdrawing his own.

'Time you were getting some sleep,' he said, putting down his glass and getting to his feet. 'And time I was getting back home.'

Zoe stood up, her eyes fixed on his now. 'You're a good man, Fergus,' she said. 'I really am grateful.'

'You know what?' he said slowly, 'Tonight has been rewarding for me as well. It's good to feel needed. So don't thank me.'

He walked out into the hall and drew back the bolts on the front door, then turned, his hand on the catch. Tears were spilling over and running down Zoe's cheeks.

He put out a hand and brushed them away. 'What's all this?' he said tenderly, touched to see the normally tough Zoe admitting weakness.

She crumpled against him, clinging to him, her voice smothered against his chest as she said 'I don't want you to go, Fergus. I don't want to be alone.'

Fergus put his arms around her and stroked her shining hair. She smelled of soap and baby powder. She was like a child in his arms.

'You'll be all right,' he said. 'He's not going to come anywhere near you. He's been avoiding you all along, hasn't he? I'll wait outside and not walk away until I hear you get all the bolts back in place.'

'I'm not talking about him.' Her arms tightened around Fergus. He could feel her trembling as he had felt so many frightened animals tremble, and in instinctive response held her reassuringly tighter in his own arms.

'You've had a hell of a day, Zoe,' he said, then, softening the words with a kiss on the top of her head, 'but you don't know what you're saying right now.'

191

'Oh yes I do.' She turned her face up so that he could feel her warm breath on the skin of his neck. 'I need somebody, Fergus.' Her hand reached up and caressed his cheek. Its pressure intensified as she made his face turn towards hers. 'So do you. Please don't go.'

She was soft against him, her lips demandingly close to his. His skin was wet with the tears from her face; her baby-soft hair butterfly-kissed his cheek.

Fergus felt his body flood with desire. The long months of banishment from the warm comfort of his wife's arms and the strength of Zoe's desire conspired with the subtle undermining of the whisky he had drunk far too quickly. Did her mouth reach up to his, or did he lower his head until he found her lips? What did it matter? They kissed, and he wanted it as much as Zoe did.

Even at that stage the blood of his upright Borders ancestors pounded warning signals through the moment's hot desire. He tore his mouth from hers and said urgently, 'Zoe – this isn't right. If I stay with you, it will only be because I'm desperate with longing for Kate.'

Zoe's lips clung to him, feathering every inch of his face even as he spoke with heady kisses.

'I don't care!' she breathed passionately into his mouth.

'You deserve better.' But even as he was speaking, her mouth was seeking his. Then, punctuating every word with kisses that clung to his lips, she whispered hoarsely, 'I – don't – give – a – damn!'

Chapter Fourteen

Kate awoke with a start to a violent pounding on the front door. She reached out to switch on her bedside lamp, screwing up her eyes against the dazzle of light. It was two o'clock. in the morning. What on earth was going on?

She grabbed her dressing-gown and stumbled down the stairs as the knocking intensified.

'I'm coming!' she called, Then, pausing, 'Who is it?'

'Me. Nat. Hurry up, Kate.'

She switched on the outside light and opened the door. It was pouring down. Nat, Barbour thrown on over the clothes he had worn last night, was soaked, his hair plastered to his head.

'There's been a fire at Lynne's,' he panted. 'Come down there as fast as you can. I've got to get back to her.' He was retreating through the gate as he spoke, slipping and sliding on the mud of the lane. 'Hurry!' he called as jumped into his car and took off, the engine screaming as the wheels spun on the treacherous surface.

Kate ran back upstairs to pull on a jumper and jeans. She snatched up her mobile – better take that. There was no phone at Lynne's. Should she call the fire brigade now? – or an ambulance? Better wait until she saw the state of things down there.

Rain turned to silver bars in the light of the torch. She was soaked through in seconds. Down at Lynne's, doors and windows were flung wide to the weather. There was no visible sign of fire, though the acrid smell of it was everywhere. Lynne was lying on the kitchen floor looking like death with Nat kneeling anxiously beside her, but as Kate walked in she suddenly convulsed into life, racked by a painful bout of coughing and retching. She didn't appear to have been burned at all but smoke inhalation was giving her a lot of trouble. The sound of Rosie's distressed crying came from upstairs.

'She's just begun to come round,' Nat said, trying to move Lynne into a position to ease her breathing. 'There's nothing much I can do. I daren't even offer her a sip of water. It might do more harm than good. I've got to get her to hospital. I've checked Rosie. She's all right. Her door was shut. The smoke hasn't got in there. What are you doing?' His voice rang out in warning as he realized Kate was starting to dial 999.

'Calling for an ambulance.'

Lynne cried out which led to an even more agonizing bout of coughing until she sank back, exhausted, her breathing rasping and the base of her throat sucked violently in with each breath.

'We can't do that.' Nat threw the mobile which he had snatched from Kate's hand on to the table. 'An ambulance would probably get stuck in the lane with neither of us able to get a car past it, and what good would that be? And use your brains, Kate. If we bring officials down here, what do you think's going to happen to Rosie? They'll have her in care straight away.'

'Shouldn't the Fire Brigade check the place, at least?'

'Not necessary. One chair burnt, and I've chucked it outside. It didn't do much more than smoulder, but that was enough to fill the place with smoke. She must have lost a cigarette down the side of it before she went over to flop on the settee. That was where I found her. If I hadn't been worried and walked down to check the state of things . . . doesn't bear thinking about.' He stood up. Lynne seemed to have lapsed into semiconsciousness again and was breathing harshly, her eyes closed. 'Can you find something to wrap her in? The sooner I get her to hospital the better.'

Kate went out into the hall and snatched a coat from behind the door, but it stank of smoke. She ran upstairs and dragged a blanket off Lynne's unmade bed. At least it smelled better than the coat.

Back in the kitchen Nat eased Lynne aside for the blanket to be put underneath her, then rolled her gently back to wrap it around her. The painful breathing went on as he lifted her carefully, getting awkwardly to his feet with her head resting against him.

'I'll come with you,' Kate said unthinkingly.

'No you won't. You've got to look after Rosie.'

She caught her breath and backed against the wall. 'I can't. I can't, Nat. We could take Rosie with us.'

'No we couldn't. I've already told you one reason why. And my car won't hold us all, in any case. Don't argue, Kate.'

'Don't leave me with Rosie.' She was verging on hysteria. 'I can't do it!'

He pushed past her, his eyes boring into hers, forcing back her panic. 'Yes, you can. Yes, you will.' Then she was following him agitatedly out through the hall, every nerve crying out in protest against the responsibility that was being thrust upon her. 'There isn't time to care about you, Kate,' he said as he stooped to lower Lynne into the passenger seat. 'Who else can be with Rosie?' The crying had intensified upstairs and Lynne whimpered as though in response.

Nat stood up and faced Kate. 'This is what you're going to do. You're going to come outside and listen for my car, and wait until you hear me turn out of the lane. If I get stuck before that, you'll have to come and push. Then, when I'm clear, you're going to go up to Rosie. She needs you, Kate. You don't have the luxury of choice about this.'

He turned back to make sure Lynne's head was back and her airway clear, then fastened the seat belt round her. He gripped Kate's shoulders as she stood speechless in the rain. 'You'll be all right, Kate,' he said, his tone allowing for no denial. 'Just get on with it. Switch your mobile on. I'll call you.'

He folded his long legs into the car and turned the key. 'You can do it,' he repeated firmly over the throbbing of the engine. Then he was gone.

Kate stood watching the rear lights on their jerky way up the rutted surface of the lane. The wheels spun wildly once or twice, but he didn't stop. The red pinpoints of light disappeared, and the sound of the engine gathered strength, gradually fading away as the car climbed the hill to the main road.

Darkness and rain. Nobody but her and the child, crying upstairs in her cot. Kate turned and went back into the house, then, her heart in her throat, she began to climb the stairs.

Rosie was squatting at the end of her cot, mouth square and rigid as she yelled her disapproval of being ignored for so long. When the light was switched on and she saw a comparative stranger in the doorway, she was shocked into silence for a moment, staring wide-eyed at Kate before subsiding on to the sagging rear of her sleeping suit.

Kate swallowed hard and said shakily, 'Hello, Rosie. I'm going to look after you for a while. Don't be afraid.' She walked up to the cot and stood looking down into the wide blue eyes, still swimming with tears. 'I expect you thought no one was ever going to come,' she went on, her voice becoming steadier as she spoke. 'Well, I'm here now. Let's see what needs to be done.'

Rosie gave a juddering sigh and seemed to debate whether she should cry again, but as Kate steeled herself and reached down for her, she allowed herself to be picked up without struggling.

Kate rested her cheek against the silky dark curls, and for a moment experienced again the heart-rending blossoming back into life of another baby, another time. She wanted to give way and howl as loudly as Rosie had been doing, but she willed herself second by second back to the present. Driven by the need to keep control of her terrified feelings, she deliberately sent her own beloved ghost child to the back of her mind. Now was not the time for wallowing in memories. Now was the time for checking the wet rear of the real child in her arms, then doing something about it.

'A clean nappy first, I think,' she said. 'Now, I wonder where they can be? Shall we go and look in the bathroom?'

Rosie gurgled in response, poking a finger at Kate's mouth, craning back to look at her with those vivid blue eyes. Practicalities took over. Kate didn't know where anything was in this far from organized house. She made a game of hunting for what she needed, and Rosie joined in, crowing with delight at each 'Oh, here it is!' At last Kate was able to lay Rosie down on her bedroom rug and clean her up. Soon the wet sleeping suit was exchanged for a crumpled but clean one from the airing cupboard.

'That's better! Now I expect you'd like a little drink to help you go back to sleep again?' she said, but Rosie was busy concentrating on trying to catch her toes.

Kate sat back on her heels, thinking through the mechanics of the situation. The chances were that she was going to be in charge of Rosie all night, for no A&E department could be relied on for prompt treatment, and Saturday night was renowned for being the worst of the week. She would need to sleep herself if she was capable of it. The sitting-room was obviously not a possible place. She hadn't looked in there, but she could imagine the pall of dirt the smoke would have left behind, and the stench that would have impregnated everything. If she took Rosie back to Barn Crest, there would be no cot to put her in, and she couldn't contemplate getting Rosie's own cot dismantled and taken up there in the rain and dark. In any case, what would she do with Rosie while tackling such a job?

No, she would have to stay here. Maybe there would be clean sheets that she could put on Lynne's bed. If not, perhaps she could wait until Rosie was asleep again and dash back to Barn Crest to pick up some of her own bed linen.

Rosie rolled over and scrabbled at the floor, trying to crawl away. 'No you don't, scamp!' Kate said, picking her up and winning a chuckle from the baby as she laughed at her. 'Let's go downstairs and warm up some milk for you. I hope you've learned to like the bottled variety by now.'

It was cold downstairs, but the cottage smelled a little less unpleasant, so Kate risked closing the doors and windows, leaving the sitting-room shut away. Soon she was sitting on a kitchen chair, with Rosie on her lap, sucking happily at a bottle.

So far, so good, Kate thought, watching the hypnotic in and out of the child's pink cheeks, and the gradual fluttering and lowering of her eyelids as sleep crept over her. The bottle was empty now, and she gently detached it from Rosie's lips and put it down on the table. Rosie startled into wakefulness briefly, but soon subsided into sleep again while Kate hummed softly to her. At last it seemed safe to attempt to take her back upstairs to her cot.

While she was doing things with Rosie it had been more or less all right. It was then, with Rosie tucked warmly up under her duvet, that the awesome responsibility she had had forced upon her really poleaxed Kate again.

This was the time, the dangerous time, when the unthinkable, the incomprehensible thing could happen. She leaned over the cot, staring tensely at the still, sleeping face, starting to tremble at the thought of the fine line between sleep that lasted for a night, and the sleep that lasted for ever. She lifted the duvet cautiously and saw the just perceptible rise and fall of the little chest. All was well. But how could she guarantee that it would stay that way?

The thought of going to get clean sheets was suddenly impossible. Trying to sleep at all in Lynne's room, equally so. She hurriedly fetched the remaining blanket from Lynne's bed and pulled the nursing chair close to Rosie's cot. With the curtains slightly opened, moonlight fell on the sleeping child's face. Huddled in the blanket, Kate settled down on the chair.

She heard the clock in the sitting-room below chime three, then every quarter until four. Rosie whimpered from time to time, turned her head on the pillow, flung up an arm. The sounds and movements brought brief reassurance to Kate.

The quarters chimed distantly on, punctuated by the longer musical marking of each passing hour. Soon after six, light began to edge the curtains, and glimmer palely in the gap now abandoned by the moon. Reassured by the intensifying of shapes in the room that her long vigil was almost over, without meaning to, Kate slept at last, but only briefly. The trilling of her mobile in the echoing kitchen roused her just after eight.

It was Nat. 'Are you all right?' he asked without preamble.

'Yes. Rosie's slept well.'

'And you?'

'Not much. But I did it, Nat. Another milestone passed.'

'Well done, you. I knew you'd be fine.'

'What about Lynne? How is she?'

'Improved, certainly. She had a pretty rough time during the night and it's going to be a few days before they let her out. She's getting oxygen which helps, and the soreness and infla-mation will gradually improve. I'm coming back to get her some oddments – night clothes and a dressing-gown and toilet things. Could you round up anything you think might be useful?'

'Will do. Did you get any sleep at all?'

'They let me have a room, so I dozed a bit once they'd got Lynne settled which wasn't much before five. But I'm afraid things have got much more complicated, Kate. I had a call from Mossthorpe at seven. There's a crisis boiling up there. A suicide, and an ugly background to it according to the lads who've talked so far. It looks all set for more trouble. I've got to go back as soon as I've taken Lynne her things. And I'm afraid that means asking you to go on being responsible for Rosie. Can you do that, Kate?'

Daytime would be easier. It was the nights that held such terror. 'You mean until Jan gets back today?' she asked.

'It's not quite as straightforward as that, I'm afraid. I rang the friends she's staying with, and they've been having the kind of downpour we had last night for days. Last night's storms caused the river to burst its banks and cut them off completely. There's no question of Jan being able to drive out of there today. So it's down to you, Kate. I'm sorry to dump this on you. You can choose to refuse. But Lynne will be eternally grateful if you don't.'

Kate was silent, fighting her demons, and he said anxiously, 'Are you still there?'

'Yes. I don't have to tell you how I feel about what you're asking me to do, Nat. But this whole situation bothers me. Are you sure we're doing the right thing, not involving the authorities? It seems to me that Rosie's at risk, and we know it. I don't know if I can cope with that on top of everything else.'

Nat sighed. 'I know how you feel. But Lynne isn't a bad person, Kate. She can hardly speak as yet, but this morning she's managed to convey that she wants help to stop smoking – they brought her a pack straight away. This has really scared her. It could kick-start her into being more responsible. Could you bear to see it all end with Rosie in care and Lynne going downhill? At least give it some thought until I get there, will you?'

Kate went back upstairs. Rosie was awake, and sitting contentedly in her cot, playing with the ears of a soft toy rabbit. She looked up at Kate and held up her arms, a smile spreading across her face. As she picked her up, Kate acknowledged to herself that there really wasn't any thinking to do. She had to give Lynne and Rosie another chance, no matter what it cost her.

Nat looked tired and strained. He had been involved in counselling the boy who had died, and was dreading that whatever had been going on behind the scenes might lead to an oubreak of serious unrest with all the potential danger that could mean.

He had thrown his own belongings into the back of the MG, and was ready for off again, calling in to drop off the things Lynne needed on the way.

'Are you going to be all right, Kate?' he asked now. For the first time, with all his other worries, she felt the need to reassure him instead of the other way round.

'Rosie and I'll be fine,' she said, with far more confidence than she felt inwardly. 'Don't worry, Nat. I might not have wanted to do this, but who can resist Rosie? She's such a love.'

Nat gripped her shoulders and kissed her on both cheeks. 'You're on the way. I know you are. This is a brave thing to do, Kate. But it's a good thing – for you, as well as for Lynne and

Rosie.' He fumbled in his pocket for a scrap of paper. 'Just checking. Yes, I've still got your mobile number. May I pass it on to Lynne? Once they decide she can come home things'll happen pretty quickly. Would you feel like fetching her?'

'No problem. I shall have to borrow a car seat for Rosie.'

'Try the Bodens at the farm on the bend on the hill. They've got children.'

'Thanks. Tell Lynne I shan't attempt to go and see her. They might not allow Rosie in in any case, but it would only upset her to see her mother and then be dragged away from her again.' She picked up a brown paper bag and put it in Nat's hands. 'Sandwiches. I didn't know if you'd have had any breakfast. They're cheese, so they won't be messy. You can eat them as you drive.'

'I'm really sorry to leave you with this situation –' he began.

'Stop worrying. Just go. Tell Lynne Rosie's a gem.'

'Bless you,' he said simply with a final hug. Then he turned and got into the car and drove off.

Rosie had had a bath and breakfast while they waited for Nat. Now she sat contentedly on a rug in a corner of the kitchen playing with her toys, barricaded in by two upended chairs while Kate washed the dishes and tidied the kitchen. She had decided to stay in Lynne's cottage, since it seemed easier than attempting to transport all Rosie's gear to Barn Crest. And there was the sitting-room to attempt to clean up. So far Kate had avoided looking at it. The smell had been enough last night.

Now was perhaps the time to take the bull by the horns. She went across the hall and pushed open the door. It could have been worse, she supposed. The real damage had been restricted to the chair. Everything else was sound, but dulled by a sooty black film, and the carpet and fireside rug where the smouldering chair had been were soaking wet. Gingerly Kate picked her way across to the back window. The chair Nat had manhandled out – how had he avoided being burned himself? – sprawled on its back in the long grass, its seat and one arm blackened and hollowed out by the fire that had smouldered there. It was good for nothing but the next bonfire.

Kate took a breath and braced herself. No time like the present for making a start. She took down the curtains and removed the loose covers, then took the smelly bundle through to the kitchen.

'Washing day, Rosie,' she said, dropping them on the floor.

Midday found the washing done, the sitting-room clean if still rather smelly, and Rosie tucked up in her cot for a nap.

Kate remembered that she ought to be at work tomorrow. She hurried downstairs and dialled Marianne's number to explain the situation, relieved to find that Marianne was sure Julie would stand in for however long she was needed.

She tiptoed upstairs to see if Rosie was all right, wondering if anxiety about a sleeping child would ever leave her. Rosie obligingly twitched her nose when Kate, smothering a yawn, looked down anxiously into the cot. She was beginning to feel the effects of last night's wakefulness and worry. And yet she daren't hope for a good night's sleep tonight. She must be there for Rosie all the time. But she would make things slightly more comfortable for herself. She would drag the mattress from Lynne's single bed in here beside the cot. Then, if she spent another wakeful night, at least it wouldn't be one that left her aching in the morning.

Get on with the grand clear-up, she told herself. Don't give yourself time to think. Quietly she left the room.

There was something else she had to do first, though. Speak to Fergus. He had not answered last night's message, and she had left her mobile switched on all the time.

Today, though, he picked the phone up at once. He sounded unlike himself, more distant than at any other time.

'What message?' he said. 'I haven't heard it. As a matter of fact, I'm getting pretty sick of messages that say nothing. I haven't bothered to check the answerphone yet today.'

'This wasn't a message that said nothing. And I left it last night.'

A wary note came into his voice that she didn't recognize.

'It's been a busy weekend.' He cleared his throat. 'You'd let me know you were coming back, in any case. How was

202

Whitehaven? Why Whitehaven, come to that? Or am I still expected to stand on the sidelines and say nothing while you do whatever you fancy?'

He was not going to make it easy for her. Kate couldn't blame him. 'I'm sorry for how things have been. I've got a lot to tell you – that's what the message was about. But I'm ringing now to say that things have got complicated here.'

'So what's new?'

'Fergus – give me a chance to explain.' She waited.

'Go on, then. I'm listening.'

'The girl in the next cottage is in hospital. I'm looking after her baby. I didn't want to do it, believe me, Fergus.'

'I can imagine that.' For the first time there was a more approachable tone to his words. 'Are you all right with that, Kate? Why you of all people? Couldn't the Social Service people step in?'

'There literally isn't anyone else at present. The Social Services were my first thought too, but Nat said—'

'Oh, Nat!' he said scathingly. 'So he's involved in it as well, is he? One step further on in the game of Mummies and Daddies now, are you? Got the baby as well?'

'Don't talk like that, please. Nat's been a good friend – to both of us, not just to me. You'll realize that when I've had a chance to tell you everything that's been happening. And he's not here. He's had to go back up north to cope with a suicide at his Young Offenders place. Fergus, I really wanted to see you today, but there's not going to be the chance now that I'm stuck here with Rosie. And if you came out here we couldn't really talk. There'd still be constant interruptions.'

'I'm on call today in any case,' he said with crushing indifference.

'So –' she went on, determined to stay pleasant, 'it'll be another day or two. Lynne won't be kept in long, I think. I'll be home just as soon as I can be.'

'Home? Don't mess me about, Kate. Don't say that unless you really mean it.'

Kate felt tears threatening in her throat. 'I do. I really mean it. I . . . I've made an appointment to see a psychiatrist later this week, Fergus. Does that show you I mean what I say?'

Still the wariness. 'It's certainly a radical change of attitude. What's brought that about?'

'It's too long a story to tell over the phone. I need to be with you when I tell you. I really want things to get back to normal, Fergus. More than anything.'

A short, fierce sigh came down the phone. 'I sometimes wonder if that's ever going to be possible after all this.'

'It will be. We'll make it possible. We've got to believe it.' When he didn't immediately answer she said anxiously, 'Are you all right? You don't sound like yourself at all today.'

'That's the trouble. We're none of us the selves we were, are we? This rotten situation has changed us all . . . Mum, you, me. . . .'

'But couldn't some of the change be for the better? Try to believe that it could turn out that way. I need you to believe it.'

'I don't think I'm capable of belief right now. I'll settle for living in hope, though the supply of that's running a bit low at the moment. But its a relief you're going to see somebody at last, Kate. I'm glad about that.'

'Me too. I must go look at Rosie, Fergus. I'm on edge when she's sleeping. Listen, I've got to charge the mobile, but once I've done that, I'll leave it on all day.'

'I'm thankful for that small mercy.'

Kate longed for some sign of warmth. 'You do want us to get back together, Fergus?'

'I'm sick of wanting. It's not easy to keep up the same level of wanting with so little sign of anything happening. Look – it's futile agonizing over the phone like this. Let's leave it until I work my way to the top of your list of priorities, shall we?'

'I love you, Fergus,' she said urgently, but the line was dead, and she didn't know if he had heard – much less whether he felt any response to her words.

Zoe frowned at the computer. Fergus had marched through Reception without speaking, just giving the briefest of nods.

Was he going to be difficult with her after Saturday? Come to that, was she going to be able to cope with the awkwardness herself? They were going to have to get themselves back into what passed for normal behaviour pretty quickly, or it wouldn't be long before somebody started adding two and two and making millions.

It had been better than she thought seeing the police yesterday, and they had been fairly encouraging, but there was still a long way to go. Becca had sounded brighter last night when she spoke to her, and good old Gran seemed to be turning up trumps as usual. They'd been to Ikea, which Becca loved, and got a new table and a swivel chair for the little bedroom at Gran's so that Becca could work up there. Zoe had a stab of jealousy at this, and told Becca not to get too fond of living at her Gran's. 'It's lonely without you,' she said, and Becca made her feel loads better by saying that she missed her, too. 'It's only until they've . . . you know,' she said awkwardly.

'Yes, got that swine where he belongs – banged up!' Zoe answered savagely.

Oh, well, it would all get sorted out eventually, she supposed. That side of things, anyway. As far as Fergus was concerned, she would have to do something about that as soon as she got the chance for a quiet word with him. Clear the air between them. Surely they were both mature enough not to let what had happened get in the way of a good working relationship. It was all very well letting your private life get out of hand, but when it came to the push, it was the wage packet your working life brought you that counted.

It wasn't until the last afternoon client had gone, his mixed-parentage dog glaring crossly from the white anti-scratch collar that framed his face, that Zoe, who had spun out her work until most of the others had disappeared for the evening, was able to catch Fergus in his room.

'Can we have a word?' she asked, slipping in and closing the door behind her.

Fergus looked withdrawn as he turned round from the sink. 'As long as it's a quick one. I want to get away now.'

'I'll get straight to the point, then. Are you going to hold Saturday night against me, Fergus?'

He concentrated on drying his hands. 'I think it would have been better all round if it had never happened.' Then he looked up at her, saw her anxious face and gave her a brief shrug. 'But I'm not quite so idiotic as to put all the blame on you.'

'And you're not going to sack me on the spot?'

'You?' A faint, rueful smile now. 'I wouldn't dare. You'd be after me like a pack of hounds for unfair dismissal.'

'Put it another way, then. Would it be better from your point of view if I got myself another job?'

'It might be easier for both of us. But I can't say it would seem at all fair to me.'

'I would, if you asked me to.'

'I'm not asking you to do that, Zoe. Forget it.'

'Then can we put Saturday down to pressure of circumstances, and get back to feeling normal around each other?'

'It would be as well for us to try.'

'Good. Let's do that, then.' Zoe straightened up. She had felt to need the support of the door for that bit of what she wanted to say to him. The rest was easier.

'I've got a favour to ask,' she began and saw his momentary wary stillness. 'Nothing much of a favour,' she hurried to say. 'Not a presumptuous favour, so don't get agitated.'

Fergus put his hands up in apology. 'Sorry. I'm not very good at this sort of situation.'

'There isn't any sort of situation. Wipe it out of your mind. What I wanted to ask is this. My washing machine packed up last night. Would you mind if I brought some washing to bung in your machine tomorrow afternoon while I'm over at your place? They can't get out to me until Wednesday.'

'Is that all?' Fergus said with obvious relief. 'No problem. Of course you can.'

'And one more thing. Becca's got to see the local police tomorrow lunchtime. Mum's bringing her over, but I want to be there with her. So if I'm a bit late turning up, you'll know why.'

'I shan't be around, so suit yourself,' Fergus said, attempting to look casual and not succeeding. 'I've got to visit my mother.'

'That's all right, then.' Zoe turned to go.

'And Zoe –' She paused and looked back. 'Kate will be back in a day or two. So tomorrow will be your last time at our house.'

'Point taken, Fergus.' She started to leave again but couldn't resist looking back and adding, as she put her hand on the door handle, 'But for goodness' sake don't hang around kicking your heels until you see my car disappear before you dare come home tomorrow. You needn't think I'm going to try to jump your bones every time I'm near you, you know. Been there, done that. Won't go so far as to say I've got the T-shirt.' Then, having had the momentary satisfaction of the last word, she departed along the corridor, her heels beating their normal triumphant tattoo.

Maggie went round the side of Gordon's house and tapped an the conservatory window. He was sitting, wrestling with *The Times* crossword, glasses on the end of his nose, and looked up. A smile spread instantly across his face and he came over to let her in.

'What a pleasant surprise. You're just in time to give me a helping hand. Seven letters. "Account-falsifying musician". Any ideas? Do sit down.'

Maggie took the wicker chair. 'Try "Fiddler",' she said.

He checked the space and beamed. 'Brilliant. It fits. Now why didn't I think of that!' He filled in the word, then put the paper down. 'You didn't come here to do my crossword. What news?'

'I came to tell you that I'm going home tomorrow,' Maggie said. Then, as he raised his eyebrows, 'Yes, home. To Fergus and Kate's.'

'Are you absolutely sure about this?' Gordon was not looking either displeased or pleased, just concerned.

'I've told Dr Lawson and he didn't threaten to keep me longer, so yes, I'm sure. I'm so grateful for your offer, Gordon. It gave me an option, and that was good. But this is what I really want.'

'Because of Fergus's reaction to my suggestion?'

'No, Fergus doesn't know which way up he is at the moment, I don't take anything he says too seriously while this business between him and Kate is going on. If he had gone to the other extreme and been desperate to get me off his doorstep, then I might have been swayed by that, but I can quite easily ignore anything else.'

'So it's back to square one?'

'No. Definitely not that. I don't want to be just the resident Granny. First of all, I very much want to go on being your friend. I hope you're not hurt or offended by my decision, Gordon.'

'A bit disappointed, perhaps, but hurt and offended doesn't come into it. You've got to make the best move for you. I realize that.' He patted her hand reassuringly, and she caught his garden-rough fingers in her own and gave them an affectionate squeeze.

'Good. And I very much want to go on learning to drive. I need the sort of freedom that my own car would bring.'

'No reason at all why you shouldn't achieve that. I'll go on taking you out as often as you want.'

'And I shall enrol on an art course – that's something else unexpected that these weeks have introduced me to.'

Gordon smiled. 'All these plans!'

'I've sat back and let myself be organized by others for long enough. But the main thing I want to do is get the family back into balance again. Losing Lucy was like experiencing some awful centrifugal force. It sent us all spinning out away from each other. I'd like us to be able to reverse that and come back together stronger than before. I believe that ought to be possible.'

Gordon smiled at her with great affection. 'If wanting it as much as you obviously do applies to the other two, then you'll make it possible. Kate's the unknown quantity, though, isn't she?'

'I've always understood Kate's behaviour. She and I both had the urge to get away from each other.'

'But you haven't seen anything of her in the past four weeks, have you? I don't want to throw cold water on your plans, Maggie, but I'd feel happier if she had shown at least some concern for you.'

'Kate had to work out her own salvation just as I had. We were no good to each other as we were. I'm only a minor figure in all this, you know. Kate and Fergus are what it's all about, really.'

'You're a good woman, Maggie.' Gordon took off his glasses. 'Now – practicalities. Want me to take you home tomorrow? Maybe have a bite of lunch at the Angel Croft on the way?'

'That would be lovely. I wouldn't ask Fergus but I could have booked a taxi. I'd like you to see where I live, though. And then you'll know where to come and have dinner with me – on Saturday if you're free? All right by you?'

'Very all right, thank you,' Gordon said, beaming with satisfaction. 'Tell you what – I've got one or two goodies coming along in the poly-tunnel. Want me to bring the veg?'

Maggie had scarcely got back to her room when the receptionist rang through.

'Mrs Callender? I've another Mrs Callender here to see you. Shall I send her along?'

'Kate? You mean Kate's actually here?' Maggie flushed with pleasure. 'Oh, yes! Send her straight along, please!'

She was waiting at the open door when Kate turned the corner. For a moment they looked at each other, then Maggie held out her arms and Kate walked into them.

'Oh, Maggie!' she said. 'Do you hate me for neglecting you so badly? I'm sorry. Truly sorry.'

Maggie held her away, looking into her face. 'Don't say that. Don't think it. Circumstances called the tune for all of us. You're here now, and it's so lovely to see you.'

She hugged Kate convulsively again, then closed the door and led her to a chair.

'How are you?' they both said together, then laughed, and the tension in the air diminished.

209

'You first,' Kate said.

'I'm better. So much so that I'm going back home tomorrow.'

'Really? Oh, that's wonderful. Does Fergus know? He didn't mention it, not that we've spoken at length yet. I've heard what good progress you've been making and about your friend Gordon.'

Maggie pulled a face. 'Fergus is very wary. But he's no need to be. Gordon's a lovely man. Odd to come to a place like this and go away the richer by one good friend. I think you'll like him. Fergus too, when he's had the chance to get to know him without needing to feel suspicious. But how are things with you, Kate?'

'Getting better. Whitehaven cast a new light on the situation for me, but forgive me if I don't go into details because I haven't spoken properly to Fergus yet. But I can tell you one thing that he does know – I've agreed to see a psychiatrist to sort me out.' She gave a shaky smile. 'You and me both, eh, Maggie?'

'Whatever it takes – that was my thinking. I knew I needed help, whatever Dr Terry said. I can't say I see quite the same need for you. My behaviour was abnormal. Yours was perfectly natural.'

'I don't think you know everything. Fergus and I – things weren't right between us.'

'I did know that. I'm not going to ask questions you can't – or don't want to answer. But I think you can guess just how much I want to see the two of you back together again.'

'I've already spoken to him about going back, but I'm caught up in a situation that puts a question mark over when that can be. He didn't exactly press me on the subject, I'm afraid, Maggie.'

Maggie sighed. 'Fergus hasn't been himself these last weeks, like us. Just between the two of us, Kate, I'm afraid my boy has had what he wanted from life for so long that it takes him time to work out how to deal with any kind of failure or rejection.'

'I don't blame him. Don't think that. I've been enough to try the patience of a saint. I hope seeing this man will be a turning point. I shouldn't have resisted help for so long. I'm desperate for things to work out for both of us.'

Kate looked thin, and there was an almost transparent look to her face. Maggie realized that her eyes were blurring, and brushed a hand across them. 'It's so good to see you again, Kate,' she said.

Kate drew in a shaky breath. 'You too.' She was playing nervously with a button on her coat. 'Believe me,' she said, looking up at Maggie, 'I really wanted to see you for your own sake, but I'd better come clean. I'm ashamed to say there's an ulterior motive to this visit, Maggie. I've something to ask you. I feel bad about this, but at the same time it seems the right thing to do.'

'This is me,' Maggie said. 'You don't have to go all round the houses if there's something you want me to do.'

Kate smiled ruefully. 'All right. You know I have this appointment I've told you about? Tomorrow afternoon at four, at the man's home in Abbot's Bromley. Well, the thing is, I'm looking after a little girl of ten months old called Rosie. Her mother's in hospital and there's literally nobody else to take care of her. What I'm wanting to ask you, is – Maggie, do you think you could possibly have her while I go for my appointment? I could-n't think of anyone better than you. I was going to ask if you could bring yourself to go back home just for the afternoon, but now that you're going home properly tomorrow it seems–' She looked up, and saw that Maggie was crying. 'Oh, it's too much. I shouldn't have suggested it.'

'It's the most wonderful thing ever!' Maggie said with diffi-culty. 'Oh, Kate! To think you can actually come to me and suggest this after – oh, Kate! Of course you can bring her to me.'

Kate visibly relaxed. 'I'm so relieved. Asking you says every-thing that needed to be said between us. It seemed such an obvious way for us to turn around and step out of the past. But I was so afraid of doing the wrong thing from your point of view.'

'You couldn't have done anything more right. I can't wait to see her,' Maggie said, drying her eyes.

'You don't have to. She's here now. Had to be, of course! One of the girls in reception is looking after her.'

Maggie jumped to her feet. 'Then what are we waiting for?'

Rosie, being spoiled rotten in reception, beamed cheerfully and won Maggie's heart instantly. Kate had a stab of painful memory as she watched Maggie bending delightedly over this child as she had over Lucy, but she was becoming more adept now at letting the memories flower and fade, and more accepting of the need to do so.

It was a mild and sunny morning, so they took Rosie out and made all the final arrangements for the following day as they pushed her round Ashfield's garden. Maggie showed Kate 'her' seat, and made her laugh at the story of the first meeting with Gordon. Kate gave Maggie an edited version of her visit to Alice, and then went on to tell her about Nat, and Fergus's early-morning phone call that gave rise to the 'It's the vicar' incident.

'Oh, isn't it wonderful to be able to laugh at things again?' Maggie said. Then her expression changed and she added anxiously, 'Please don't think I'm unnatural and unfeeling to say that. It doesn't mean that I could ever forget Lucy.'

'I know you couldn't. And nor can I. But I'm beginning to realize that if I allowed memories of Lucy to crystallize into nothing but pain, it would be a denial of the huge joy she brought me. Those were three shining months, Maggie. It's not easy to be thankful for them and not give way to raging against the brief time we had her, but it's a lesson that has to be learned.'

'How has it been with Rosie?' Maggie asked tentatively.

Kate looked down at the bright biue eyes, watching her intently. 'I didn't think I could do it – and if I'd been given the choice from the outset, I'd have refused. But it was forced on me, and I've done it, and gained by it.'

They had reached the car park. Maggie waved them off down the drive, a feeling of deep satisfaction inside her. Everything was coming together as it should, at last. It just remained for Fergus to pull himself together – and he would. He wasn't a Callender for nothing.

Chapter Fifteen

The lane had dried out quite a bit over the past few days but its rutted surface jolted Rosie awake with a little bleat of protest.

'Nearly home.' Kate told her.

It was not until Kate was opposite the hawthorn hedge that screened Lynne's cottage from the Barns, that she saw first Jan's car, and then the glowing windows of the cottage.

She was prepared to find Jan indoors when she let herself in, but was surprised when Lynne came running out of the sitting-room, reaching out eagerly for Rosie who kicked frantically and went into her mother's arms in a flurry of hugs and kisses.

Jan said she had called in at the hospital and found Lynne ready for home.

'We're absolutely gobsmacked at the great job you've done in there,' Lynne said, nodding at the sitting-room. She buried her face in Rosie's neck again, and when she looked up she had to blink back tears. 'I owe you, Kate. Have you been all right?'

'Better every day,' Kate said. 'She's been good as gold. My mother-in-law had her this afternoon because I had to go somewhere, and she's joined the Rosie fan club. I'm to tell you that once she's passed her driving test, she'll be willing to come and babysit any time. But how are you, Lynne? How's the throat?'

'Just a bit sore still, but nothing like it was.' She pulled her sleeve up and displayed the patch on her arm. 'No more smoking for me. I've got all the kit, and the doc's keeping an eye on me.'

Jan made tea and they sat and talked while Rosie kicked happily on the newly cleaned rug, then Lynne took her off upstairs to be bathed. Glad though she was to give up the responsibility of the past three days, Kate felt sad to say good-bye to Rosie. But it was time to concentrate on her own life.

'I'm going back into town to see Fergus now that I'm not needed here,' she told Jan in the kitchen.

'That sounds like progress. Have you sorted things out?'

'Just beginning to, I think. I'll know more after tonight. Keep your fingers crossed for me, Jan.'

'And everything else. You've been great, Kate. You deserve your reward.'

'Tell Lynne, will you? I'll see her tomorrow at some point. She's all right for food for the time being.'

'You've done your bit and more. Get off to your man,' Jan said, adding in typical Jan fashion, '– but don't be a pushover.'

The traffic had slackened and the hectic atmosphere of earlier on given way to calm on the roads. Kate's pulse quickened as she passed the Cathedral Close with its fleeting glimpse of the Christmas tree and floodlit West Front, and slowed down for the turn into Gaia Lane. It beat even faster when she headed up the drive for the second time that day, but to her own house now.

Fergus was just coming out of Maggie's. He raised a hand as she passed, and waited on the doorstep while Kate drew up alongside his car and got out.

'I wasn't expecting this,' he said.

'Lynne was home when I got back just now. I didn't want to wait any longer.' She hesitated, then reached up and kissed him. He let himself be kissed but didn't make any attempt to touch her. She thought bleakly that he might as well be a stranger.

'You'd better come in, then.' he said, unlocking the door.

It felt strange to be crossing the threshold of her own home again. Was it still her home? She looked round, becoming aware of the smell of polish and orderliness of the place. That was unexpected. Fergus held open the sitting-room door. 'Go along in,' he said with cool politeness, as though to an unexpected guest.

Kate held up the bags she was holding. 'I called in for a take-away. Is that all right? I'll just put these in the kitchen.'

The kitchen too was bright and shining, with no dirty dishes in the sink, just a bowl, mug and plate in the drying rack from Fergus's breakfast. Middy approached her warily and sniffed the hand she held out to him, but ducked away when she attempted to stroke him.

'He hardly seems to remember me,' she said, hurt by this unexpected rejection.

'His memory's linked to his stomach – and someone else has been taking care of that.' Fergus said matter-of-factly.

Kate stood up and faced him. 'You seem to have been managing extremely well, Fergus. Everything looks well cared for.'

'Were you expecting chaos?'

'I don't know what I was expecting. Just not perfect order.'

'Someone from work has been coming in. Before I set that up, things had begun to slip a bit.'

'I'm glad you got some help.'

'Are you?' Fergus said in an odd way. But then, everything seemed odd. He took his coat off and threw it down on one of the chairs. 'If you don't mind, I'll go up and have a shower and change before we get down to business. Bit of a messy afternoon.'

'Fine. I'll lay the table and put these in the microwave.'

Business. He'd referred to her as business. We could be strangers, Kate thought desperately. When are we going to say anything that means anything? Does Fergus even want to hear what I've got to say? He seems so detached and distant. For the first time she began to feel afraid of the damage the past weeks might have done. She had been so obsessed with herself, and now she was being made unpleasantly aware of the dangerous course she had been following. The Fergus she left had been desperate for her to stay, pleading with her not to leave him. The Fergus she was attempting to come back to hardly seemed to care what happened.

She shivered, then determinedly began to lay the table. When everything was ready, she wandered round the rest of the ground floor. There were fresh flowers in the sitting-room – button chrysanthemums in bronze and gold. The thought of Fergus bringing flowers home to a house his wife had left was a statement of indifference to her presence or absence that was almost unbearable. She went back to the kitchen and sat staring at Middy's back view as he crouched over his bowl of biscuits, crunching noisily.

Fergus didn't keep her waiting long. She heard him coming along the landing and set the microwave to reheat the takeaway.

'I realize I mustn't press you, but are you thinking of staying?' he asked with hurtful politeness as he came into the kitchen. 'I could fetch your luggage if you are.'

'I didn't bring anything. Just didn't think of it. I only knew that I had to come and talk, now that it was possible.'

The microwave pinged and Kate started taking out the cartons.

Fergus removed lids and dropped them in the bin. 'So what have you got to say?' he asked, sitting down.

Not now. Not like this, between mouthfuls of Indian food, Kate thought desperately. 'Can we eat first and talk after?' she asked.

'That suggests that you're either extremely hungry, or what you have to say is bad enough to put me off my food. Could you pass me a poppadom?'

'I'm glad you can joke about it. I don't find any of this funny at all,' she said quickly.

He looked at her – really looked at her for a moment, then gave a slight, apologetic shrug. 'I'm sorry. I didn't mean that to come out quite the way it did. OK. Let's eat, then.'

It was an uncomfortable meal for which Kate had little enthusiasm. Fergus's appetite seemed unaffected by the atmosphere. She gave up on her own small helping and scraped the chicken from it into Middy's bowl, then started to clear the dishes, but Fergus put his hand on hers and stopped her. It was the first voluntary touch. She looked up at him. For a moment he looked back at her, then he said, 'Come on. Leave this. Let's talk. I'll get coffee later.'

In the sitting-room she sat with her back to the flowers. Fergus sat on the end of the settee furthest away from her.

'So how did you get on with this guy this afternoon?' he asked.

'I think I'd better start with Whitehaven,' Kate told him.

'You know best. Whitehaven, then.'

He had listened intently to her story. She had begun hesitantly, gathering confidence as she went on, aware of bewilderment, incredulity, sympathy even, but not, she thought, hostility to what she was saying.

'Have you still no shred of real memory?' he asked when she had finished.

'I can remember beginning to dread that I might be pregnant. I've no memory at all of the day I knew for certain.'

'So strictly speaking, you've only Alice's word for the pregnancy.'

'I believe it. If you had seen and heard her, you would know she was speaking the truth. Besides—'

'Besides what?'

'There was something else that bore out what she said. Before I went to Alice's house, I called in at a pub for coffee.'

'The one where you used to meet him?'

'No. But he was there. Same trade, same town, different pub.'

'You spoke to him?'

'No. He came in to see the barman. The sight of him nearly made me pass out. I've never fainted in my life, but I almost did when Jamie Bragg came into that room. Why should I do that if there weren't some reason for such a reaction?'

Fergus rubbed his forehead. 'I feel lost in all this, Kate. What good is knowing all this going to do? It's so long ago. . . .'

'That's what Robert Stevens is going to sort out, I hope. As I understand it from what he's said so far, my feelings about what happened eight years ago have been getting mixed up

217

with what I felt about losing Lucy. Complicating matters, confusing my reactions. I need to get both times well separated in my mind — which I couldn't do while I wasn't consciously remembering the Whitehaven business.'

'But you don't remember it now, do you?'

She shook her head. 'He asked if I'd be willing to try hypnotism. I don't know about that. I don't fancy that idea much. But I suppose I ought to go along with whatever he suggests.'

'What did you think of him?'

'He seems to be thorough, the careful sort. He's sending to Whitehaven for my medical records so that he knows exactly what kind of injury I had. He told me it would all take a while. "We're not as quick as the cut and stitch brigade," was what he said.'

'Did you tell him about us?'

'Of course I did.' She closed her eyes and rested her head against the chair back. 'I'm sorry, Fergus. Sorry that our private life has to be talked about.'

'It's better than not talking about it and no progress being made.' He was silent for a few moments. Kate opened her eyes again and looked at him.

'Fergus . . . do you despise me?'

He sat up. 'Why on earth should I feel anything but sorry about the whole wretched business? You weren't much more than a kid. He sounds to have been an absolute shit.'

'It isn't exactly a good thing to discover about yourself – or your wife.'

'You weren't my wife then, were you?'

'I just feel that . . . I don't know. As though I'm not the person you thought I was.'

She looked exhausted, he realized. He held out a hand towards her. 'Come here,' he said, his voice soft.

Kate looked hesitantly at him, then she moved over to sit beside him on the settee. He put his arm round her and pulled her close to let her head lie against him.

'What are you going to do?' he said after a moment.

'Do? Go on seeing him, I suppose.'

218

'Not that. What are you going to do tonight? Stay, or go?'

She turned her face up to read his expression. 'What would you like me to do?'

'Whatever seems right.'

'This seems right.' she said, her voice faint.

'Then stay.' They sat in silence, afraid to do anything to shatter the beginnings of understanding. Eventually Fergus gave her shoulder a squeeze and said, 'You're all in, aren't you?'

'The last three days haven't been easy. I was so scared to be responsible for Rosie, Fergus. I've hardly slept.'

'What about a milk drink and bed? Better idea than coffee?'

'I'd like that.'

'Go on up, then. We can talk again tomorrow. I'll bring you some Horlicks.'

She went up to the bedroom and found herself a nightdress. Fergus brought her drink and told her that he had one or two things to do downstairs. He would try not to disturb her.

She was too tired to read into that whatever was there to be read. She drank the milky drink and lay back in her own bed in her own room, and felt to be at the end of a mammoth journey.

She turned on her side, facing Fergus's place and wondered how long it would be before he came up, but that was the last conscious thought she had. She was not awake to hear or see him when he did.

Halfway through the night Kate awoke and sensed first, then saw the shape of him lying there, his back towards her. She felt a wave of great thankfulness sweep over her. Carefully, so as not to rouse him, she reached out and placed her hand against his warm back, her palm and fingers absorbing the feel of him. Then she slept again.

It was half past six when she woke next, needing the bathroom. She got out of bed carefully and went silently across the room, only putting the light on when she had closed the door.

I'm home, she thought, looking around at the familiar things. She was putting the towel back on the rail when she saw something caught behind the radiator, near the floor. She pulled it

out, and stared at the flimsy scrap of silk and lace she was holding. It was an all-in-one undergarment, black, something she
had never worn, put off by the ridiculous names given to that
sort of thing. Body . . . teddy . . . silly names.

Second by second the glow of thankfulness to be home
faded. The conclusion for her to draw was glaringly obvious.
She registered it with unnatural stupefied calm at first. It
seemed inevitable that something like this should have
happened. She supposed it could be said that she deserved it.
She had shrunk away from sex for months. Not just not wanted
it – been repelled by the thought of it, and let her feelings
show. She had walked out on Fergus. The door had been wide
open for whoever had been here.

But there was more than her own attitude to blame. Fergus
had to have been ready and willing to turn to someone else.

She went back into the bedroom. The light from the bathroom fell on the bed that had seemed such a safe haven in the
night, and now was something it hurt her to look at. Fergus had
rolled over on to his back, and he was waking up, his arm flung
back on the pillow, the knuckles of his hand rubbing his eyes.

She switched on the main light, no longer stupefied, no
longer calm. A sense of outrage was building up in her. She held
out the thing she had found, the finger and thumb of each hand
displaying it distastefully by the fine shoulder straps so that he
could see what it was.

'This was behind the bathroom radiator,' she said coldly.
'Whose is it?'

Fergus sat up, looking mildly puzzled, his face giving nothing
away. 'Yours, I guess. Certainly not mine.'

'Not my style,' she said, throwing it contemptuously down in
the corner. 'Try again, Fergus. You can do better than that.'

'Wait a minute!' he said, alert to her tone now and getting
out of bed, pulling on his towelling robe. 'What are you implying?'

'What do you think I'm implying? You haven't been normal
since I got here last night. Seems I've stumbled on the reason?'

'Don't be so ridiculous, Kate.' Understanding suddenly

flashed over his face. 'I know what it is. It's part of Zoe's wash-ing. She had stuff all round the house on Tuesday, drying on the radiators.'

'Zoe's?' Kate asked, the name registering more than the explanation.

'Yes. She's the one who's been helping out here.' He was avoiding her eyes, 'Her washing machine had packed up, and she asked if she could bring her stuff to do over here while she was working.'

'Why on earth Zoe? She isn't a cleaner.'

'She knew something was up. She kept ferreting away until she found out that you'd gone. She suggested it. You know Zoe. . . .'

'No I don't. But you obviously do. Tell me about her.'

He was walking aimlessly around the bedroom, still not look-ing at her as he spoke. 'I wasn't eager for the others to find out about us, so when she offered to come here on her afternoons off, I took her up on it.' He stopped and spun round to face her. 'I wish you wouldn't look at me like that, Kate. I swear that nothing like you're imagining has gone on here. How can you think that I'd -' he gestured wildly, 'I mean – our bed for God's sake. She really did bring her washing to do. That thing must have slipped down the back of the radiator and been missed. I hadn't noticed it.'

She gave a mirthless laugh. 'Obviously.'

'It's the truth!' Anger suddenly flared up in him. 'It was your decision to go. You're lucky I'm still here for you to come back to. What right have you to question what I say?'

'About as much right as you had to jump to conclusions about Nat. You weren't exactly cool and mature about him, were you?'

'Well, now you know how I felt.'

'And I hope you're as unjustly accused as I was.'

The fire went out of him. 'Oh, you're right to accuse me of not being myself. I don't feel to know where I am since you left. I used to feel so sure of who I was and what my standards were. I'm certainly not that any more. Your going shook me to the roots, Kate. I'm not proud of the way I've been these last weeks. Far from it.'

'What are you trying to tell me?'

He hesitated, hands thrust into the pockets of his robe. At last he said, 'That I came close to getting more involved than I should have done with Zoe.'

'I bet she played you like a prize salmon,' Kate sneered, choked by jealous anger. 'I never trusted her. I knew from the start that she meant trouble.'

'Don't turn her into the villain of the piece. She's not a bad person. She's on her own in her early thirties. She's got problems and nobody to share them with. She'd reached a low point.' He gave her a look that was full of bitter reproach. 'And I've never felt more alone in my life.'

'My heart bleeds for the pair of you,' she said viciously. 'I was having a ball at the time, myself.' She wanted to run at him, pound him with her fists, scratch and kick. She had never felt such rage, such a sense of betrayal. 'So if it wasn't here, where was it – this sordid little involvement?' she said scathingly.

'Nowhere. Nothing happened. She rang me on Saturday to say that her daughter had been caught shoplifting, not a one-off thing, something that had been going on for a while. I went over to try to help – it was good to be asked to help – and I did. I got Becca to talk to me. She'd been got at by her father, made to steal for him. You don't want all the details, but the upshot of it all was that we took Becca over to Zoe's mother to be out of the way of her toerag of a father. It was after we came back that . . . I could have been tempted to stay that night. I didn't want Zoe, Kate. I wanted you. I've never wanted anyone but you. That night, though, I just needed to be wanted by somebody.' He looked up at her. 'But I didn't stay. I didn't stay. I couldn't. Before all this happened, though, I wouldn't have believed myself capable of even thinking of it. And I can't deny that I did. And I haven't been able to stop thinking about that every time I've looked at you.'

She took a step closer to him, not knowing what she was going to do, only drawn to him by a fierce possessiveness stronger than she had known for what felt like a lifetime.

'I'd have wanted to kill you if you had,' she said passionately. 'You're mine, Fergus Callender. Not somebody else's consolation prize. And don't you forget it.'

'I've always been yours,' he said, and without knowing who made the first move, they were in each others arms, pain, relief, anger and desire fighting for supremacy.

'Come back to bed . . .' Kate said breathlessly.

'Do you really mean—?' But he didn't finish the sentence.

She was backing up the side of their bed, cheeks flushed, eyes blazing with life, tugging him after her, half laughing, half crying.

'Fergus – do I have to spell it out for you?' she sobbed.

The scent of spring flowers was in the Cathedral . . . daffodils and narcissi, pussy willow and mimosa. Evensong was over, and closing time fast approaching.

The girl was standing by the monument to The Sleeping Children. Her dark hair and the still intentness of her reminded the verger of someone he had seen there before, some time ago, well before Christmas, he thought.

She looked round when he came closer, and he saw that it was indeed the same girl, dressed in a flower-sprigged cotton frock today in honour of the mild Easter weather. He had a brief mental picture of a dark winter coat and something red on her head the time before – a beret, he thought. He didn't usually remember people as clearly as that. There must have been something special about her.

'Hello!' he smiled. 'I've done this before – told you it was time to go – haven't I?'

'So you did – quite a while ago.' She had a bunch of violets and primroses in her hand, and she held it up towards him. 'I'd like to leave these here with them,' she said, gesturing towards the sleeping figures. 'Is that possible?'

He took the flowers from her and leaned over the brass rail to put them on the floor below the inscription on the monument. 'Best I can do, I'm afraid,' he said. 'Can't put anything on the marble. And I can't promise that somebody won't whisk them away tomorrow.'

'Thank you,' she said. 'They've been put there, that's all that matters.'

She turned to go, and as her dress caught on the barrier, the light fabric momentaiily pulled tight against her swollen stomach and he realized that she was pregnant.

First baby? he wondered. Feeling a bit nervous about it?

'Good luck!' he called after her.

She turned round and nodded slowly, then gave him a smile of great happiness. But there was a trace of vulnerability there too. His guess had been right, he thought.

'Thank you. We all need that, don't we?' she said, and went off towards the door.